SPLICE

EXPERIENCING TRUE PURPLE
BOOK 3

L. S. SILVERTHORNE

AWARD-WINNING AUTHOR
L.S. SILVERTHORNE
3

SPLICE
EXPERIENCING TRUE PURPLE

***Antarans overrun Civilization
As ancient ruins light up across the system.
Triggered by Peter Mitchell's DNA.***

The war converges on Civilization as ancient ruins light up across the system. Triggered by Peter Mitchell's DNA. As Peter unravels the tangled truth about his existence and the enigmatic secrets encoded in his DNA, Antarans assault the planet while UCOE government operatives demand answers about Dr. Orlando Constantine.

As betrayals emerge and Dr. Constantine's mysterious plan takes shape, Peter becomes an unwilling pawn when he discovers the shocking fate of the lost UCOE colonies on Naharra and Ballese.

When hidden code in Peter's DNA activates, he discovers that he carries a genetic key to an ancient alien machine that could turn the tide of the war. A key that both factions will stop at nothing to seize.

A key spliced into Peter Mitchell's DNA.

Splice

Book 3 of the ***Experiencing True Purple*** series

Lisa Silverthorne

Copyright © 2023 by Lisa Silverthorne

Published by ElusiveBlueFiction.com

Elusive Blue Fiction Logo designed by Samantha Romage

Cover Design by Lost Souls Studio

Additional Cover Elements licensed by Creative Market, Deposit Photos, Shutterstock

ISBN-13: 978-1-955197-48-9 (Hardcover)

ISBN-10: 1-955197-48-2

ISBN-13: 978-1-955197-49-6 (Trade paperback)

ISBN-10: 1-955197-49-6

Novels by L.S. Silverthorne

Experiencing True Purple series:

RECOMBINANT, Book 1

HELIX, Book 2

SPLICE, Book 3

Standalone:

REDISCOVERY

Writing as Lisa Silverthorne

A Game of Lost Souls series:

Contemporary Romantasy

THE CINDERELLA HOUR

THE PRINCE CHARMING HOUR

THE EVER AFTER HOUR

THE FALLEN HEARTS SEASON

THE RISING SPIRITS SEASON

THE ETERNAL SOULS SEASON

THE ROYAL WEDDING HOUR

THE HEAVENLY HONEYMOON HOUR

THE DIVINE NEWLYWEDS SHOW

THE CELESTIAL COUPLES SHOW

THE ENOCHIAN APOCALYPSE SHOW

THE ANGELIC ANNIVERSARY SHOW

THE PERDITION PICTURE SHOW

Complete Series!

Curse and Crown series:

Epic Court Intrigue Romantasy

THORN & BLADE

STORM & STEEL

The Spiral series:

Dark Contemporary Fantasy

BETWEEN

REPRISE

AVENGE

The Resurrectionist Papers

Paranormal Romystery

GRAVE RECKONING

Standalones:

ISABEL'S TEARS

LANDFALL

PACIFIC BLUE TATTOO

Short Story Collections

THE SOUND OF ANGELS

THE MAGIC OF ORDINARY THINGS

TIMELESS

WINTER'S EMBRACE

1

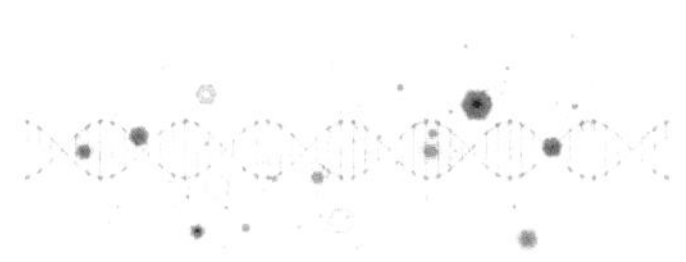

THE BODY WAS LIFELESS, lying face down in the line of scraggly yellow brush surrounding UCOE's training grounds where Field Sergeant David Temple trained a unit of recombinants. Wind blew across Civilization's dusty red and amber plains as twilight settled into the dry, cracked ground like spilled ink, stretching dark, shadowy fingers across the landscape, turning it a deep, dusky purple. The air was hot with dust and tart with ore, baking the terrain in an unyielding heatwave. Pulling the moisture out of everything.

Turning bodies left in the sun too long into mummies. Except this one.

A ruddy-haired recombinant soldier, part of Earth's cloned army training planet-side for the warfront, stopped and dropped down on his haunches. He brushed umber dust off his dull green uniform, a hand against the sunbaked clothing on the corpse as his unit rushed ahead past David.

Laughing, and shouting, they ran toward the boxy grey shuttle crouched on the paved runway. The engines fired, kicking up clouds of dust and debris, giving the air a sharp, chemical smell. But the recombinant lingered.

"Hey, Sarge! Over here," shouted the ruddy-haired recombinant over his shoulder, motioning at David.

"Report, Moody," David ordered, moving behind the private.

Was Moody stalling? Or did he have a good reason to delay the shuttle's lift-off?

David's tan field camos and chukkas were dusty and heavy in the heat, his short brown hair damp from exertion as Moody motioned for him again.

This unit was fresh from RDC in record time, producing training-ready recombinants in less than three months now. He hoped they weren't cutting corners, making these soldiers' short lives even more difficult. They already dealt with MRCs and other brain-controlling hardware in their heads. Memory Replacement Chips hijacked their ability to create memories, removing anything that impeded performance—a.k.a. their ability to kill—and replaced them with carefully crafted fake memories. The MRC was also an AWOL tracker. In case they decided to try and escape the military.

UCOE had zero tolerance for escaped recombinants. They were shot on sight or if captured, sent back to RDC for washout. A polite term for euthanasia. It made David sick.

"Sarge, you really need to check this out," Moody called, not realizing David was behind him. "Look!"

David squinted in the dying light as Moody pointed at something long and dark in the brush, but he couldn't make it out.

"Check what out, Moody? You need to fall in and get aboard the shuttle. Move it!"

David sighed. It was probably some dead lizard-like creature or a desert rodent. They outnumbered the people ten-to-one on this sparsely populated mining planet. Except near the poles where the planet cooled enough to build more comfortable accommodations for corporations and upscale colonies that charged a fortune for the right clientele. David was glad they were far from the pole colonies, so he wouldn't punch their smug, elitist faces with his dusty, commoner fists.

His job was to prepare recombinants for the Antaran war front, but after Ku'Tal and Ballese, he no longer believed in the Recombinant Defense Program that sent thousands and thousands of cloned young men and women to their deaths. So, no citizens ever had to die in a war again. UCOE didn't stop anyone from dying. Just people they knew dying. Even he'd been okay with it—until he met Peter Mitchell and John Stingley.

A nice sentiment that got politicians voted into office. But hollow —and dangerous when UCOE produced cloned soldiers like commodities. Requisition a rifle, rations—a replacement human being to fight a war in your place. It was still wrong.

Recombinants weren't androids. They were humans.

The overwhelming number of dead recombinants made him ill, but the automatic washout of recombinants after five years infuriated him even more. After surviving five years of hell, UCOE destroyed them, like expired cans of peas.

He squinted toward the darkening horizon, a hand over his eyes, barely making out Moody crouched in the brush. The shuttle's engines vibrated, clouds of dust swirling over the ground, smelling dry and acerbic with ore dust. Moody was good with a plasma rifle but easily distracted when there weren't any targets to shoot—virtual or otherwise. No telling what the young recombinant had found.

"Sarge, trust me. You need to see this."

David dropped down on his knees in front of the line of amber brush that separated the training grounds from Civilization, the mining town in the distance.

As he got closer, Moody let out a shout and fell backward, scrabbling away from something.

David reached out to the young recombinant trainee, hand on his pistol as he glanced from Moody to the thick yellow grass. Immediately, he saw the fear burning in Moody's brown, wide-eyed stare. With a shaking hand, Moody pointed at the brush.

"There, Sarge! Look! It moved!"

David turned toward the brush, squinting at the shadows

lengthening and darkening in the warm twilight haze. He let out a hiss.

The body was face down in the dust and dirt, dark hair short and cut in a fade up the neck and sides, greying at the temples. The green camo uniform was torn, burned (plasma fire?), rusty, and stiff with dried blood. The man's chest didn't rise and fall. There was no movement. He was a corpse.

Something gold glinted on the right shoulder.

David sucked in a breath as his heart began to pound, stomach dropping.

Officer insignia—captain's spirals. Rising and falling. What the hell?

This body wasn't dead anymore. And now, it was breathing.

Moody kept his distance, eyes still wide, face pale. His hands shook as he pointed at the body again.

"Sarge, it wasn't moving—or breathing—when I called you over. It was dead! I swear it!"

"Calm down, Moody," David said in a quiet, reassuring tone, his voice steady as he watched the man's thready breathing stretch into regular, even breaths. "We need to get this man some help. Moody, get our shuttle pilot to request a field medic and emergency transport to Civilization's hospital. Now, go!"

Nodding, Moody scrambled to his feet, running hard toward the shuttle.

David turned back to the man and laid a hand on his shoulder.

"Sir," he began as he slowly turned the man onto his side. "We're going to get you some help, okay?" He spoke softly and gently took hold of the man's right arm and shoulder, shifting the man slowly onto his back. "Stay with me now. I've called for a medic and medical transport to a hospital. I just need your name, I—"

David gasped, fear icy cold, his body frozen, mouth hanging open. His insides twisted into knots and all he could do was stare at the name on the uniform.

Captain D'Angelo!

The man lifted his head and stared through David, a dazed expression in his hard, grey eyes. A blackened circle stretched across his chest, the uniform burned through to blackened skin where he'd been shot point blank with a plasma rifle.

David shuddered, the image of D'Angelo's stiff, greying corpse still burned into his brain.

Three of four recombinants also died that trip. Antarans had turned Private Tanner into a recombinant hybrid. He returned to camp to wipe out the recon team, managing to kill D'Angelo and himself. David felt bad about D'Angelo's death. But after the man had recognized Peter Mitchell from Ku'Tal and ordered the young recombinant to be immediately sent back to RDC for washout, David was relieved when D'Angelo took that information with him to the grave.

How was he alive? And here? On Civilization! After UCOE nuked the planet.

"I...remember you," D'Angelo spoke in a thin, gravelly but unsure voice as he stared at David. "My field sergeant." He pulled in a shallow breath. "Temple, right?"

D'Angelo had been out of his mind when he sent three recon missions to Ballese—all of them suicide missions. All three teams invoked Naharra rules, requesting immediate nuclear bombardment of the planet and its long-murdered human colony. Half of David's recon three team died that day on Ballese and D'Angelo's mental state had deteriorated to a point that David had to relieve him of his command.

The man had already been dead on Ballese when David returned from the hellish Antaran research facility with Mitchell and Stingley —and some rescued recombinants. Rigor mortis had set in, D'Angelo's body stiff with death.

Nothing moved. Nothing lit his eyes with life.

They were forced to leave his body behind and barely escaped the planet as an orbital strike force bombarded Ballese, dropping nuclear warheads on the Antaran structures, their genetic repository, and the ruins of Earth's first successful colony in the Taus system.

It was physically impossible for D'Angelo to be here. Alive.

Chills raked David's spine, fear cold against his fingertips.

"Don't try to talk, sir," said David, his skin crawling.

His brain raced, trying to come up with some plausible explanation—no matter how far-fetched—for D'Angelo to be alive, but every possibility was more horrible than the last.

It was impossible and it made his brain scream.

But the worst part of this situation was Peter Mitchell. D'Angelo recognized him on Ballese. Would the man still remember that detail somehow? Would he send troops to hunt Mitchell down now and wash him out?

David couldn't take that chance.

Peter Mitchell was the love of his sister, Diana's life and Peter was head over feet in love with Diana. Besides, the damned kid was like a brother to him. David would do anything and everything to keep Mitchell safe and out of the military's hands.

Especially D'Angelo's undead hands. Or whatever the hell he was—lich or human. He shuddered. Or something else entirely.

And that safety included Peter's best friend, recombinant John Stingley. Peter moved heaven and earth on Ballese to find his best friend and save him from the Antarans. Bring him home. Here. To Civilization.

All of that was in jeopardy now. Especially Mitchell's life.

D'Angelo frowned, the lines on his face deeper and more pronounced. Guess being dead tended to make people age a bit and look older. Who knew?

"Temple, I need your final report from the recon mission to Ballese," D'Angelo ordered, a hard edge to his voice. "I'll expect it on my desk tomorrow, Temple. That's an order."

"Sir," he said, shaking his head. "That was filed weeks ago. After the nuclear bombardment you called in—remember? You invoked Naharra rules."

"Then I'll look at it as soon as I'm back at my desk," D'Angelo muttered, gazing around the terrain, like he wasn't quite sure where he'd landed.

A white shuttle appeared on the dusky purple horizon as blue and white stars appeared in the velvet dusk, heat softening, wind dying down. The shuttle set down behind the transport shuttle as Moody thundered up the stairs and closed the hatch.

A medic in tan camos and two other soldiers stepped out of the medical shuttle as the transport buzzed down the runway and shot into the sky. The recombinants were headed toward the shuttle port where UCOE's transitional base had been set up. After the Antaran attack on the training station that orbited Civilization. Still in ruins, but somehow maintaining a stable orbit around the planet. No one knew if the station could even be repaired or if UCOE planned to replace it.

The medic, light brown hair short and shaved up the nape, dropped down beside David, laying open his medical kit. Two soldiers in dull green uniforms, plasma rifles drawn, flanked the medic. Guarding him, David realized.

"What happened here, sergeant?" the medic asked, reaching out with a medical scanner to take D'Angelo's vitals.

This ought to be good.

David shrugged. "Honestly, I don't really know. One of my trainees found this man unresponsive in the brush. He wasn't breathing when I first tried to check for a pulse, but then he just started breathing and moving, like nothing had happened. Then he regained consciousness and started talking to us."

The medic frowned. "That's very strange. I'll scan for anoxic brain injuries when we get him stabilized at the hospital."

"I don't know quite how to explain this," David said with a sigh, "but this man led a recon mission to Ballese and I was his field sergeant. Half my recon team saw D'Angelo shot point blank in the chest with a plasma rifle. They saw him die. The next day, I saw his body. Rigor mortis made the corpse board stiff and his skin was cold and grey."

He watched the medic's eyes widen with a mixture of disbelief and horror.

David pulled the medic away from D'Angelo, so the man couldn't hear the rest of their conversation.

"We left D'Angelo's corpse at the campsite where he died when we left Ballese ahead of the orbital strike team," said David, his voice barely above a whisper. "They bombarded the planet with nuclear warheads, obliterating the colony ruins and everything surrounding it. Where we'd set up camp. Where we left his body. How the hell does a dead man come back from the dead, from a nuclear strike, and we find him alive and breathing on Civilization?"

The medic couldn't even speak. He just shook his head, fear still sharp in his hazel eyes.

"We'll get him to the Civilization hospital and I'll get a team to investigate all of your claims."

Claims? Oh, great! Now, he sounded like the crazy one.

This guy could see for himself the burned uniform, the clear evidence of plasma fire. He wondered if the wound was still there on D'Angelo's chest. He had no explanation for any of this and every possibility was terrifying.

The Taus system had gone crazy since UCOE had bombed Ballese as Antarans grabbed toe holds on the agricultural worlds, Farnas and Karaba. From there, the only place standing between the Antaris Nation and the Sol system was Civilization. But the most terrifying aspect was that Antarans were able to drop D'Angelo, unseen, on Civilization. They'd destroyed the orbital training base and now, they'd covertly returned D'Angelo to the military.

What had they done to D'Angelo? Reanimated him? Used some sort of medical procedure or process to bring him back from the dead? Or was this some whacked-out necromancer shit that he'd only read about in some fantasy novel?

But the bigger question was why.

Why did they heal or reanimate the dead captain? Just what had D'Angelo become? And what was still present in his brain? The man recognized him, so his brain hadn't been wiped? Had they installed some brain hardware like UCOE did to their recombinants? Or had they used something like their biodrone processing facilities to somehow bring him back?

David watched the medic and his staff slide D'Angelo onto a transport board and carry him to the medical shuttle. The shuttle lurched down the runway and shot into the sky, banking toward Civilization.

He turned toward the small silver skimmer shadowed behind a thick stand of yellow brush and slid into the seat. He lit the engines and skimmed across the dust and sand toward town. He needed to talk to someone about D'Angelo's second coming and figure out a way to contain this situation. Before they all woke up to Antarans and their army of biodrones on Civilization's doorstep.

Or worse. They all woke up dead. Like D'Angelo.

2

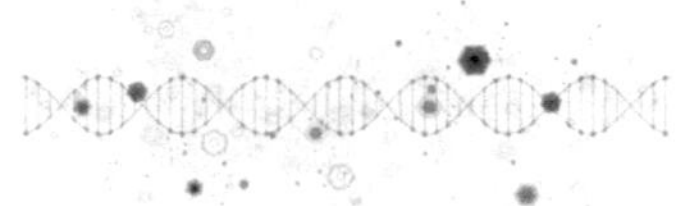

HEAT ROILED across the hilly ochre terrain, sun high and bright, giving Civilization a polished sunny glow as ex-Private Peter Mitchell landed Mimi Constantine's shuttle. His landing was abrupt and a little rocky, but he'd flown the shuttle all the way from Karaba to this little canyon on the outskirts of Civilization. He'd even picked up Mimi's supplies, including a restock of Karaban coffee.

Diana looked tense in the cramped cockpit, gripping the co-pilot's armrests to his right, her grandmother's purple scarf bright against the green and red and blue lights that filled the U-shaped cockpit. Her intense, fiery brown eyes and warm brown hair reflected the blue and red glow like colored highlights as she stared at the instruments, not looking at him.

He felt his stomach drop. Had he messed up again?

He glanced left. At John *Sting* Stingley who slouched in the navigator's chair, that devious grin creeping across his face, framed by tangles of light blond curls. His green eyes were bright as he glanced over at Peter and gave him a thumbs up.

Peter was afraid to look at Diana's face. Fearing her reaction to his takeoff and landing. This was his second attempt to fly a shuttle solo. His first flight got aborted because he'd forgotten to file his flight plan with the spaceport, prompting a fifteen-minute lecture from Diana on how the spaceport shut down rebels fast when they didn't file flight plans. Or shot them out of the sky.

He'd been training for two months to become the newest pilot in Mimi's underground operation. He wanted to join Diana and some of the underground pilots in flying rescued recombinants out of hot zones—and back to Civilization. He wanted to be more useful to the operation than washing—and breaking—dishes and picking up recombinants at the spaceport. Besides, Mimi always needed more pilots, so he'd hoped to give her one more that could carry recombinants from safe houses across Taus and back to Civilization.

He was tired of breaking dishes and being the backup of last resort.

"Well?" Peter said finally, glancing over at Sting who gave him a deep, decisive nod. "Did I get it right this time?"

He glanced out the cockpit as the brilliant sunlight disappeared from the horizon, twilight descending. Dust blew across the alien ruins ahead. This was one of many old sites that dotted Civilization and appeared on every planet in the Taus system. The dark spires were stark against the yellow landscape and purple horizon, smooth metal glinting against the sea of sand and umber rock. They looked like long skeletal fingers sticking out of the ground. Tall and tapered, about ten feet tall.

Diana sighed and Peter slumped against the pilot's seat, smashing his eyes closed. Feeling defeated and ashamed.

Why couldn't he get this right? He'd done every sim they'd thrown at him without a single mistake. Why was the real flight so different?

He went through his shutdown procedure, purple cast still on his right hand. He flicked levers, tapped buttons, and turned off switches until most of the lights winked off on the dashboard. He made sure that he transmitted his flight log and that the locator beacon was set to transmit until all but two green lights, one blue, and two white lights remained in the cockpit. That was it. He'd given his best effort.

But it hadn't been enough.

Disgusted, he unfastened his restraint harness and threw it open, wanting to get out of this cockpit and away from another failure. His chest ached, still bandaged from Ballese, the tight harness hurting more than he'd realized.

"I'll be outside," he said with a growl and jumped up from the chair, but Diana grabbed his arm.

"Peter, wait," she said, turning at last toward him.

"Why?" he said. "I failed again, didn't I?"

At last, she smiled, shaking her head as she stood up from her chair and pulled him into a steamy kiss that left him a little lightheaded.

"Congratulations," she said in a quiet voice. "You just passed your solo flight requirements. I was afraid you'd forgotten to do the shutdown procedure, but you remembered. That was the last required procedure for your solo flight."

He could barely process the words as they touched his ears. He'd passed.

"I passed?" he said, studying her face, her beautiful brown eyes, but she wasn't kidding or trying to trick him.

Diana never did things like that to him.

A smile crept onto his face as she nodded and threw her arms around him again.

"You passed, Peter!"

Sting let out a whoop and pounded him on the back.

"Way to go, Pete! Knew you could do it."

Diana reached up and caressed Peter's cheek. "I just signed off on the data and sent it to the spaceport for processing. That was the last requirement. They'll contact you as soon as your license is ready to pick up. You did it, Peter."

Sting ruffled his hair as Peter stared back at the cramped shuttle compartment. But he couldn't hold in the grin or the shout.

"I did it!"

"Come on," said Sting, tugging him toward the exit doors. "Let's go celebrate!"

"I've never been to this set of ruins before," said Diana, taking hold of his hand. "Let's go explore."

He'd never seen these ruins either. They were north of Civilization. He'd never been this far north before. And there were twice as many spires at this site than at the smaller ones to the south and west of town. He appreciated this warm, bright landscape after the hell of Ku'Tal's swamps and Ballese's burned-out, haunted buildings where so many colonists had died. Where he, Diana, Sarge, and Sting almost joined them.

Where Mimi's brother had disappeared—or died.

It had never been clear to Peter what had happened in that lab on Ballese.

The three of them rushed out of the shuttle and walked through the spires that poked up through the sand. A network of honeycomb-shaped metal tiles interspersed with smaller clusters of spires covered the ground and connected the spires in a triangular arrangement. Most of the two-foot-wide tiles had been buried beneath the sand. This site was about the size of Mimi's dining room.

Peter held his hand over his eyes, blond hair blowing in the hot breeze as he watched Diana and Sting walk through the ruins that perched between the mines and the bustling town bisected by the steamy, silt-laden river. Three of the tallest sets of spires stood at three points, forming a triangle. The honeycombs were laid out between the clusters of spires in some sort of pattern that only the aliens that built this structure understood.

Sting wore a tan bucket hat, his blond curls peeking out, a pair of khaki pants, military-issue black chukkas, and one of Peter's T-shirts —a faded blue one with distressed, blocky letters that read, Civilization, Taus System. He'd taken Sting to a shop in town to buy the pants. Sting was taller and more muscular. Couldn't wear any of the pants in Peter's footlocker. They were all given to him by Mimi when he'd first escaped the military. They'd belonged to someone else. But Peter wanted Sting to experience going into a store—and buying something that was just for him.

Peter wore heavy blue pants that Diana called jeans, grey boots she called Chuck somethings, and a charcoal grey T-shirt. His tan bucket hat was tucked into his back pocket. He didn't like hats. They reminded him of military helmets and made him feel claustrophobic. Everything about the military made him feel claustrophobic now. He laid his left hand against his chest and moved with slower steps toward the edge of the ruins. Watching Sting and Diana goof around.

No matter how much his hand and chest still hurt, he'd do everything all over again to rescue Sting. A strange sense of peace had settled on him now that Sting was with him again. The closest thing to a brother he'd ever known.

Diana left her black flight suit in the shuttle, revealing a lavender tank top and tan shorts. She put on a floppy lavender hat. A hint of her warm vanilla cologne softened the pungent ore smell and the dust.

Calmed him. Made him smile.

"These ruins look like alien stone circles to me," said Diana, holding out her hands toward the stout, tapered metal pillars that poked through the sand around her. "Made of metal, not stone. Wonder what all these pillars and columns meant to the people that erected them here. And the honeycomb-shaped plates on the ground. What do they do? Do they mark a place? Represent a religion? Or run something?"

Sting walked around the spires, a hand against his chin, and studied the strange structures.

"I've never seen anything like these before," he said finally and glanced at Diana. "They look almost functional. Not mystical. Like they did something mundane like light up a park or something."

"Those honeycombs look like solar charging panels to me," Peter added.

Diana and Sting nodded.

"Yeah, exactly, Pete. Just wonder what they power."

"Me, too," said Peter.

"Well, they still remind me of those old stone circles back on Earth," said Diana with a chuckle as she wandered toward the closest spire, gazing up at it, a hand on her hat. "So many mysterious formations and nobody knows who built them."

"Circle or triangle, they both form a circuit, don't they?" said Peter, pointing at the three points where the spires stood in a triangular pattern. "Connected by those honeycombs."

The air was tart with traces of ore and pungent with salt grass that waved long, spindly yellow blades in the wind as Diana swished through the grass, that bright purple scarf fluttering around her neck.

Peter smiled. The edges were a little bit frayed from all those months when he'd carried her scarf against his heart in Ku'Tal, fearing he'd never see her again. And here, the three of them stood together at last, exploring the ruins that stood against a huge, ochre rock formation and its six, shiny metal spires: three tall ones and three shorter ones.

"These spires out here look brand new!" Sting called across the rocks as he walked between them, chukkas kicking up dust as the wind buffeted the stones. "Not like the others closer to the restaurant."

Diana laid her hand against one of the three taller spires, the glossy, dark grey metal looking like polished stone.

"This metal looks like obsidian or onyx," said Diana with a nod. "And they do look new compared to the ones to the south. Like someone just installed all of them. They've been here a very long time, Stingley and archaeologists say they're older than the Earth."

Older than Diana's home world?

Peter's eyes widened and he almost couldn't process Diana's statement. He'd been devouring every optical and video stream that the restaurant had access to, learning about where Diana and Sarge had come from—a neighboring system with eight planets. But the more he watched and read, the more lost and overwhelmed he felt.

Like he didn't know anything at all because there was so much more to learn.

"I can't even imagine that," said Peter as he moved beside Diana, laying his palm against the smooth, bright metal.

It felt cool against the heat and the sand surrounding them. He'd expected it to blister his hand, but it didn't hold onto the heat.

"I know," she said in a soft tone. "It's hard to wrap your brain around billions of years. Especially since you've only been alive for a little over a year."

He winced. Would he ever measure up and be worthy of her attention? Would he ever understand all the things that she and Sarge took for granted? That they'd learned as children? Or would he be an uneducated noob in Diana's and Sarge's eyes for the rest of his existence? One that required constant supervision.

Sighing, he let that thought go as he slid his arm around Diana's waist and held her close. He loved her more than his own life. For her, he'd keep trying.

She leaned up, kissed his lips, and then brushed his windblown bangs out of his face.

"Where's your hat?" she asked.

"In my pocket," he answered with a shrug.

"It blocks the sun much better on your head, Peter," she said with a chuckle.

He couldn't explain about how wearing a hat made him feel like he couldn't breathe. Besides, it was almost dusk.

Then he squinted, realizing that one single spire in the triad was taller than all the others clustered in the sand.

"Why is one of the spires taller than the others?" Peter asked, moving toward it. "Does it serve some function that the other pillars don't?"

Diana shrugged. "Good question. Lots of researchers have studied them, this group in particular, but no one has answers. The metal blocks most of our scanners. Most scholars think these structures are ceremonial or spiritual rather than having some sort of function."

Peter laid his hands against the cool surface. Why wasn't it scalding hot like every other metal thing on Civilization? This metal was the opposite. It kept things cool. Was there some sort of electronics or circuits inside this thing? Were these spires protecting some sort of alien tech inside?

Sting frowned, but that devilish grin curved across his face as he ran around the perimeter of the ruins, blond curls bright beneath his hat.

"What good are these things anyway?" Sting asked, tagging each spire with his hand as he ran past. "They don't even do anything."

"He's right," said Peter as he stepped around the tallest spire, staring up at it, still puzzled by the strangely cool metal.

The sun's full glare beat down on these structures every day, yet its surface was as cool as those cans of cherry soda in Diana's cooling unit.

"Do they mark some sort of burial place?" Peter asked. "Or do they just brighten up the dust and the rocks?"

Diana leaned against one of the shorter ones that came up to her chest.

"No one knows what they symbolize or who built them. But I do know that there are ruins like this on every planet in the Taus system."

Peter turned to stare at her. "Even Ku'Tal?"

Sting grabbed him around the shoulders and pulled him toward the rock wall, messing up his hair.

Peter couldn't help but laugh. He hadn't seen Sting so happy and relaxed before. And right now, Sting burned hotter than Civilization's sun. Every single thing here was new to him and he loved seeing it all. Peter looked forward to showing him the colors sparkling along the river and the pub where Diana played darts. Even the rush of wind as the city shuttle took off from the platform. He never thought that he and Sting would ever be free from the military, much less here, exploring Civilization.

Together.

"Yes, Peter," said Diana, laughing as Sting smeared dust across Peter's face. "Even Ku'Tal. There are more of these little alien fairy rings on Civilization, too."

"More?" His eyes got wide and he stared at her. "Uh, what's a fairy ring? These are more fairy...triangles."

Diana laughed and moved toward him. Smiling, she brushed the dust off his face. "Back on Earth, they were rings of flowers or mushrooms that grew around trees in the forests. People liked to say those rings were magical, created by fairies."

He grimaced. Fairies? Magic? He glanced at Sting who shrugged.

"No clue, Pete," he said.

"They're just stories, Peter," she said, a wistful look on her face, brightening her warm brown eyes. "But they're fascinating."

"I don't know what magic or fairies are," he said and laid his hand against her flushed cheek, caressing, "but I think so, too. And I want to know all about them."

She squinted at him, tilting her head so the setting sun didn't hurt her eyes. "Why do you want to know about them?"

"Because your whole face lit up when you talked about them," he said, smiling. "If they're that special to you, then I want to know about them."

She studied his face a moment and her smile turned into a grin, making those warm brown eyes sparkle.

"I'll have to show them to you in books and videos," she said, squeezing his hand. "You'll love them."

"I can't wait," he replied, leaning over and kissing her.

Sting's cackle rang out across the rocks, echoing as Diana's hand jerked to her neck. She whirled around, smirking at Sting.

He held her purple scarf in his hands.

"Give it back, Stingley," she said in a bright singsong tone, holding out her hand.

He shook his head.

"I don't know, Diana," he said, backing away from her. "Pete held onto this for a long time. Like it was special or something."

"Stingley!" Diana shouted and lunged for her scarf, but Sting was too fast.

She chased him around the ruins and toward the dusty yellow rocks that towered above the sand, framing the alien ruins. Through waves of pale, yellow salt grass. Sting's cackle echoed against the spires.

Peter leaned against the tallest spire and watched Diana chase Sting around the rock wall. The metal was almost cold against his fingertips. It felt so good in the stifling heat.

Sting pounded across the sandy ground, that purple scarf gripped in his fist. He was too fast for Diana. She laughed and veered left, cutting him off. He lost his footing and tumbled headfirst into the sand.

Diana's sparkly laughter pealed across the landscape like wind chimes, so clear and musical.

Peter laid his face against the cool metal, letting her laugh wash over him like a skimmer wake as he enjoyed the view of her gentle curves and lean body in those tan shorts and lavender tank top. He loved every soft curve of her. Every clear note of her voice.

This metal was so cool. It felt so good against his overheated skin.

Until the vibrations startled him.

He felt them deep in the pit of his stomach, rising through his chest, into his shoulders, and surging down his legs like skittering insects. It was an almost aching thrum that shook his entire body.

He sucked in a breath, the vibrations rolling in waves across his skin, and into his teeth and bones. Deep bass notes ached through his brain. He felt them into his feet.

But he couldn't let go of the metal.

With a groan, he fought against the rhythm pounding through his head. Until his fingers released from the metal.

He rolled his shoulders, leaning until he could rock his body away from the spire's cool, shiny grey metal.

When his bare skin no longer touched the surface, the vibrations faded and then subsided. Leaving him shaking and shuddering in the wind and the heat as Diana yanked her scarf out of Sting's hands. His cackle rattled in the wind and brought Peter out of the chill and remnant pulses that shuddered down his calves and into his feet.

Like aftershocks.

The spires looked dark. Abandoned. Dead. Like nothing had touched them since they were built. But he was certain that overwhelming force had come from these ruins.

His breaths came in gulps as he backed away from the metal structures, trying to get his bearings. And the feeling back in his arms and legs. He scrambled backward, trying to get as far away as he could from these unnerving artifacts.

Until he ran into the rock formation behind him.

He pulled in a deep breath. Held it. Another breath. Held it. And turned around.

Sting's laughter echoed across the plains as Diana put the scarf around her neck, grinning at Sting, saying something, but Peter couldn't hear her over the thrumming that began in the pillar ten feet away from him. The sound built, like the pillar was gathering energy —like just before the battlefield sims materialized in the trenches when he'd been training for Ku'Tal.

The thick, resonating sound disturbed him. Deeply.

And it made him ache all over. Deep into his bones.

Diana had just said these things were billions of years old. Dead. Dormant. Ceremonial not functional. The metal structures had stood here stoic and dark like stone as long as anyone had been on the planet.

How did this one suddenly possess some sort of resonant energy inside it? The one he had chosen to lean against?

Like the whine of a plasma rifle charging, the other two tall pillars began to hum, the pitch insect-like. Frenetic. Buzzing. Electric. Reverberating against his body. Into his brain.

He grabbed his head, the ache beginning again as Diana snatched Sting's hat off his head and ran with it. Laughing, he chased her away from one of the tall alien pillars and across the sand.

Diana squealed as he grabbed her around the waist and wrestled the hat out of her hands. She giggled hysterically, her musical laugh carrying through the ruins as three tones pierced the silence, one from each of those tall pillars. In a chord that throbbed up his spine and pulsed into his brain.

Pain radiated. Piercing his temples.

He gasped, smashing his eyes closed as the chord rolled over him, causing his limbs and muscles to twitch and shudder.

Muscles cramped. Nerves burned. Limbs trembled.

Until a fourth tone vibrated down his spine, through his feet, and into the sand.

His eyes snapped open as a harmony exploded through his head. Throwing him backward into the dust.

Sting laughed, Diana's voice pealing above the wind as they ran back toward the spires.

Peter pressed his palms against his forehead, trying to cool the fire burning through his brain. The fading sunlight seemed so bright that it nearly blinded him, eyes tearing from the intensity.

"Peter?" Diana called, her voice growing louder. "What's the matter?"

He felt her drop down on the sand beside him. Hands gripped his shoulders as a shadow fell across him.

Diana cried out. "Peter?"

"I'm okay," he said in a quiet voice.

Already, the pain was dissipating.

"Holy shit! Pete, what's happening?"

"It's just a headache," he mumbled.

"No, Pete—this!"

Peter opened his eyes, but the light was so bright it hurt as Sting grabbed hold of his wrists and shook his hands, including the one in a cast.

Both his hands glowed with cyan light.

He stared at the blue-green light, confused and frightened as his gaze flicked to Sting.

"I—I don't know, Sting," he answered.

What was happening to him?

"Oh, God...look."

Diana's voice trailed off as Peter's gaze shot past Sting. Diana wasn't looking at him or Sting. She was staring at the ruins.

Pulsing bright with cyan light. All of the spires. The same blue light illuminating his hands.

3

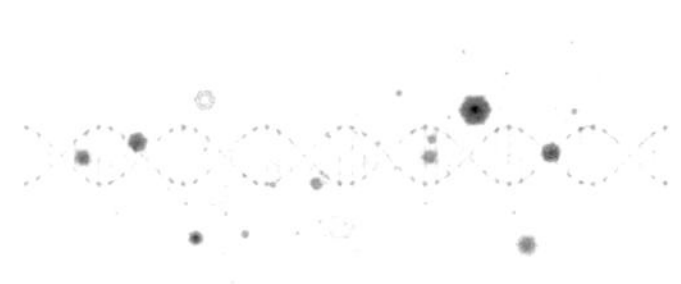

BEFORE HE HOPPED INTO A SKIMMER, David called Diana and told her to meet him at the Treehouse Pub. She'd been upset when he called, mumbling something about Peter and lights and the alien ruins, but David wasn't in the mood to listen. Not with zombie D'Angelo roaming Civilization and about to get reinstated—like nothing had happened on Ballese.

Sand and umber rock rushed past on both sides, the fading sunlight at his back, ore tart in the back of his throat as the sand and dust kicked up around the sleek silver puddle jumper that whined like a methed-up mosquito across the desert toward Civilization.

His tan helmet's sun shield wrapped around his face and kept the dust out of his eyes. A lock of dark brown hair fell onto the shield, reminding him that he needed a haircut. Didn't want to get written up for a non-regulation haircut. Although with the chaos in the Taus system and the warfront shoved much closer to Civilization now, he doubted anyone would even notice. He swept his bangs off the shield and gunned the skimmer.

Couldn't get D'Angelo's sudden rise from the dead out of his head right now.

UCOE had nuked Ballese and every Antaran installation in proximity to the destroyed colony only minutes after David and his crew had managed to find both Mitchell and Stingley. They'd nuked D'Angelo's corpse, too. It was still at ground zero after the biodrones tore him apart. After David and his team managed to escape Ballese ahead of the strike force.

UCOE was desperate for more forces and more tech, but not desperate enough to reinstate zombie D'Angelo. Were they?

The thought made him ill.

And now, he had to break the horrible news to Diana and poor Mitchell.

D'Angelo would recognize Mitchell. The captain wouldn't hesitate to arrest the kid and wash him out for being an escaped recombinant. Somehow, he and Diana needed to smuggle Mitchell and Sting off Civilization. Away from D'Angelo. But where? The whole system had gone crazy. Antarans had pushed the warfront back from Ku'Tal. Way past Karaba. Toward Farnas now. David shuddered. Toward Civilization.

After he broke the bad news to Diana, Mitchell, and Sting, they needed to talk to Mimi Constantine. Fast. See what the recombinant underground could do for Mitchell and Sting. Keep them away from D'Angelo somehow.

And that would break Diana's heart.

David hated to separate his sister and Mitchell again, especially after everything they'd already been through. But hiding Mitchell and Sting was the only option right now. Unless Mimi had other ideas. Regardless, she'd know what was possible and where they'd be safe from UCOE.

And the Antarans.

He and Diana would have to trust the underground until zombie D'Angelo had been dealt with—and right now, he had no clue how to handle D'Angelo.

David slowed the skimmer to a crawl and lurched along the edge of the river into Civilization, the air gritty with ore dust and sand, heat beating down from a purple sky as he parked the skimmer beside the two-story wood and glass building that looked like an old tree house.

He pocketed the starter and shuffled through the heat and dust toward the heavy, polished wood door. The door thumped open and he shoved through the opening, turning left at the massive polished wood bar that curved around the entire right side of the building. The honey-colored wood sparkled against the dark mirrored shelving behind it, stocked with an array of colored liquids and unusual bottles that made him want to try some of the exotic drinks the pub sold. But the mirrors reflected constant movement.

Making David uneasy.

Like he was being flanked.

He pulled in a deep breath, held it as he moved past the snarls of green plants and draping vines that adorned the room and tangled across the ceiling where fans whirred overhead. Cool air sank around him and swirled through the airy space. Tall wooden booths lined the room, glass tables in the center. On the far wall, beneath a loft area that overlooked the main floor, hung four dartboards.

Where Diana and Sting flung darts at the black and white targets on the wall. Mitchell sat alone in a booth to the left, hands covered in dusty old work gloves. He looked frightened. Confused. Worried.

If it hadn't been for the work gloves, David would have assumed Mitchell was in one of his pensive moods. Worrying about something he couldn't control. And that included the people he loved. David knew that the news he carried would upset the young recombinant even more.

David sighed. He just hoped he could protect Mitchell and Sting this time. Keep D'Angelo—and any other UCOE military officers—from washing out Mitchell and Sting both.

It was a priority to get Sting and Mitchell under wraps. Before D'Angelo lumbered into them on Civilization, with the training base relocated here permanently now. And hauled them away before David could hide them. That thought terrified him.

4

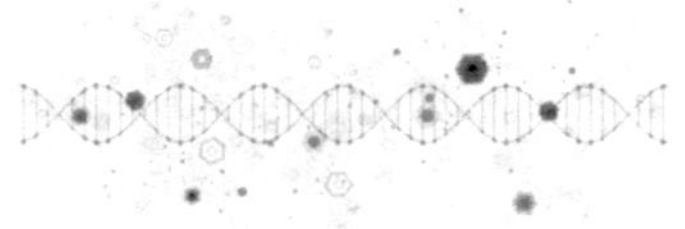

PETER SAT BACK in the wooden booth of the Treehouse Pub and watched Sting and Diana fling darts at the nearby dartboard that hung on the adjacent wall, honey-colored wood smelling like oranges and polished until it glistened. He didn't know what an orange was—or how it tasted—but Diana said it kept the wood looking shiny.

"You're good, Stingley," Diana said, sounding a little distracted, "but I'm better."

He wondered if she was still upset about what had happened in the ruins. And he worried that she thought he'd done something he shouldn't out there. Touched something. Messed with something. Turned something on. But he hadn't done anything. Everything had been enclosed in that cool, sleek metal. There was nothing to mess with or turn on in those ruins.

It was almost like those pillars and structures had reacted to his touch somehow. To his body.

"We'll see about that," Sting replied and glanced over at Peter.

Checking to make sure he was all right? Or to make sure he still had on those old work gloves that Diana had shoved on his hands. They were dusty and sun-bleached a dull grey. She'd insisted on hiding the strange glowing light that still rippled along his palms and across his fingers.

Didn't they see that he hadn't done this on purpose? That he hadn't done anything to cause this?

He stared at his purple cast peeking out from beneath the right-hand glove, anxious for it to heal. And the chest wound that still hurt when he slept on his stomach. Sarge said he hoped they reminded Peter of how close he came to losing everything on Ballese. The thought still made him shudder.

But he couldn't stop smiling as he watched Diana and Sting spar at the dartboard. Like brother and sister. Rescuing his best buddy had been worth the risk of going to Ballese. Peter had no regrets. If he had to make that decision again, he'd still go there and rescue Sting. No matter what anyone else said.

"Loser buys the next round of beers," said Sting, smirking as he leaned against the wall, green vines curling down from the wooden rafters of the high ceiling where yellow, blue, and fuchsia birds chattered and roosted.

"You're on, Stingley," Diana replied.

Sting's curly blond hair had grown past his nape while imprisoned on Ballese, his green eyes regaining their familiar sparkle. This time, he'd kept his hair longer. Sting picked up a red dart and approached the dartboard. Sting still looked a little thin in the new tan pants and Peter's faded blue T-shirt, but those black, UCOE-issue chukkas made Sting look more like his old self.

He was finally ex-Private John Stingley. The best friend Peter had ever had in his life—all eighteen months of it. He reached up to the god symbol around his neck. Sting had given him the half-black, half-white circle on the Ku'Tal shuttle ramp before Antarans had carried him off to Ballese. Now that Sting was safe, he didn't feel guilty about wearing the god symbol anymore.

A recombinant like Peter, Sting had lived a year longer and done two tours on Ku'Tal. Then he'd renegotiated Peter's deal with the Antarans, saving him and Sarge. Unable to live with Sting's sacrifice,

Peter risked everything to rescue his best friend by stowing away on a recon team led by Captain D'Angelo bound for Ballese. Half the recon team died on that mission. Peter, Sarge, Diana Sting, and the rest had managed to escape the planet—with more than a dozen recombinants rescued—before UCOE's nuclear bombardment from orbit began.

After D'Angelo died invoking Naharra rules.

Diana flung a green-tailed dart that thumped against the board, embedding the point dead center in the small, yellow bullseye. She rubbed her bare arms, her grandmother's purple scarf covering her shoulders and lavender tank top like a shawl. She was cold. The pub was always cold and she'd left her jacket in the skimmer. He watched her give Sting a hard time, but his gaze kept returning to the work gloves. He was afraid to see what was underneath the gloves now.

Diana Temple was the most beautiful person he'd ever met. She still took his breath away. All he wanted was to hold her in his arms, against his body forever and ever.

He hoped she still felt the same about him. Especially after what had happened in the ruins earlier. She seemed angry at him. Frustrated. And now, she was goofing around with Sting, almost ignoring him, like she was trying to forget what had happened out there.

He winced. Did that include him, too? Sometimes, she seemed more comfortable with Sting than him. Like now. And sometimes... he sighed...sometimes, it hurt. He wished she would have fun with him like she did Sting.

"Aw, tough luck, Stingley," she said, giggling, the sound soft and musical.

He'd carried her scarf against his heart through his entire tour on Ku'Tal and into the safe house where he'd carried Sarge, her badly injured brother. According to Mimi Constantine, the deep, true purple was a symbol of long life and he'd brought that scarf back to Diana. Just like he'd said he would. And the scarf brought them luck when she wore it as the pilot of D'Angelo's secret suicide recon mission to Ballese.

He hoped that he wouldn't need Diana's purple scarf for protection a third time. He wanted it to protect Diana. Always.

"Sure you really want to bet on this game, Stingley?" she asked with a smirk. "You're gonna lose."

"Sure do," Sting said with a chuckle as he gripped a red-tailed dart between thumb and index finger and nodded at Peter. "Because I've got my good luck charm back." He glanced over at Peter, grinning. "Pete was the best thing that ever happened to me. So, see, Diana—I can't lose."

Sting's voice cracked a little and it choked Peter up. "You're the best friend I've ever had, Sting—you and Diana. Couldn't stand you not being here."

Peter scowled at the stupid, dusty work gloves, but he was afraid to take them off. Would he find that glowing blue light enveloping both hands? It was so strange not wearing a uniform after Ballese. These faded, loose-fitting pants Diana called blue jeans looked so strange to him, but they were soft and comfortable, almost familiar like this dark grey T-shirt and his black UCOE-issue chukkas. But Diana had talked him into wearing the grey canvas boot things she called Chuck somethings. And the jeans. Diana liked how he looked in the jeans. For her, he'd wear them.

Sting walked over to the table, frowning as he pointed at the gloves.

"How are your hands?" Sting asked.

Peter shook his head. "I don't know," he said. "I'm afraid to look. They don't hurt or anything."

"Keep the gloves on until Sarge has had a look," said Sting, squeezing Peter's shoulder. "Just in case, okay?"

"I will," said Peter with a nod.

Sting returned to the dartboard.

Mid-afternoons were quiet on Civilization, the mines' shift changes still a few hours away. The half-empty pub smelled like cooked onions, salty and buttery with something Diana called popcorn. Peter sighed. And Diana's soft vanilla scent, her hair smelling like the first drops of rain, like a warm blanket he wanted to wrap around him and hold onto forever.

He stared at Sting. Seeing him standing here still seemed so surreal. Peter couldn't believe that he'd managed to find Sting and get him aboard ship. Or that all the people he cared about had managed to escape Ballese that day. Including the rescued recombinants. Sometimes, it all felt like a dream. A datadump from the recombinant headgear he'd been forced to wear every night as a recombinant soldier.

Peter had been unconscious and in incredible pain when they'd lifted off from Ballese that day. He winced, his chest still aching. Sometimes, he feared that if he closed his eyes, Sting would disappear when he opened them again. Was it all a UCOE datadump distracting him as he lay dying on the roof of that Antaran genetic repository?

He shuddered and struggled with the stupid gloves to pick up his cold pint of golden ale, the clear glass frosty as he took a long drink. The cold, malty liquid tasted like grain. It was smooth and icy against his tongue, but it warmed his belly. And it cooled Civilization's late-day heat, fogging up with painful memories of the Recombinant Development Center and Ku'Tal's swamps as they waited for Sarge.

The ale blurred the pain of losing Sting that night on Ku'Tal and all those long months not knowing if his best buddy was alive or dead. He winced. And that horrible moment when D'Angelo recognized him. Peter had never wished death on anyone, but he'd felt only relief when he learned that D'Angelo had died, taking Peter's escape (and Sting's) from the military to his grave (as Sarge put it).

Regardless, it would take Peter a long time to put all of this behind him and let it go. He felt a little like that tiny rodent he'd saved from Drake during training. That loud-mouthed, violent recombinant had tried to stomp the little mouse to death in the training base's launch bay, but Peter had coaxed it out with a cracker and gave it to Diana to release on Civilization. Diana said that the little guy had been frozen stiff with terror long after she'd released it into the brush. Eventually, the little rodent skittered away. Even though Peter took a painful beating over it, he didn't regret saving the little guy.

A red-tailed dart thunked against the board, past the black and white spokes stretching to the circle's edge, past the narrow blue ring, and slammed into the bright yellow bullseye.

"Yes!" Sting's infectious laughter filled the half-empty pub as he cheered. "How about that, Diana?" he said with a snicker. "Sorry you taught me how to play yet?"

"A lucky shot, Stingley," she said with a shrug, her smile still bright.

Peter grinned. Like moonlight on water.

Sting chuckled, but he couldn't hold in his infectious belly laugh. It echoed through the pub, making Peter laugh out loud.

Diana laughed, too, her smile electric, lighting up her face and the room like sunlight drenching storm clouds. Filling his heart with warmth and feelings he'd never felt before. Smiling, she flung her second green-tailed dart with a sniper's accuracy, slamming the dart point right next to Sting's, almost knocking Sting's dart off the board.

Peter pulled in a breath. Her smile set his skin alight, filled his senses with heat, like a hot shower on a cold night, a glass of garnet-colored wine warming his whole body with every sip. Diana Temple had an intoxicating lightness that made him feel like he was floating on air whenever he was with her. Like those colorful earth insects she loved. The ones with delicate, sky-blue wings that flitted on the wind. She called them butterflies. His heart thrummed with the flutter of hundreds of those butterfly wings whenever he was near her.

Diana threw her hands in the air. "Yes! Bullseye!" she cried and rushed toward the table where Peter sat. "Did I mention that Peter Mitchell's my good luck charm, too, Stingley?"

Sting grimaced as Diana pressed against Peter, sliding her arms around his neck, and kissed him in a long, urgent kiss that made

Peter's whole body turn to rubber. The beat of her heart vibrated into his chest until their rhythms combined in a rush of hot, staccato heartbeats that hurt when she let go of him, moving back to the dartboard. The damned work gloves made him feel like he had flippers for hands.

He sighed. God, he ached for her!

"Great toss, Diana!" Peter shouted and glanced over at Sting who was frowning. "Right next to an amazing throw by Sting." He ran his fingers through his light blond hair. "This isn't fair," he said with a sigh. "Why can't I root for my best friend AND the love of my life?"

He gasped and clamped a dusty glove over his mouth. He hadn't meant to say that out loud! He and Diana hadn't even talked about what came next yet. What if she didn't feel the same way about him?

Had he just ruined everything?

Diana moved toward him, stopping an arm's length away, cheeks flushed as she gripped his forearm, big, caramel brown eyes wide and filled with tears. She looked deep into his eyes as if she could see into his soul.

Was she angry at him for saying that? Embarrassed because she didn't feel that way about him? Especially after what had happened in the ruins today?

He bowed his head and smashed his eyes closed, afraid to look at her, afraid to see her expression change, terrified that he'd see anger—or revulsion. Why would a beautiful woman like Diana Temple want to spend the rest of her days with a naïve, uneducated recombinant like him?

"Peter?" she asked in an achingly tender voice. "Did you—really mean that?" She laid her hand against his face, tilting up his chin as his eyes opened to slits. "Am I really the love of your life?" Her voice was so quiet and uncertain.

Peter laid a dusty glove against her hand on his cheek, but the cloud of dust made him pull it back.

"Diana...your smile changed my view of the world. Your love..." He exhaled, closing his eyes to slits again. "Your love changed my life.

Changed me. Forever...and I don't want to live a single moment without you in it. I want to hold you in my arms for every single moment that the Recombinant Defense Program gave me." He let out a sharp breath, squeezing her hand. "Forever."

Tears threaded down her face and fell onto her lavender tank top and purple scarf, her lips trembling. She shook her head, opening her mouth to speak, but nothing came out. He reached out with his right hand, still covered in the old work glove and wrapped in the purple cast underneath it. Gently, he stroked her hair and then laid his hand against his chest. His heart was too full to say anything else.

"Peter," she said in a tight, shaky voice. "You're my forever. My everything." She pulled in a breath as more tears streaked down her face. "There will never—be anyone but you—for me. You are the love of my life, Peter Mitchell. And I love you so much it hurts."

He slid out of the booth and enfolded her in his arms, stupid gloves and all, holding her so tight he couldn't breathe for a moment. He kissed her softly in gentle sips that became a long, urgent connection crackling like embers through dry leaves, stoking his need, making him ache for her all over.

Sting stood beside them both now, grinning, arms folded against his chest, his gaze scrutinizing them through a tangle of curly blond bangs.

"Does this mean you forfeit and I win, Diana?" he asked and let out a cackle that made all three of them laugh.

"You wish, Stingley," said Diana, grinning as Peter let her go.

"Go," said Peter, motioning her toward the board. "Finish it."

She pressed a soft kiss against Peter's lips and moved back to the dartboard. Taking a deep breath, she picked up her second dart.

"And Pete...you're the best friend I'll ever have," said Sting in a quiet voice, his back to Peter. "I'll never take your presence beside me so lightly ever again."

"Thanks, Sting," he replied. "I won't either."

Diana stepped up to the dartboard and sighted her target—that yellow bullseye. She smiled. And Stingley's red-tailed dart.

Pulling in a deep breath, she held it and drew back her arm, taking aim, dart poised.

"Mitchell! Stingley! Fall in!"

Peter and Sting both snapped to attention and then let it go when Sarge walked toward the booth as the pub's wooden front door banged against the door frame. He didn't break stride, an intense expression burning in his warm brown eyes. And he didn't crack a smile, making Peter nervous.

Diana halted in mid-throw and turned toward her brother. Sting was beside Peter now, concern tightening his features.

"David! Thank God!" Diana cried, tossing the dart at the wall.

Sarge took the last few steps toward the booth in the corner, right beside the dartboard, and wedged himself into the booth. He wore a dusty, green field uniform flecked with umber and rust-colored plains dirt, his dark brown hair damp with sweat, and plastered against his forehead.

Diana hurried over to the booth. Sting looked anxious, fidgeting, drumming his fingers against the table as he slid into the booth across from Sarge. Peter slid in beside Sting, his gaze fixed on Sarge. Diana looked worried, her face tense, lips pressed into a grimace as she sat down beside her brother.

Sarge looked like he'd spent the day at the virtual combat simulators, where recombinants were tested for combat readiness. A place Peter hated. But after Antarans had destroyed the training base orbiting Civilization, the entire operation had been recreated on the planet's surface. Sarge's face was unusually pale, his warm brown eyes looking haunted.

Like he'd seen something horrible.

Peter pulled in a breath, wondering what could have horrified someone that had spent six months in the hellish swamps on Ku'Tal, fighting biodrones, the elements, and caregivers. Someone who had seen dozens of recombinants eviscerated and torn apart by cascade mines. A man that had seen the aftermath of Antaran attacks on the former UCOE colony on Ballese and the atrocious experiments the

Antaran monsters had performed on captured recombinants. Sarge had returned from that hellscape, too.

"Sarge?" Peter asked in a low voice. "What's the matter?"

Sarge motioned for them to lean closer as his voice got deadly quiet, his face a mask of fear.

Dreading what his former training sergeant was about to say, Peter folded his hands together, tired of these stupid, bulky work gloves that had been bleached grey by the sun.

"Something really bad happened at the VR training sims today," said Sarge, his voice barely above a whisper, brow furrowing as he cast his hard-edged stare around the pub and then around the booth.

Peter and Sting exchanged confused looks, shrugging at each other. The worst thing that happened when Peter had been in training was Drake swapping out his holo charges for live rounds. Peter took a live round to the shoulder, saving them from failing their training sim—and washing out.

"What does that mean, David?" Diana asked, frowning at her brother.

"Today was the first round of field sim testing," Sarge explained to Diana, his gaze settling on her and then Peter. "So, you can imagine all of the nervous training sergeants pacing the control room beside their stone-faced COs."

Peter nodded, remembering his own struggles through those training sims. Sarge's heart must have been in his throat throughout the entire exercise while Peter struggled below in the trenches to kill on command. Killing still sickened him, but Sting had kept the exercise together while protecting him from washing out—and from Drake. Peter didn't miss those days at all. He smiled—only the ones with Diana and Sting in them.

Sarge cleared his throat and leaned back against the wooden booth, rubbing his forehead. Ore dust clung to his uniform and tinged the pub's dry air with a tart scent. But Diana's soothing cotton and warm vanilla scent floated around the booth, settling against Peter's face. He reached across the booth and smoothed the light, airy fabric of her purple scarf against her shiny brown hair.

She looked up from her hands, deep in thought, and smiled at him, but it quickly faded when her gaze fell onto the gloves covering his hands. That made him feel sad. Like she was disappointed in him somehow. That combined with Sarge talking about training sims made him sad and anxious. He bowed his head.

"Go on, Sarge," Sting replied with a nod, his green gaze unblinking as he watched Sarge's every move.

Sting patted Peter's shoulder. His best buddy knew that, even now, the memories of those training sims still distressed him.

"Just as the last groups finished," Sarge continued, "one of the recombinants hovered near some brush at the edge of the simulator trenches. Pointing at something." Sarge ran his hand through his short, dark hair, frowning. Fidgeting. "So, I left the control room to get a closer look. When the recombinant saw me, he motioned me over. So, I followed him toward the northern edge of VR trenches."

"Sarge, did you know this recombinant?" Peter asked. "Or his CO?"

Sarge chuckled, shaking his head. "Didn't even know which unit he was in, Mitchell. I just followed him blindly. Trusting him and everything around me like it was all true. Like Ballese never happened."

Sarge's voice was bitter and thick with anger.

"Sarge, don't," Peter said in a half-whisper. "Don't beat yourself up over Ballese. This...corruption took a long time to recruit so many people."

"Good point, Mitchell," Sarge replied, studying him a moment. "You always see something the rest of us miss."

Peter shrugged, staring down at his gloves as Sting ruffled his hair. "That's my best buddy, Sarge. Smartest recombinant I ever met."

Diana reached under the table and slid her hand into Peter's. His heart beat faster. Maybe she wasn't ashamed of him. Stupid gloves. He couldn't feel the heat of her hand because of these damned gloves. And he couldn't take them off if his hands were still lit up like the lights along Civilization's waterways. How could his hands light up anyway? He didn't have LEDs underneath his skin.

With her other hand, she rubbed his calf.

He pulled in a heavy breath, closing his eyes and losing himself in her touch. He wanted to wrap his arms around her and forget about what had happened at the ruins. But he felt Sarge's unease and knew that something bad had happened. Peter felt queasy.

"So, what did you find, David?" Diana asked, letting go of Peter's hand.

Sarge ran a hand across his face, shaking his head. "A–A body, Diana. A corpse...no movement, no rise or fall of the chest. Not a single breath." He sighed. "The skin was cold and grey."

"Sarge, did one of the recombinants die during the training sims?" Peter asked with a gasp.

Sting's brow furrowed. "Sarge, how could anyone that died in those sims be cold and grey in that heat?" His face was animated, his brain already chewing on Sarge's story.

"Exactly, Stingley," said Sarge, his gaze encompassing Diana and Peter now. "I thought it was one of the recombinants and I was so confused. There was no way a recombinant's body could be in that condition that quickly. Much less cold. This man had been dead quite a while—and nothing stays cold on Civilization—unless you're rich and live near the poles."

"So, it was a man," Diana repeated.

"Sorry, I should have given all the vital information up front," said Sarge, shaking his head. "I was mid-sentence in dismissing the recombinant that found the body when—the dead man's chest began to rise and fall. Breathing now. Like normal."

Peter shook his head, confused. This didn't make any sense to him. Why would Sarge be terrified of one body?

"So, it just starts breathing like nothing was wrong?" Sting asked, his green eyes fixed on Sarge. "That's really creepy, Sarge. And it makes no sense."

"Agreed, Sting," said Sarge, sitting up straighter as he propped his elbows on the table, his gaze fixed on Peter now. "So, I started talking to this suddenly breathing corpse as I turned him onto his side and then onto his back."

Sarge shuddered, swallowing hard as his hands began to shake. He covered his face with his hands.

"You okay, Sarge?" Peter asked, watching Sarge's jaw muscles tighten and his breath quicken.

Whatever was coming next, Peter knew that Sarge had already struggled through it as a field sergeant.

As Sarge pulled his hands away from his eyes, Peter saw the sharp realization in Sarge's brown eyes. The man had suffered a good deal of emotional trauma over it. He wanted to help Sarge, like the man had done for him so many times.

But the worst part was coming, the part that Sarge hadn't said yet. The part that directly involved Peter. Somehow, this corpse affected his future. He was certain of it.

That's why Sarge was staring right at him now.

The thought made Peter shudder. He swallowed hard, pulling in a deep breath, his hands beginning to shake. He looked at Sarge, unblinking, knowing something terrible was about to affect his world.

Sarge's face twisted into a deeply painful mask. He glanced at Diana and then his gaze moved back to Peter. His eyes glistened with moisture.

"Dear God, Mitchell," Sarge said with a hiss, his face screwing up. "The corpse was D'Angelo. Alive and well. Remembered me and everything." He shook his head. "Like nothing had happened."

"David, that's impossible," Diana replied, shaking her head as she laid her hand on his arm.

"D'Angelo took a point-blank shot to the chest with a plasma rifle! I saw the whole thing. I sat with him until he passed. He was dead, David. His body was cold and stiff. Like that recombinant named Tanner. We left D'Angelo's and Tanner's corpses in the ruins when we ran for the shuttle."

Peter studied Sarge's fearful brown eyes. He felt sick. D'Angelo could expose him as an AWOL recombinant now.

"But Sarge...UCOE bombarded those ruins, every single Antaran building, and everything around them with nuclear warheads," said Peter. "That should have destroyed everything on the planet's surface, right?"

Sarge nodded, his face turning pale. "Yes, Mitchell—it should have. UCOE reduced every structure to rubble and ash." He looked weak, the honey-colored wood's glossy sheen reflecting Sarge's dusty uniform and the concern etched into his pale face.

"You need to take a break from all of this stuff, Sarge," Peter said in a quiet voice. "Take a deep breath and hold it. Then we can talk about—" He sighed. "D'Angelo tomorrow."

Sarge nodded, letting a breath out slowly. "Maybe you're right, Mitchell?

He inhaled sharply. Held it. Exhaled. Paused. Drew in another breath. His bangs were damp, eyes shadowed from lack of sleep as he tilted his head back and sank against the booth. He laid a hand over his warm brown eyes, a troubled look on his face.

Sting looked unnerved as he watched Sarge and then Peter. He shook his head.

"Pete, this is bad," the curly-haired recombinant said in a half-whisper and slid into the booth opposite Sarge.

Peter nodded and slid in beside Sting as Diana slid closer to Sarge. Sting gave Peter's shoulder a quick rub.

"David," Diana began in a soft voice, her eyes wide as she gripped his hands in hers. "How can D'Angelo just show up on Civilization like nothing happened?"

"Because he's undead D'Angelo now," Sarge said with a sneer. "That's why."

Peter sucked in a breath, unable to process all of this information. Regardless of how or why, if D'Angelo was back from the dead, he probably also remembered that Peter was an escaped recombinant. What would the man tell the base commander? Would the soldiers hunt him down and ship him off to RDC to be washed out? Or would he be shot on sight as a deserter? For being AWOL?

Peter looked Sarge square in the face.

"Sarge, none of us has talked about Ballese since we came back. Shouldn't we have had something like a debriefing?"

Sarge laughed and laid a hand against Diana's face, cupping her chin. "My kid sister here made such a fuss about keeping you alive, we put off all the reviews and reports until you were back on your feet, Mitchell."

Sting snickered. He reached over and ruffled Peter's hair. "We brought you in half-dead and unconscious, Pete. And that was after a medic treated you on Farnas."

Peter winced. "I don't remember much after I climbed out onto the dome with the repository keys."

"You were completely out of your head, Mitchell when we carried you back to camp," said Sarge in a matter-of-fact tone. "Slipping in and out of some real bad stuff all the way to Farnas. We weren't sure you'd even survive."

"I—I don't remember that," said Peter, shaking his head, frustrated by the gap in his memory.

He frowned, shaking his head. Why didn't he remember anything after that? Sighing, he rubbed his temples and tried to locate the memories. He didn't have an MRC chip anymore, so UCOE hardware wasn't hijacking and purging his memories deemed unproductive or preventing him from forming new and dangerous (according to UCOE) memories. Why weren't there at least pieces of memory from those events somewhere inside his head?

"Of course, you don't, Pete," said Sting in a soothing tone as he slid his arm around Peter's shoulders and pulled him into a hug. "You were badly injured and runnin' a high fever—" Sting's voice cut out, green eyes welling with moisture as he sucked in a quick breath, his face pinched with concern and anger. "Tryin' to—break me outta there all by yourself."

"Peter, you were delirious," said Diana. "Barely conscious even after we landed on Civilization."

Sting nodded, his arm still around Peter's shoulders. "The whole trip, you were shouting for me and your girl," said Sting. "For a week, you fell into this deep, deep sleep, Pete. As quiet as death and we couldn't wake you."

"You couldn't?" Peter asked with wide eyes, staring at Sting and then Diana.

Sarge shook his head.

Diana reached across the table and held his hand, reassuring him, he realized. "Peter...you almost died!" Peter felt her shaking. "We were afraid you'd never wake up again. It's only been a week or so since you regained consciousness."

"And now, D'Angelo's back," Peter replied, unable to wrap his brain around the fact that D'Angelo survived a nuclear planetary bombardment and returned to his post—from the dead—like nothing had happened.

"Good thing those reclamation specialists were on holiday on Civilization," Sting replied.

Peter's brow furrowed. Reclamation Specialists? What was Sting talking about?

"What specialists?" Peter asked.

"Reclamation Specialists, Mitchell," Sarge replied. "Dr. Kingston and her colleague, Dr. Kai Drew."

"Do you remember Dr. Kingston, Peter?" Diana asked. "She treated you a few times on the training base."

At last, Peter smiled, remembering the kind, patient woman with short auburn hair that had treated him like a citizen. "I do remember her," he replied. "I like her. She treated me like a real person."

Diana nodded. "She was wonderful to work with at the base. She and Kai are back at their reclamation station, but she's scheduled a meeting with Mimi to discuss MRCs, genetic batches, and a bunch of anomalies."

"That sounds scary," said Peter.

"You said it, Pete," Sting replied, swiping at a tangle of blond curls hanging in his eyes.

The conversation lulled into an uneasy silence that made Peter even more nervous. The handful of patrons in the pub had emptied into Civilization's afternoon heat, just ahead of the mining shift changes.

He glanced around the booth at Sarge then Diana, and finally Sting. They looked so tired. Frightened. And unnerved. They'd all been worried sick about him, fearing he'd go off and do something foolish and impulsive. He'd come so close to losing all three of them and they were all still worried sick about him.

And now, D'Angelo had made a creepy return from death.

Peter didn't know how or why D'Angelo was alive, but he was certain he knew who was responsible. His anger deepened. Caregivers. What terrifying technology had brought back D'Angelo? To do what?

Had it been some sort of Antaran dark ritual? One that required a sacrifice—human? Or something else? Had the ritual required a great deal of death—or something—to bring D'Angelo back to life? Or was it just a routine task from the Antarans' biodrone production technology? Something they could do anytime they felt like it? He'd learned more than he ever wanted to know about those monsters. He wondered what sort of gods they prayed to—and what their god symbols looked like.

But he wanted to know why the caregivers had brought back a UCOE captain from the dead. What was the point? D'Angelo wasn't a general or part of a special operations squad. He was just another soldier. And like Sarge, D'Angelo followed his troops—even his recombinants— into battle. He didn't spend his time behind a desk. Or leading anything. What did they gain—or hope to gain— by bringing him back to life and sending him back to his home base?

It made no sense, but regardless, Peter knew they had to find out why. Fast.

As long as D'Angelo was back on base, the captain could get him and Sting washed out for being escaped recombinants. Who knew what else lurked in the man's mind, just waiting to slide off his tongue? As long as this undead D'Angelo lived and breathed, he was a danger to everyone Peter loved and cared about.

And worse, one comment from D'Angelo and UCOE would end his life.

"Sarge," Peter said, his gaze falling onto his field sergeant. "What possible reason would the Antarans have to bring D'Angelo back from the dead?"

Sting and Diana turned their attention to Sarge. They wanted an answer to that question as much as he did.

Sarge sat up in the booth, staring at Peter and then Sting. "I keep asking myself that question, too, Mitchell. Besides D'Angelo being able to spy on UCOE forces, I just can't come up with any other reason for his reanimation and return. Maybe they intend to watch our every move through D'Angelo? Maybe D'Angelo will be their saboteur? Maybe he's the latest test of their biodrone-recombinant hybrid process?"

Silence descended again, all of them deep in thought. Peter wasn't certain about much, but he knew that those horrid caregivers were behind D'Angelo's return.

"D'Angelo didn't behave like one of their hybrid recombinants," said Sarge, staring at the table, "so I don't think the man was returned to infiltrate our armed forces."

"What about the caregivers, Sarge?"

Sting and Sarge bristled. Sting's mouth pressed into a tight, thin line, anger sparking in his green eyes. He rubbed the vertical scars on his wrists where the caregivers had intentionally inflicted wounds and drawn blood to attract their biodrones. Sarge bit his lip and clenched his hands into fists.

"What about those monsters, Mitchell?" Sarge snapped, his gaze becoming a glare.

"Could D'Angelo be a plant by the caregivers?" Peter asked, glancing from Sarge to Sting. "I don't know what he'd be doing, but

Sarge, my gut is telling me they're behind bringing D'Angelo back to life."

Sarge smiled. "Peter Mitchell going on a gut feeling? How did that happen?"

Sting cackled, his infectious laughter traveling around the table until even Peter was laughing out loud.

"Seriously, Sarge," Peter said, the smile leaving his face. "D'Angelo recognized me. If his brain and memories are still intact, he could send me back to RDC as a washout. As a deserter. But he doesn't have any incriminating information about Sting or Diana. Well, he does know that you helped me, Sarge. But that's it. Since I'm the one that blew up their repository, maybe they sent him back to get rid of me?"

Sarge shifted toward the table, propping his elbows on it as he leaned toward Peter, worry in his kind brown eyes. "What are you getting at, Mitchell?"

He sighed, staring past Sarge now. "I killed two caregivers— maybe more when I entered their repository on Ballese."

"There were lots of deaths on both sides," said Sarge. "I killed a caregiver, too. In self-defense."

"Both caregivers I killed were trying to kill me first, too," said Peter, feeling uneasy even talking about caregivers. They made his skin crawl. "One of them was in charge of the repository. And I bombed it to rubble."

"Pete, I killed several caregivers in self-defense when I was their prisoner on Ballese," said Sting, patting him on the shoulder. "So did the other captured recombinants. Other recombinants killed those sneaky little bastards for sport. What are you getting at?"

Peter sighed and leaned forward, his voice growing soft, almost a whisper. He glanced at Diana, seeing the fear building in her eyes. She'd barely said a word since Sarge arrived. Her face was pale, her mouth pressed into a taut line as she absorbed every word. He felt guilty that he couldn't tell what she was feeling right now and he hadn't even asked.

"Come on, Mitchell, tell us if you know something," said Sarge, nodding toward him, his tone a little sharp.

"When I climbed onto the repository dome, I had their three door keys to the repository. Only by using those three keys simultaneously could they close the repository doors and protect their genetic specimens from the smoke and fire. I took the keys deliberately, so the caregivers wouldn't shoot me on sight. Several of them came at me inside the dome, but only one followed me onto the roof. It was one of the higher-ranking caregivers. It climbed onto the dome after me, trying to kill me, and take the keys back."

Sting studied his face a moment. "Which caregiver was that, Pete?" he asked. "It matters."

"I think his name was...Tevihu," said Peter.

Sarge's face burned red with anger, his brown eyes turning hard as he gritted his teeth. Sting's eyes narrowed, his upper lip curling into a scowl as his green eyes burned with fury.

"Tevihu," Sting said with a growl as he chewed his bottom lip. "I dream about killing that bastard."

"Same here," Sarge snapped through gritted teeth.

Sarge's eyes narrowed, frustration evident as he brushed thick brown bangs off his forehead and tried to hold back the tide of anger that surged through him. Sting never seemed to feel the need to rein in his emotions, but Sarge always kept his in check. Right now, Sarge couldn't stop his hatred and fury from surfacing, something that surprised Peter. Even at his most extremes, Sarge appeared to be in control.

Peter glanced at Diana again. She was staring at Sarge, her face a mask of concern. He worried how she would react to what he was about to say. He doubted Sting or Sarge would appreciate it either, but they had to talk about it.

Before anything else happened.

Peter cleared his throat and pulled in a deep breath. "Sarge? Sting? Uh, what if the Antarans...sent D'Angelo here. After me. As payback for killing Tevihu?"

He glanced over at Diana. Her wide-eyed gaze settled on him for several moments, turning glassy as she shifted her attention back to Sarge. She reached out to Peter, gripping his forearm. Squeezing. He smiled. Her reaction was clear. He lifted her hand to his mouth, dust rising from those old gloves, and pressed a soft kiss to the back of her hand.

"I love you so much, Diana," he whispered as he leaned across the table. "With my whole heart."

Her warm cotton and vanilla scent brushed across his face, intoxicating, like an autumn breeze carrying the memory of summer's last handful of wildflowers.

"I wouldn't put it past them, Pete," said Sting, letting go of his anger as he settled back against the booth. "But how'd they survive the nukes? That's what I want to know."

"I wouldn't put it past them either, Stingley," said Sarge. "I'll keep that possibility in mind, but I think there's more to it than that."

Sarge began to fidget, looking uncomfortable.

"Sarge?" said Peter. "What aren't you telling us?"

His former training sergeant winced, his eyes looking sad. "Dammit, this might all be my fault."

He kicked the table, startling Diana who cast a frightened gaze at her brother.

"David?" she said, shaking her head, looking frightened. "What is it?"

"Yeah, spill it, Sarge," said Sting, leaning toward Sarge.

"On our way out, I...I..."

He pulled in a deep breath, looking upset now.

"Sarge, what is it?" Peter asked.

"Dammit, Mitchell," he said with a moan. "The caregiver, Nikoam helped us. Saved you. Us. Got us out of the repository and into the woods. If it hadn't been for Nikoam, we all might have died there."

A chill rushed down Peter's spine. "What's that mean, Sarge?"

Sarge covered his face with his hands. "When he told me he'd rescued Antaran civilian DNA and put it in the vault, I told him to get supplies and get in the vault. It's probably my fault that D'Angelo's back from the dead and here."

The silence around the table was heavy. Painful. Peter remembered Nikoam. He'd been the only caregiver that Peter hadn't wanted to kill. And he remembered Nikoam even showing how much he despised Tevihu.

"Sarge, no," said Peter, laying his dusty gloved hand against Sarge's forearm. "Nikoam hated Tevihu almost as much as the recombinants. If you warned Nikoam about an attack, he would have let Tevihu roast. Besides, Nikoam probably had minutes to get to the vault. This isn't your fault."

"Pete's right," Sting added. "Nikoam wanted to stab Tevihu in the face like the rest of us. He wouldn't have helped that bastard. He'd have fanned the flames as Tevihu burned. Roasted marshmallows over his corpse. Like the rest of us."

At last, Sarge uncovered his face, chuckling at Sting's comment. His expression was calmer. The pain in his eyes had been replaced with a hint of relief. Peter knew that Sarge agreed with him and Sting.

Sarge patted Peter's gloved hand and sat up, glancing around the booth. "Mitchell, you and Sting are right. It was clear that Nikoam disagreed with Tevihu on everything. Regardless, D'Angelo may be targeting Mitchell. So, we can't let him out of our sight."

Diana looked worried as she stared at Peter, her eyes welling with tears. Peter saw the pain and fear burn in her soft brown eyes.

Sting grinned and poked Peter's shoulder with his fist. "No worries, Sarge. Pete's not gonna leave my sight."

He turned to Diana.

"I'm gonna guard Pete 24/7, so don't you worry about him, Diana. I'm not gonna let anyone separate the two of us again. He's too important to me."

Moisture stung Peter's eyes and he swallowed a breath. Sting was like a brother to him and he would protect the curly-haired recombinant with his life. He wouldn't lose Sting a second time. He turned toward Sting, sliding his arm around Sting's shoulders and pulling him into a hug. Leaving a dusty patch on his T-shirt from the work gloves.

"You're my best buddy, Pete," Sting whispered. "I won't let those bastard caregivers touch you."

Peter grinned, hugging Sting tighter. "I won't let anyone take away my best buddy—never again."

Sarge's comunit chimed. He flicked it on and held it against his ear. "Training Sergeant David Temple," he said into the com. "What? When?" His voice hung in the air, worry spreading as Peter and Sting shared a confused glance and returned their attention to Sarge.

"Are you certain?" he asked. "Absolutely certain?"

A moment of silence ended with Sarge clenching his eyes closed, teeth grinding.

"All right. Yes, I understand—right away. I'll see you shortly." Sarge glanced around the booth until his gaze fell on Peter. He nodded. "Right, I'll make sure he's there. Temple out."

The heavy sense of dread settled like a lodestone as the sense of quiet deepened. Intensified.

Everyone turned to stare at Peter.

"Why are all of you staring at me?" Peter asked.

Sarge's eyes were filled with pain as he reached out and patted Peter's sleeve. "The way station between Civilization and the Reclamation Station Hub was attacked early this morning. Completely obliterated."

The silence was palpable this time. Peter's stomach roiled. What did it all mean? Did it mean that the Antarans were advancing toward Sarge and Diana's home world?

"There's more," said Sarge, rising from the booth.

Peter unfolded himself from the back of the booth, Sting scrambling out behind him. They moved toward Sarge as Diana huddled close to her brother, following him out of the pub.

Peter hurried toward Diana. When she saw him, she turned and leaned into his embrace as he wrapped her in his arms and held her despite the work gloves. Sting stood close beside Peter, the curly-haired recombinant's shoulder pressing against Peter's shoulder, his gaze tracking around the room. In a protective stance, Peter realized with a grin. Diana and Sting wouldn't let him out of their sight, no matter what.

"What else has happened, David?" Diana called to him before he got to the front doors, her caramel-brown eyes wide and glassy with worry.

The heavy sigh that escaped from Sarge's lips terrified Peter. Sarge's posture stiffened, back straighter as Peter waited for a response.

"Reclamation Station Three Four Three Alpha Omega Delta was also attacked," Sarge announced.

"Why is a reclamation station important, David?" Diana asked, gripping Peter's arms tighter against her.

"It's the closest reclamation station to home system," Sarge said in a dark voice. "Government agents will be swarming all over that station now." He sighed. "It's right beside Dr. Kingston's station."

"No," Diana murmured and pulled in a breath.

Peter felt a sharp stab of pain against his chest. "Not Dr. Kingston."

Sting bowed his head, sighing.

Peter really liked Dr. Kingston. He hoped she was okay and that her station hadn't been affected. But from Sarge's demeanor, Peter knew that there was still one more bad thing to reveal.

"But that's not the most important reason, is it, Sarge?" said Peter, a lump in his throat.

Sarge slowly shook his head. "Nothing gets past you, does it, Mitchell?" he said with a deep sigh. "Mitchell's right though."

Everyone turned their attention to Peter again.

"What's Peter's referring to, David," Diana said, her grip on Peter's arms tightening as she glanced from Peter to Sarge.

Sarge's gaze didn't leave Peter's face as he spoke. "The station was destroyed in an Antaran attack, but the worst thing is that the last and only secured location left in the Taus system is Civilization."

Sting's mouth fell open and he whispered some curse words that only Peter heard.

"We're screwed," Sting said finally.

Peter nodded. "We have to fight the Antarans here—on Civilization. And win. Otherwise, they'll roll over Civilization and be on your home planet's doorstep in two or three months. If that long."

Sarge turned around, nodding, and patted Peter on the back. "Everything the kid said is true," he said, his tone sounding so dark.

"Who contacted you, David?" Diana asked.

"Mimi," he replied. "She's expecting all of us at the restaurant within the hour."

Diana frowned. "What for?"

"For the fight of our lives, sis," Sarge said in a soft voice. "The Antarans will be coming here next, to Civilization. We need to end them here. Now. Otherwise, Earth and all her descendants are doomed."

"Lead the way, Sarge," said Sting, a twinkle in his green eyes.

Sarge's expression brightened as Peter, Sting, and Diana followed him out of the pub and down the dusty street toward Mimi's restaurant, End of the Line. But he stopped, frowning, and pointed at Peter's work gloves.

"All right, what's with the miner's gloves, Mitchell? I've been meaning to ask you since I got to the pub."

Peter started to respond, but Sarge grabbed one and yanked it off.

Wincing, Peter glanced at his right hand, dreading trying to explain his glowing hands to Sarge. His right hand was encased in a purple cast. But his hands looked normal. No bright blue glow clung to his fingers.

He grinned. It had stopped!

Peter slid the other glove off. Left hand was also dark, not even a glimmer of light there. Whatever had happened today at the ruins had only been temporary. He exhaled sharply as the tension drained out of his body.

"It was cold in the pub," he replied.

Sarge rolled his eyes. "Cold enough for dirty old mining gloves? Where'd you get these anyway?"

Peter shrugged and cast a wide-eyed look at Sting. "Found them."

"Get rid of them," said Sarge. "They could be radioactive for all you know."

Gasping, Peter dropped the other glove in the street and followed Sarge and Diana toward the restaurant. Sting followed beside him, giving him a wary but relieved look.

Peter glanced around at the busy mining town with its three parallel streets and the colored lights lining the buildings. Civilization was the only place he'd ever known. His stomach twisted into knots. Unless they stopped the Antarans here and now, Civilization's days were numbered.

But he couldn't let go of what had happened today, after he'd passed his shuttle flight trial. At the ruins. They were all over the planet. He'd seen several. They were supposedly all over every planet in the system, but he didn't remember seeing them on Ku'Tal or Ballese. There was even another smaller set of ruins just south of the restaurant.

As soon as everything got settled with Mimi, he planned to slip away and investigate the other, smaller set of ruins. For a little while. To make sure his hands weren't going to light up again. He needed to understand what had happened to him today. Maybe he could get Sting and Diana to come with him? Help him make sense of it.

WASHING DISHES HADN'T BEEN Peter's idea of contributing to Mimi's operation. Peter grumbled, terra cotta tiles slick underneath the grey boots that Diana had given to him. Steam rose in the long, narrow dish room beside the kitchen, turning the little white room into a sauna. He wore a white apron over his jeans and grey T-shirt and shifted two trays of water glasses into the dishwasher.

In the kitchen, Mimi worked with Diana and a couple of underground operatives that were helping her cook food tonight. They were all busy preparing a bunch of food for some gathering that Mimi had planned for tonight about 2000 hours. Tasting food and discussing the stations that had been attacked.

And Peter was supposed to be there.

Peter's blond hair was plastered against his forehead, the smell of lemons and soap heavy in the air as he shifted a stack of ceramic burgundy platters off the stainless-steel counter. They were hot and heavy and he struggled to get them into the kitchen before they burned all his fingers off. But he managed to stack them on the silver shelving beside the grill station and the two operatives. Marinated meat and fish sizzled across the steamy grill.

After he'd stacked a tray of gold coffee mugs beside the coffeemaker that sat across from the sauté station where Peter smelled garlic and butter browning, he picked up a slick grey tub of dirty dishes and carried them into the dish room. He loaded them into the compartment behind the glasses and turned on the machine. Finishing everything Mimi had asked him to do.

Sting was outside fixing one of the skimmers with Sarge.

It was just after 1800 hours. He had plenty of time to visit the ruins before Mimi's gathering.

He tossed his white apron smeared with tomato sauce and something nasty and purple into the bin and hurried away from the dish room. For a moment, he paused outside the kitchen, the savory spices and grilling marinades making his stomach growl as he watched Diana rushing around. Trying to finish the food in time for the gathering. He sighed. She was too busy to come with him to the ruins.

He'd tell her all about it tonight. After he got back. After the gathering.

Backing away, he hurried into the dining room. Toward the front doors. They were locked on the outside, but he could still leave through them. No one would miss him for an hour or two.

Casting a last glance back at the restaurant, he made sure no one was there to stop him. He groaned. Or make him wash more dishes. But everyone was way too busy to notice him slip out the front doors and hurry through the rocks into the desert landscape beside End of the Line. Toward the small set of ruins that was about a five-minute walk south.

He turned left beside a tall rock formation that cast cool black shadows across the prickly brown and yellow brush that grew stiff and tall against the rocks and headed across the sand. Toward a rock face in the distance. And the umber and sandstone formations behind it that ringed a small set of spires. A triangle formation. Three short spires connected with those honeycombed plates, most of them covered in dust and sand. And tumbleweeds as Diana called them.

The sun glared overhead, making him sweat as he plodded away from the southern edge of Civilization. Where thin patches of stringy yellow grass grew, looking grizzled and sunbaked, the air gritty and smelling of dust and chalky with ore residue. Mining shift would change about 1900 hours, sending shuttles and skimmers shooting across the desert as the sun sank low on the horizon. Far from where he walked, but visible from every part of town as the colored lights flickered on behind the white arc of the shuttle track and miners filled up the pubs and bars.

Shadowed in crisp late afternoon shade, the small triangular structure rose out of the sand and rocks. That smooth, cool metal defied the brutal sunlight that never stopped shining on the desert sand and grass.

When he got about a hundred feet away from the ruins, he felt the soft thrum of vibrations in the sand. Shuddering. Coming in waves that rolled through the brush. And vibrated into his chest, down into his hands.

He held them up, expecting them to glow again, but no lights colored his skin. His hands.

But as he got closer, he felt the ruins fluttering awake. Something he'd never felt before today. Before they lit up his hands.

The rhythm continued, deepening as he reached the closest point of the triangular layout. Even the honeycombed plates began to vibrate as he walked across them. Toward the next set of small spires pointing at the sky.

He hesitated a moment but then reached out to the closest spire.

The metal was cool. Soothing against his fingers. Dampening the heat building through his body from the bright, burning sun that baked the landscape. Everything except the strange metal of these spires.

The rhythm in the honeycombed plates quickened. And he felt it deeper in his chest. Beating. Pulsing. Like his heart only faster. More frenetic.

He squinted at the plates. At the spires. At the whole structure as he turned north. He could just make out End of the Line in the distance. Just past a few rock formations and some scraggly brush.

The first bright cyan light lit the spire he touched. Startling him.

It bled down the length of the spire and spilled into the other two. Pulsing in time to the rhythm in the honeycombed plates.

He stared, stunned, watching the light seep across the honeycombs, peeking through the dust and sand as it moved into the next point in the triangle. Lighting up that cluster of short spires. Flashing in unison with the first bunch.

"Pete? What are you doing?"

Sting's voice startled him.

He jumped, turning around.

Sting stood there, face smeared with black grease, tan camos dusty, faded blue T-shirt smudged with dirt, his blond curls loose around his face. Sting's green eyes were wide and intense as he stared at the lights.

"I just touched them, Sting," he said and held out his hands, sounding apologetic. "I swear, I didn't do anything else but touch them."

Sting watched the lights travel across the plates and reach the final point in the triangle formation. Turning it bright cyan. All three points flashed together and then the lights began to strobe, rushing across the structure in a strange pattern of movement. Like it had been programmed to follow a certain path through the spires.

"What's happening to it?" Sting asked with a gasp as he watched the light show.

"I wish I knew," said Peter, shaking his head.

For a moment, the ruins went dark and then they lit up with that cyan light again. And stayed lit.

"It's...on now," said Sting who turned back to Peter. "The light. But Pete—what else turns on with the lights?"

Peter shook his head. "I have no idea. That's what scares me, too."

Sting gasped and pointed toward the west. "Pete, look!"

In the distance, across the desert floor, cyan light burned as the sun slipped closer to the horizon.

"There's another ruin lit!" Sting cried, squinting. "There, across the desert." He whirled around and grabbed Peter by the shoulders. "Pete, you tell me what you did!"

Peter shook his head. "Sting, I didn't do anything but touch the ruins. Honest."

"Your touch apparently makes these things come to life," said Sting as he glanced at the ruins across the desert and then the ones beside him. "But what do they do?"

Peter sighed. He had no idea what these things did. Or where those lights had come from. Just that they had responded to his touch and turned on.

"And look, way in the distance!" Sting pointed again. "Another one."

"Sting, they turning on all across the planet!" Peter gripped Sting's shoulder. "Why? How could I do that? Me? I'm just a recombinant."

Sting pulled him into a hug and ruffled his hair. "Wish I knew,

Pete. But we ought to get back before we find out what these things do after they're lit up like this."

Sting had a good point. What if it was a beacon of some kind? Drawing the Antarans to Civilization? That thought terrified him.

"Let's get back to the restaurant," said Peter as Sting let him go.

Sting walked close beside him as he hurried away from the ruins. He hadn't expected them to light up like this. He'd expected his hands to light up, but not the whole structure like this. Much less ruins all across the desert. He winced. The planet.

"Fast," Sting said. "Before something bad happens."

Something surged across the sky, engines lit bright orange, its vector tight as it streaked north toward the shuttle port. Leaving a trail like the tail of a comet behind.

"Whoa!" Sting cried and stopped, pointing at the sky. "You see that?"

Peter nodded. "What was it?"

"Doesn't look like any craft I've seen land around here," said Sting, watching it fall out of the sky.

Another strange object shot across the sky toward Civilization, a burning trail of smoke rising. Like it was on a collision course for the stretch of desert west of town.

All around them, like meteorites, a bunch of those strange objects fell out of the sky in bursts of orange and red. They had a round shape. But they weren't meteorites.

"Those aren't ships, are they?" said Peter as they reached the little footpath that wound back toward the restaurant.

Sting shook his head. "Don't think so."

At the foot of the restaurant steps, Peter saw Sarge and Diana watching the sky. Sarge had a pair of binoculars pointed at the sky.

Peter and Sting ran toward them.

"Sarge? Diana?" Peter shouted. "What are those things?"

"My God," Sarge said in a quiet voice as he lowered the binoculars, staring at them like it was the end of the world. "Those are escape pods."

Sting frowned. "From where, Sarge?"

"Looks like the escape pods used at our orbital bases," said Sarge, looking sick. "Has there been another attack?"

Diana shook her head as she glanced back at the restaurant. "No one's mentioned another attack. Mimi would have said something."

"C'mon," said Sarge, motioning them into the restaurant. "We'd better check with the underground and with the nearby bases. What if it was Dr. Kingston's station? It was right next to the one attacked earlier."

Peter slid his hand into Diana's and followed Sting and Sarge into End of the Line. Those escape pods meant that there had been another attack. And this one had to be close. Was it the station that Dr. Kingston and Dr. Drew worked at? He hoped not. And he hoped they were both okay.

5

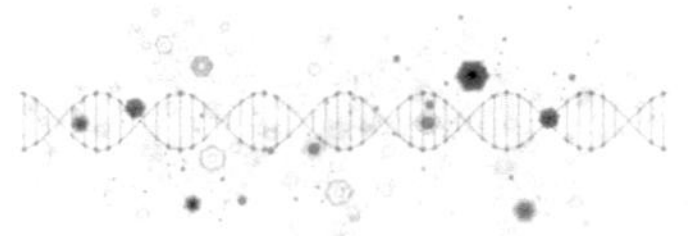

DR. JEANETTE KINGSTON glanced up at the large digital clock perched high on the tall, composite grey walls of the cavernous reclamation chamber. It was 0254 station time. She groaned.

Twenty-six minutes until third shift ended.

She stared at the shiny grey walls reflecting light and the clock's green numbers onto the dark grey floors and the chamber's high ceilings. The endless sea of grey made everything blend together, but third shift felt like shining a flashlight into a black hole. Especially now that she'd had her MRC removed.

Sometimes the light even reached the enclosed observation deck above that seated about two dozen people or so. Always empty, it overlooked the *reclamation theatre* (as Kai called it) below as the grim tasks of recovery and exhumation went on 24/7, 365 days a year in the belly of Reclamation Station 343-AOD. Throughout the cavernous room, the theatre grid, comprised of endless quads of exhumation and recovery stations, clustered around a complex maze of conveyor belts that circled above the floor and ran down to each quad. Bright white lights scalded the greyness, the rumble of the conveyor belts constant as they brought a steady but complex influx and outflow of body bags.

Jeannette had no idea where the bags went after leaving the reclamation theatre. And she didn't want to know either. She'd seen enough dead recombinants and citizen soldiers to last a lifetime.

She shifted one red body bag onto the conveyor belt and then another one, her last of the day, onto her exam table. Her unit only had four specialists mixed in with the techs on the grid this shift. Unusual, but she wouldn't argue with Stanton over something like under-scheduling specialists. No, she'd take her observation to the data and see what the numbers said about Stanton's decision to understaff her shift.

Thousands of recombinants and citizen soldiers passed through stations like this one every single day. Dozens and dozens of human specialists exhumed, processed, and routed patented and secret mission-critical hardware to classified hands while techs handled the unclassified tasks. Specialists also routed copyrighted artificial nucleobases and genetic sequencing tracking data from recombinants to other secure locations. Despite the high stakes, highly complex genetics, and technology, Stanton seemed to have fewer and fewer specialists on the grid. Like it was no longer important.

Jeannette wanted to know why.

She glanced up at the clock again. 0259. Twenty-one minutes until shift change. Her stomach began to flutter, her nervousness spiking.

And her first date with Dr. Kai Drew.

She unzipped the red bag down to the recombinant's shoulders. Red for recombinants. Blue for citizens. Scanning the attached tag, she checked the basic information against visual observation, looking at the recombinant's face, ensuring that everything matched the bag's tag. If they still had a face. She'd looked into so many of their faces, her MRC removing the pain of seeing so much death.

Recombinants had been developed and cloned by the thousands, protecting Earth, and keeping the Antarans on the farthest edge of the Taus system. But it still hurt every time she looked into their eyes and stared death in the face. They were human, so they still felt emotions, they still bled, and they still hurt when they died.

This recombinant was female. Five-foot-seven, short curly dark hair. Dark skin. Dark brown eyes. Her frozen, coffee-brown stare was empty, looking past Jeannette's left shoulder. At first look, the recombinant's injuries appeared minor, but the bag felt too light.

She pulled down the sleeves of her grey lab coat, butter yellow scrubs clinging to the goosebumps rolling across her arms and legs. Her short, dark red hair was netted and covered by a warm grey skull cap. The reclamation chamber was always so cold.

The station clock reflected 0303 on the aft wall—seventeen minutes until shift change.

Her teeth chattered as she daubed lavender oil under her nose and then completely unzipped the bag. Peeling back its flaps.

The recombinant's dark curls were heavy with black, congealed blood and spongy remnants of...she groaned...brain matter. Despite the clean scent of lavender and her clear protection visor, the stench of death slipped through dried blood, decaying flesh, and the sharp, bitter scent of germicide.

Everything felt so different without her memory replacement chip. Degrees different. But despite the sensations and feelings being genuinely different—and deadlier—had the Antarans created something larger? Deadlier?

Overcoming her gag reflex, Jeannette tilted the recombinant's chin to the left, her eyes narrowing to slits as she picked up forceps and worked through separating the woman's dark curly hair from the spongy bits of brain and hard slivers of bone from any UCOE hardware that had survived.

When Jeannette got deeper into the tangles of hair, her stomach dropped. Hair and bone were tangled, grey matter everywhere.

Her stomach twisted into knots, clear latex gloves squeaking against the tissue resin separator as she flicked on the power. Its brilliant blue-white beam glimmered against the minty germicide constantly misting the aluminum exam table.

Reaching up to the virtual computer interface that floated above the table, she flicked her index finger across the search parameters for locating MRCs. She set the beam's width to its thinnest possible setting.

As she calibrated the beam, she tested it against a sim setting. Satisfied, she turned on the separator.

Station time was 0310.

This case would take longer than ten minutes. At least Kai would understand her reason for being late.

The separator trilled at its highest pitch, a soft soprano warble as Jeannette held her breath, steadying her hand. With slow, deliberate movements, she cut through hair, the resistance lowering the pitch and turning the laser light a pale blue.

The smell of burnt flesh mixed with the stink of hot, congealed blood as she cut through the layers. She concentrated on the hint of lavender oil under her nose, the one she daubed before opening each body bag. It didn't eliminate the awful smells, but it blunted the profound stench of death and distanced her from the raw reek of decay.

She'd just cut through the skull remains, the laser's pitch whining a quiet alto note, the beam a deep Pacific blue, when the separator warbled up the scale to a steady soprano note as the laser light's deep blue faded to a crisp white light. All resistance stopped as the sensor located one single shard of the recombinant's splintered MRC.

Everything else was gone.

She sighed. This young recombinant had been twenty-two when UCOE progressed her into a soldier and then sent her to a training base bound for Ku'Tal. Eleven days after passing her training sims and landing on Ku'Tal, she was dead. Eviscerated didn't even begin to cover it. The damage was way worse than that. Biodrones AND cascade mines maybe? No. She winced. This recombinant was torn apart by something far worse and far deadlier.

What had done this?

She thought about when Diana Temple had worked for her at the training base, asking the recombinants with affected MRCs questions. Of all those recombinants, only two had data points for being gentle and emotional, qualities she'd only seen twice in recombinants so far. She remembered Peter Mitchell, that sweet, kind young recombinant that had just wanted to live, to experience everything the world offered—and love Diana, the fiery young shuttle pilot that had helped Jeannette gather recombinant data. The other was Mitchell's loyal best friend, John Stingley, who had defended Peter like a mother grizzly with cubs.

And later, after Jeanette had listened to Mimi Constantine's experiences and interacted with recombinants they had rescued, she realized that none of them were rabid killing machines like she'd been told.

Like UCOE wanted them to believe.

Jeannette's heart rate quickened at the memory of entering Private Peter Mitchell's status as just another dead recombinant on Ku'Tal. And his friend, John Stingley, as KIA. Peter and Stingley mattered and Jeannette loved the fact that she'd helped Peter escape the military—into Diana Temple's arms. With John Stingley finally at his side—or so she had learned from a trusted source. A recombinant she would be meeting with soon. Jeannette smiled. About a job.

Well, she cared and so did a lot of others. And she wanted to know what they'd done to this recombinant on her table. The one she'd just labeled Rena 7221. She named the women Rena, after her daughter, and the men Dylan after her dead ex-husband. Because all these recombinants mattered.

What had this recombinant seen before she died? She wanted to acknowledge this recombinant's life. Rena 7221's life. RDC didn't include recombinant given names when they died, just a barcode and a corpse number. But Jeannette wanted to recognize that this young woman had lived, even if it was only for four months and eleven days.

Jeannette turned the young woman's face to the right and picked up the tissue resin separator. Using slow, precise movements, Jeannette guided the separator laser, its blue and white beam whining through hair and bone, the burning smell upsetting her stomach. Using slow, precise movements, she cut through more thick tangles of curls, skull remnants, grey matter, and hardened tissue until, beneath those shiny curls the color of walnuts, she found the other side of the body bag.

The back of the young woman's head was missing.

Wincing, Jeanette bit her lip and looked away. No, it was gone!

There was no adequate way to say it. Or describe the moment of realization. Everything that made humans feel, react—love—was missing from Rena 7221's head. Three pounds of flesh shredded and scattered. Where she had once created, connected, and collected the moments of her short life, events, people, and places inside this three-pound storage compartment. Where she had conjured, cherished, and contained the dreams and actions that made her human. Like every other human being, she had caressed, cared, and crusaded for the people she'd loved, for a place she called home—even if it had been a barracks and a cot. She'd fought—and died—for the human right to live and love.

Jeannette shuddered. How could she have ever agreed to insert brain hardware that stole all these memories from her, all these feelings, and all the people she'd loved when losing them hurt the most. Even with all the pain and loss and emptiness.

Grief was the final act of love—even if Jeannette had delayed it all these years, storing it away in another compartment when she couldn't handle the raw, stabbing ache rising out of the blackest holes of loss and the physical stab of pain that came from every memory and every regret. Grief was like rereading the best book of her life— about the one she lost—turning page after page of its beginning, middle, and end. An end that she knew would rip her heart out with every memory leading up to that last breath.

But as time blunted the sharpness and acuity, she found that she could go back and read it again. And that it wouldn't hurt quite as much as did the last time. Until finally, she could read it cover to cover and remember why she loved it, what she lost, and what she carried away with her when she closed the book.

By letting her MRC capture the memories and lock them away, Jeannette had let go of the one thing that had helped the most. Time to heal. And remember.

Good or bad, she'd remember this tomorrow.

With all its judgments and uncertainties. And all those conflicting emotions. At the same time, she'd remember how numb her fingertips felt using the tissue resin separator. How intense the bluish-white beam was, making her eyes water.

She glanced over at the reclamation station across from hers, her heart fluttering as she watched Dr. Kai Drew input his observations for the recombinant on his table as he reported the facts. His jet-black hair peeked out from his blue skull cap, shining in the white light, those intense blue eyes laser bright. A layer of interaction she hadn't even noticed was missing in him until she'd had her MRC removed. A layer that said so much about the man he was, the man she needed.

"Cranial cavity—compromised," she spoke into the computer. "No, it isn't compromised, it's freaking missing. Like the back half of her body. She wasn't just killed. She was massacred. This wasn't a cascade mine—it was a damned crate of cascade mines carried in by a platoon of biodrones!"

She felt the room go quiet until only the thump and whirr of the conveyor belts echoed through the cavernous space and across the grid. Amber Bao, Amit Gravinder, and Kai Drew, the reclamation specialists in her unit for third shift, were staring at her.

The station clock read 0313. Seven minutes to shift change.

"And magically," Jeannette continued her ridiculous required verbal analysis, "one teeny tiny little shard of Rena 7221's MRC was found where her brain stem should have connected to her diencephalon. I took real good care of the MRC shard, too. Yes, I did. Wrapping it in layers and layers of anti-static film and labeling it oh, so carefully and clearly. Rena number 7221, aged four months and eleven days. Cause of death: shredded like cheddar."

Specialist Amber Bao, at the station in front of Jeannette, glanced up from her exam table, looking more amused than shocked.

"Can't rule out the presence of a wood chipper on the battlefield," Jeannette continued. "Just like the last dozen or so recombinants that came through my station. Like the excessive damage we've all been reporting for weeks and no one's advised or even responded. Address this! Now. Before Earth wakes up one morning to find Antarans on their doorsteps, right next to the Almond Milk and cinnamon scones. And this analysis easily completes Stanton's quota. Which wasn't needed or necessary. End record. Close."

She zipped up the red body bag and slid it onto the conveyor belt. The last reclamation of her shift.

She pulled off her grey cap and protective visor, freeing her short, reddish auburn hair. It fluffed around her face as she removed her gloves, throwing them into the round, green bio-hazard bin that stood at the end of her station.

"Reclamation Specialist Kai Drew. Reclamation results for 7491, male," Kai began, the tension in the room draining as Amit's deep voice joined Kai's as they completed exhumation reports.

Kai zipped up the last red body bag he'd slid off the aluminum holding shelves and slid it onto the ubiquitous conveyor belt. His deep blue scrubs hugged his leanly muscled body as the bag squeaked and rasped, the belt tugging the bag into the endless line of bags headed toward the main tract. His matching blue skull cap hid his thick, jet-black hair that she longed to run her fingers through and feel the silky locks against her cheeks. His big blue eyes were LED bright and mesmerizing as he turned back to the computer.

Jeannette saw the clock change to 0316 as she stepped into his cube in the unit's quad, her pale, yellow scrubs complementing his deep blue scrubs—and those leading man eyes, lush dark eyelashes framing them with mischief as he smirked at her. He motioned her over to stand beside him.

She shuffled her feet, still muffled by sterile yellow shoe covers that kept them from passing harmful bacteria and viruses throughout the station.

"Hey, Kai," she said, smiling at his handsome face, sexy stubble shadowing his strong jaw, giving his oval face a soft expression. "Just finished my quota."

"Same," said Kai as he reached up to the floating computer interface.

He leaned against the empty exam table, his pale blue eyes electric in the pools of stinging white light that drenched his reclamation station (half of them unused and vacant on third shift), so brilliant against the grey walls and dim lit reclamation station's belly where only third shifters (and staff that had pissed off Stanton) worked.

He looked tired, watching the lone red body bag disappear onto the main belt where the bag merged with the line of hundreds of other red bags above them and disappeared into the endless sea of dead bodies. The main conveyor belt thumped and whirred as it climbed up toward the observation deck with its invisible watchers seated like spirits at the opera. It chugged along, moving in and out of the maze of body bags as it moved through the bowels of the station on an unending journey. Probably to the morgue bay's ships.

She cringed. Or the incinerator.

Kai crossed his arms, looking disgusted. Barely thirty-one, Kai was six feet tall and soldier-lean from his days as a front-line medic and years as one of UCOE's top fighter pilots. Dr. Kai Drew was hotter than fireworks in Death Valley. He took her breath away.

"Y'know, I'm not sure if I should feel insulted or relieved by Stanton's quota." His voice was barely above a whisper.

He smiled as he slid off his skull cap, thick jet-black hair almost blue in the clear white light bathing his reclamation station. God, she wanted to drown in that silky black hair, faded up the sides and at his nape.

Like her, he'd left his safe place on Earth and volunteered. Because he'd believed in the cause. Not the thriving war economy that made a few people rich while so many young men and women died. Even though they were created in a lab.

"Definitely insulted," said Jeannette. "Over half these recombinants are missing their MRCs. And most of their heads and torsos. The rest are obliterated and beyond extraction."

He sighed. "So, Stanton's just trying to waste our time," he said with a growl. "Hoping we'll quit."

Kai had been one of UCOE's best and youngest fighter pilots until everything came apart at Ku'Tal. Antaran technology rendered most of UCOE's war front and bleeding edge technologies useless. He returned to practicing medicine, this time as a front-line field medic and being part of the med-evac squads. Captured and tortured by the Antarans, he managed to escape by stowing away on a freighter. Someone had told Jeannette that story, but she wanted to hear it from him. Maybe that's why he'd kept his MRC? Not wanting to remember those days?

"Guess she doesn't realize who she's dealing with, does she, Kai?" Jeannette said with a grin.

"Got that right," he said in a soft voice, his eyes brightening. "We still on for tonight, Red?"

She nodded. "We are. I've got a nice bottle of Merlot for the occasion."

"Real wine? My favorite. Oh, and nice analysis on Rena 7221. I'm feeling inspired." The corners of his mouth quirked into a grin as he pulled off his gloves and tossed them in the small green bio-waste bin at the end of his station. The clear plastic lid opened just wide enough for the gloves and then closed.

He turned back to the computer interface above the table.

"Unpause report. Recombinant number 7491's analysis is

complete. This report puts me easily over the imposed and insulting quota by more than fifteen recombinants, making said quota look ridiculous and unnecessary."

She grinned. That was the Kai she knew. Didn't take shit from anyone. And didn't pretend things like stupid quotas were acceptable. It had been about two weeks since Stanton had moved them both to third shift and imposed an insulting quota so low a specialist on her first day would easily achieve it. And she'd demoted Kai from shift coordinator to specialist. Stanton said it was insubordination, but Jeannette and Kai knew better.

But tonight was their first date. After third shift ended.

Still, she and Kai should have gotten a medal for performing extensive research on live recombinants to assess the batches of MRC errors they'd encountered while extracting UCOE technology. The results were clear. RDC had been reissuing and reusing old MRCs rather than implanting new ones.

With disastrous results.

Together, they had decided to use Stanton's disciplinary action against her, gathering insertion (and reinsertion) data from every MRC as well as observational data from cloned soldiers. Together, she and Kai had gathered reams of data from the cloned soldiers, hoping to find more errors—and more Antaran code.

They had even managed to gather data from Stanton herself and her cadre of advisors.

Jeannette glanced up at the clock and groaned. Damn! 0318. Two minutes. This shift was never going to end!

"Due to the unforeseen complication," Kai continued his report, "of this recombinant losing his cranial cavity, both lobes of his brain, and well, most of his limbs and internal organs, cause of death has been very difficult to determine. MRC failure due to the device and its accompanying organ failing to operate while missing, all data-gathering procedures have also failed. But not my quota! Still, I have determined that for 7491, I've named him Steve by the way, his cause of death is: shredded. Like Mozzarella. You know, the fancy kind. No hardware enclosed. End record. Close."

Kai let out a belly laugh, the sound warm and infectious.

"Like the fancy kind," Jeannette said with a laugh. "Stanton will be fuming when she hears that."

"Mission accomplished then," said Kai. "It's now 0322," he said in a soft voice.

"And this shift's finally over," Jeannette replied with a sharp exhale. "Let's get out of here."

"It sure is," Kai said with a nod. He moved so close to her that his lips brushed against her ear, sending chills down her back. "Race you to detox?"

"You're on," Jeannette replied.

"Just let me launch a sanitize and shutdown on my station first," said Kai, rolling his eyes as he reached up and tapped through the task lists visible on his overhead display.

He highlighted several tasks and his finger hovered over *initiate*.

"Wouldn't want to get written up. But maybe I should just shut down the life support systems and conserve oxygen in case we get called down to her storeroom office."

Jeannette rolled her eyes. "You can't shut down life support from here."

"Can to," he snapped. "But just down here in the theatre and store room."

"Prove it," said Jeannette.

He motioned her over to his station, sliding open the menu's maintenance option. Right there on the screen was the life support systems shut down.

Jeannette shook her head. "That shouldn't be part of maintenance."

Kai just shrugged. In a moment, his smile returned as he pivoted around the edge of the exam table and turned his body toward the double doors leading out of the chamber and to the lift.

"Loser buys the first round."

Jeannette laughed as the sanitization sequence launched across his exam table, its shiny silver surface and bright overhead lighting misting all the surfaces with sterile compounds as the fine minty spray of bitter germicide at his station turned off. Overhead, the last two body bags disappeared on the conveyor belt into the station.

Tonight, the last body bag was blue—a citizen. She wondered if that citizen had been like the other recombinants tonight. Shredded like cheddar. Missing their brain and half their body.

The last two reclamation exam stations' lights snapped off, the clear white afterimage trailing like smoke that disappeared across the chamber's smooth grey composite walls as germicide misters shut down, the strong mint and germicide smell beginning to dissipate. At last, the room became dark and cavernous again. The muffled tick of shoe covers shuffled up the lit aisle, the sound rising in thick layers above the steady thump and whirr of conveyor belts as the dozens and dozens of third-shift staff members headed toward detox and the exit. The reclamation chamber was so eerily quiet at this hour with only half the number of specialists on duty and half the number of techs to support them.

She glanced at the large shift clock reflecting 0324 in green throughout the room as Specialist Amber Bao walked beside Jeannette, grinning as she removed her protective visor and hot pink skull cap, her hands bare. She wore baggy hot pink scrubs, her thin, five-foot-two, barely twenty-three-old body hidden beneath the scrubs' loose, wrinkled folds. Her thick, straight bob was a deep metallic blue, framing her oval face and brown eyes.

Specialist Amit Gravinder walked beside her, a white lab coat over his tan scrubs. His hair was chocolate brown like his kind, wide-set eyes.

"Best thing that ever happened to me was getting you and Kai on third shift," said Amber. "We always finish on time now. And we have three times more fun, too."

Kai laughed, bowing his head.

"Amber, what were you saying about those ruins," said Amit as he shut down his computer and turned off the systems in his pod, hurrying to catch up with them.

"Just that they found more on Farnas and Civilization. Tangled in the brush on Farnas. Under the sand on Civilization."

"Under the sand?" Kai replied. "On Civilization? That's all that's on Civilization. Well, that and miners."

"Wish they'd find out what they do instead of finding more ruins," said Amit.

"Agreed," said Kai.

Jeannette glanced up as the clock flashed 0326. Moments before an explosion ripped through the station.

Everything went dark. Station tilted violently.

Jeannette and Kai fell backward into Amber as Amit rolled toward them.

Station stabilizers wrenched back on like the twist of rusted screws. The station rolled back upright again. Tossing all four of them against the far wall. Beside the double doors—the exit.

Metal rasped metal. A deep moan echoed through the station, the sound growing sharp, echoing in layers through the structure like the angel of death reciting last rites.

Kai grabbed hold of the door handle and pulled Jeannette against his side, his left arm like a steel band around her waist. Amber and Amit grabbed hold of the other door.

Red and white lights streaked past the rows of tiny portals, leaving trails of dust and plasma as glowing lights flashed in yellows and reds. Small bullet-shaped ships zipped past the portals from all sides, in all directions as the station rocked forward and back again. The screech and twist of its structure as it tried to resist the plasma cannons and missiles pounding the station from a hundred different directions.

The massive strike force of bullet-shaped fighters surged toward the reclamation station, unleashing hullsplitters that cut through the unshielded station walls during the few moments of blackout caused by the explosions.

Lights and forcefields flickered green and went dark for only moments at a time. But those fleeting moments were enough to split the station's hull in strategic locations and plant more explosives.

As the protective shield fluttered blue and held, the hullsplitters and fighters rushed off, drawing fire away from the small, dark grey bioinjector ships that injected the first wave of biodrones onto the station.

Two of the stations' upper levels buckled and collapsed. Two levels below them imploded.

Half the reclamation station went dark and silent, the silence spreading like a deadly virus through the station as whole sections collapsed in thick black coils of smoke that swirled through the passageways as each section lost its artificial gravity and comfort controls.

Including the reclamation theatre grid.

Jeannette felt her body floating as the station tilted, tossing her toward the exhumation stations.

"Attention, all personnel, please report to your assigned escape—"

The comm went dead and silent.

"Kai! Where are you?" Jeannette called out to her shift partner as dust and darkness filled the dim-lit cavernous reclamation chamber. "Kai! Answer me!"

The silence was deafening, her whole body taut and aching at the silence.

Former fighter pilot turned reclamation specialist wasn't responding.

Another cascade of explosions rippled through the station as it began to bob like a fishing lure.

Jeannette grabbed hold of the body bag conveyor belt and used it to pull her weightless body down to one of the reclamation stations.

"Techs! Specialists!" she shouted. "Everyone, report. Now!"

Jeannette gripped the shiny exam table like a life preserver, watching the ghostly images of techs struggle toward her in torn, dusty orange scrubs. Weathering out the station's sudden, nauseating shifts.

"Amber and Amit, report!" Jeannette called. "KAI!"

"I'm—right here, Red," said the weak, frail voice somewhere behind her, floating through the clouds of dust and debris to settle near her left shoulder. "I'm…on your six."

Thank God there were only four reclamation specialists and six technicians on duty from her unit tonight.

"Dalinta, Pearson, Specialist Bao, and Specialist Garvinder," Jeannette shouted, her voice cutting through the thick dust and heavy fear. "Respond."

All four responded with *here*. Four accounted for. She made five and she'd heard Kai's voice nearby. Still four left.

She counted the others as they gathered around her station, holding onto it. Lin and Rubesh joined Specialist Bao. Toliver and Garcia floated out of the darkness and crowded around her as body bags floated off conveyor belts and dead recombinants rose from exam tables.

Then she saw Kai holding onto his reclamation station. Relief washed over her.

She had visuals on all ten. They were all safe.

Another explosion ripped through the station's central shaft. Shock waves rolled through the orbital base.

Groaning, the entire station shifted forward and back again.

Lights flickered. Kai looked up from his station as a red body bag floated off the conveyor belt and into the darkness.

Kai was hurt. She saw the pain in his face.

"Jeannette!" he called out as systems and equipment began powering up and down all around them.

"Kai, don't move," she called. "I'll come to you."

"Careful, Red," he replied through gritted teeth, his voice echoing across the expanse. "Take it slow."

She liked it when Kai called her Red, but his dire tone made her heart race with fear. For years, she'd colored her hair ash blond to hide her natural red-auburn hair. Her MRC had helped her forget why. Now that she'd gotten Mimi Constantine to remove hers, she remembered her decisions—and all the times that Kai had flirted with her over her *red* auburn hair.

In moments, gravity returned. Her feet thumped against the floor, crew falling against tables as she grabbed hold of a cart to steady herself.

And turned toward Kai's station.

Alarms screeched, red lights flashing as she struggled toward him, the composite grey floor slick.

Again, the station shifted, stabilizers kicking in until the structure had leveled out.

Techs bolted away as the corpse carts toppled over, red and blue body bags sliding off carts and shelves. More body bags launched off conveyor belts, skittering across the floors. Dust mixed with darkness and blue emergency lights that lit paths to exits or shelters.

Com channels crackled with terrified voices. Silenced floor by floor as bulkheads slammed shut.

Jeannette's gut twisted into aching knots. They were closing bulkheads, cutting off compromised sections to preserve the rest of the station's integrity.

She winced. All those people...she smashed her eyes closed...were—they just gone now? All those prominent specialists and their years and years of expertise in Antaran physiology and technology. She shuddered.

Just—gone.

If she and Kai hadn't ninja-investigated those anomalies in batches of recombinant hardware (including their memory replacement chips), Stanton wouldn't have moved them to third shift. She and Kai would have been on those upper levels right now.

Asleep. Trapped. Asphyxiating.

She rubbed her eyes. They'd both be dead now.

The station rocked forward and back. As gravity evaporated again.

She closed her eyes and hugged the struts anchoring the exam table to the grid floor.

Behind her, Amber and Amit tried to calm six techs as she struggled toward Kai's station. He was the only one in danger right now.

She had to get to him. Alive. She had to!

Metal scraped metal. The sound was almost deafening.

She grabbed her protective visor that hung around her neck and slid it onto her face. it provided minimal protection, but for a few moments, it distracted her as she held onto her exam table.

As the station rocked forward and back again, she held tight to the shiny, L-shaped exam table bolted to the floor between two shelving units.

She looked at her feet dangling in the darkness, the Observation deck a pale light near the ceiling which was the floor now. It was a long way down to the ceiling. If gravity kicked back in now, a fall from this height would be fatal.

"Kai! Please—answer me!" Her voice echoed in sharp, thin layers all through the chamber. "Make some kind of noise—anything—I need to know that you're still alive."

Sulfur and polymer burned. Drying blood congealed. The stench permeated walls, clothes, everything—even the darkness—as the bitter, minty smell of germicide floated through the abyss. Making her gag.

But the silence was deafening.

Thump and whirr of conveyor belts in the maze had gone silent and still as the station's grey chasms burned.

Bullet fighters screeched past the tilted, burning station, lasers and plasma fire strafing anything still lit and operational.

The rumbles and squeaks that had been a steady cacophony of movement and activity were absent now. The maze of conveyor belts was dark and silent. The remaining body bags were now an unmovable, frozen stream of endless dead. Most of the bags had floated off and had been flung through the cavernous chamber when gravity returned.

Somewhere in the distance, a single conveyor belt rattled and whined.

"Kai, where are you?" Jeannette called out through abyss, her heart slamming against her rib cage, desperate to hear his voice. "KAI!"

Was he lying below? Dead at the bottom of the cavernous, inverted space. The ceiling?

No, no, no! She pressed her hand over her eyes. She couldn't take it if she found Kai dead. He was the last thread that had kept her fighting, kept her opening one more body bag. The thought of losing him terrified her.

She was completely alone in the world, all her family gone. After Rena died, her marriage fell apart, her MRC picking up the pieces until she didn't remember the things she needed to recall.

The station rumbled and moaned as it listed to one side, metal grating metal. Explosions shook the station with bone-rattling force. Ships rushed past the port holes.

UCOE forces!

Jeannette couldn't hold back her grin. "Those were UCOE ships!"

"Oh, my, God!" Amber cried out. "Really?"

She nodded. "Yes! The tide on this battle just turned."

At last, the station's emergency structural leveling system activated, keeping the station from pitching forward into a death spiral. The whole station tilted like a weather buoy in an Atlantic super'cane—like Earth's constant storms that had long made much of its historic coastlines uninhabitable.

"Kai! Answer me!" Jeannette shouted across the cavernous room as debris floated past. "Where! Are! You!"

Pale blue emergency lighting winked out and kicked in again, outlining walkways and exits as the conveyors along the perimeter ground against metal and debris and hung as blue and red body bags rolled off more belts.

Another explosion shuddered above her.

Lights flickered. Power stations whined off and on.

She wrapped her arms tighter around the L-shaped exam table, holding onto it as the reclamation station's composite frame moaned and shifted. Shifted with the upper decks. Jolting into a violent ninety-degree angle.

That's when the strange thought entered her head. Had Stanton somehow planned this attack? Just to kill two specialists who knew too much about her operation? An attack that would quickly and conveniently wipe out all the data scattered between her and Kai.

Would this woman go that far, killing hundreds of people to cover up some sketchy data they'd collected? Or maybe she and Kai had found something else?

Something they didn't know they'd found. Yet.

First, Stanton instituted a ridiculous quota that had to be met every day. Something extremely low, like five or six bodies a day. And kept raising it. Then, to make it difficult, Stanton removed them from the coveted first shift and shuffled them into the station's belly because of the unsanctioned data-gathering mission she and Kai conducted, trying to uncover answers about batches of malfunctioning recombinants' brain tech (including their memory replacement chips).

A column of acrid black smoke spun out of several conveyor belt connection points. Unable to shift tagged and bagged bodies and reclaimed hardware into the huge, multi-bayed holding storage for incineration or burial, the machinery got hotter and hotter until the whole system began to smoke and catch fire.

The structure moaned again, rolling slowly through metered angles as the stabilizers struggled to hold position and bring the station back to its original position.

"Red...do you—hear me?" The sound of his weak, frail voice was barely audible.

"That was Kai again!" Amber's voice cut through the smoke and darkness.

Jeannette ripped the visor off her face and it hang around her neck. "Kai! Keep talking!"

She glanced around the grey darkness and searched for the direction of Kai's voice. How would she find him in all of this space?

"I'm—I'm here," he answered. "Right. Up. Here—Red."

The voice was behind her, floating through clouds of dust and debris to settle near her left shoulder.

"Where, Kai?"

"On—your six."

Jeannette whirled around, her right arm still gripping the table's struts that kept it bolted to the floor.

Through the thick dust, sharp smell of sulfur mixing with the intense burn of mint germicide, Jeannette saw the debris swirl in the air. And a hand reached through it.

"Kai, I see you! I see you!"

Reaching out as far as her body would stretch, Jeannette's fingers brushed across the tips of his fingers. Missed!

Amit grabbed hold of the struts and reached his hand out to her. "Amber, make a chain," he said.

Amber gripped Amit's hand tightly and stretched out into the darkness, floating.

"Jeannette, take my hand and you'll be able to reach him." Amber nodded toward her outstretched arm.

"Brilliant, Amit and Amber!"

Jeannette held onto Amber's hand with all the strength she could summon and reached out into the grey, gritty dark. Her hand wrapped around Kai's hand, his grip weak and shaky. She held onto him for all she was worth, pulling as hard as she could until Kai sailed through the thick, dusty air toward her.

"Kai—you're safe now. It's okay." Jeannette said in a quiet, comforting voice as Amit and Amber pulled the two of them in tandem toward the exam table.

"Looks like we're about to freefall through this bad boy," Kai said in a rough voice, ducking his head under the table.

Amber let out a shout as Amit bent beneath the exam table, his body covering her as things began to fall, the station struggling to tilt upright again.

Jeannette held Kai tight against her chest with her free arm and he gripped her body like a life preserver. His face was swollen, cuts and bruises mottling his handsome face. He closed his eyes, shuddering as one of those bullet ships screamed past the portals.

He looked so vulnerable, both his arms wrapped around her waist, those pale, electric blue eyes filling with moisture. It was pain, she realized, as he held onto her. With a quiet touch, his hand shaky, he reached up and traced his fingers over her cheekbones, down her nose, and across her lips. His touch was so soft and gentle as he stroked her short red hair, entwining the shiny strands around his fingers. He cupped her chin in his hand.

She smiled. "I had to find you," she said in a soft whisper.

"Why?" he asked, the corners of his mouth rising into a quick grin.

"Because, I don't want to fight the Antarans—or Stanton—alone, Kai," she said.

"Hearing my name on your lips was like poetry." His gaze studied her eyes, her face as he laughed. "I wanted to keep hearing it—over and over—but the pain in your voice kept me fighting to get to you," he said, his voice gravelly. "So, I don't have to fight Antarans alone either. Red."

He leaned into her, his body heat burning across her skin, reaching flashpoint as he kissed her so hard on the lips that the sensations vibrated into her feet.

Until a deep rumbling quaked through the station. Shaking everything until glass shattered. Cardboard containers crumbled.

"What's happening?" Amber shouted, clinging to Amit.

A horrible moan cut through the dark silence of the weightless abyss.

Dozens of ships screeched past the portholes. Bearing the UCOE green flag.

"More of our ships!" Jeannette cried out.

"Suck it, Antarans," Kai shouted in a thin, weak voice.

The silence faded as the familiar thump and whir of the conveyor belts spun up in a desperate whine of structural stabilizers that moaned like a great door creaking opening.

In an instant, the weightlessness disappeared and the station crept in small increments toward some semblance of equilibrium. With every jolt and twist, the world got heavier and heavier. Jeanette and Kai kept their position wedged underneath the exam tables with Amber and Amit and the techs.

Messages began to broadcast through the station.

"Please go to your assigned escape pod location and depart the station immediately."

As the message repeated, Jeannette glanced at the double doors that led out of the basement's recombinant theatre. To the right was a clear polymer screen frosted with red and white stripes. Behind that wall were the spherical escape pods with hazard harnesses and oxygen supplies that held about a dozen evacuees. The pods were programmed for the closest habitable site for touchdown. Most likely, they would land on the planet Civilization.

As soon as the station had settled enough for them to reach the exit doors, they had to get out of here. And get to the escape pods.

Walking felt odd after so much time in weightlessness. Jeannette felt clumsy and uncoordinated as she staggered with Kai behind Amber and Amit, the six techs buzzing around them like orange dragonflies, helping anyone struggling to walk.

Now that he was on his own two feet again, Jeannette saw how labored Kai's breathing was and how his gait looked like a drunk failing a field sobriety test. She slid her arm around his waist, letting him lean on her as they moved with slow, deliberate steps toward the double doors.

With every step, those doors felt farther and farther away. Kai needed medical attention and he needed it now. No, he needed a hospital and some much-deserved bedrest.

At last, Amit shoved open one of the double doors. A tech caught the door and held it open so Jeannette could get Kai through without causing him more pain. She felt him leaning on her more and more. By the time they entered the dim-lit hallway, they were under a full-on beige assault: beige tile floors, beige walls, and beige doors. To the right, a sign blinked red: *escape pods are loading now* on the frosted polymer wall.

"This way," Jeannette said, leading Kai and the others behind the frosted glass wall.

All along the wall were numbered portals with their hatches open. Revealing sixteen silver pods, the numbered hatches continuing around the hallway.

"Our unit's in B6," said Amber, pointing to the right.

Jeannette and the techs followed, Amit helping her get Kai inside the pod labeled B6 in bright white letters. She and Amit took turns lifting and swiveling Kai through the hatch and down into the dark pod. Inside, the dashboard with a com was off to the right and six drop harnesses were affixed on both sides of the pod walls.

"Sorry, Red," Kai said with a moan. "Guess I'm not much help, am I?"

"You're fine, Kai," she said, patting him on the shoulder. "It's just hard to maneuver inside this thing.

Jeannette locked him into a harness as Amber and Amit sat down across from him. The six techs slid into the seats in back and locked into a harness.

Two seats left.

"You should close your harness, Red," Kai said in a weak voice.

"In a minute," she said, staring at the two empty seats across from each other.

If those seats didn't get filled, someone had to manually start the launch sequence.

It seemed like forever before two reclamation specialists from first shift jumped into the last two seats opposite the escape hatch. First shift? They sat down across from one another and pulled down their drop harnesses. And stared straight ahead.

Jeannette frowned. She didn't hear their harnesses snap closed.

She didn't know either specialist. The young, red-haired second-shift guy called Arlen Greer was from somewhere in the Taus system. Greer was pale and stocky. Pelham was a thin, porcelain-delicate fortyish woman from Lunar Colony. Both were first shift. Pelham's hair was a tawny mix of blond and brown cut just below her chin.

The lights inside the pod began flashing red.

"Is that the thirty-second launch warning?" Kai asked, sounding so exhausted as he looked over at Jeannette and smiled. "Hold tight, Red. It's a rough ride. We'll be out before the station buckles around us. Landing's worse though."

She reached over, brushed the jet-black hair out of his eyes, and caressed his bruised cheek.

"Helluva first date, isn't it?" he said with a smirk.

Jeannette grinned. "It's one I definitely won't forget, Kai."

"Now, we'll be on Civilization and we can finally go see Mimi and ask those questions you want to ask."

"What questions?" Jeannette asked, shaking her head as she watched his expression.

Kai was still smirking. "From your MRC, remember? You wanted to know about your work on the Recombinant Defense Program with Mimi's brother, Orlando Constantine."

Jeannette felt the air leave her lungs, feeling like she'd been sucker-punched. Had she really worked on the Recombinant Defense Program—and at the Recombinant Development Center? With Mimi's brother? She had no memory of either of those activities, but the thought of helping produce a barbaric program that cloned soldiers and let them die for humanity made her sick.

"I sent you the relevant EVF captures weeks ago, Red," he said, worry darkening his eyes. "I marked them urgent, so they'd pop to the top of all your data feeds."

She sighed. She hadn't been able to watch any part of her past yet. It was all still so raw and hurt in ways she hadn't even dreamed of hurting.

Jeannette glanced up at the open hatch. Why hadn't it closed when every seat was full?

"Kai, the hatch is still open," she whispered, leaning toward his ear.

His expression slid from relaxed to apprehensive. "Thirty-second countdown hasn't even started yet," he whispered back.

"I'll check the control panel by the hatch. See what's up."

Jeannette rose from her seat and moved toward the hatch, grateful that she hadn't locked down her drop harness yet.

Pelham and Greer turned their gaze toward her as she paused.

Fear coiled around her spine and slithered a cold trail down her back. She paused, glancing at Greer and then Pelham.

Then the control panel.

Red intercom light blinked *off* beside its toggle switch.

She glanced at Pelham. Then Greer. But the red message that flashed on the screen made her glance back at it.

Launch command paused. Station critical. Estimated implosion in five point five minutes.

Her mouth went dry, her hands shaking.

"Waiting for someone?" Pelham called to her.

Lie! Make something up. Don't make them suspicious.

"Yeah, my tech isn't here yet. He's on B7."

"Maybe he arrived after you checked?" Greer offered in a flat voice.

"Maybe," she mumbled. "I'll give him another minute just in case."

"Don't wait too long," Pelham said. "The pod won't launch until everyone's in their seats."

Jeannette looked past the warning. Seeing a yellow message.

Sensors that detected harness lock overrides were on for seats six and twelve. Pelham and Greer.

Her skin crawled with goosebumps. Something was very wrong here.

The override/launch initiation button blinked blue on the console. Beside the general lockdown override button, flashing orange.

Blue and orange. Manual overrides because the system didn't recognize Pelham and Greer.

"John Stoneman, where are you!" she called, taking a long stride past the control panel. To the escape hatch. She poked her head out of the pod.

All the other pods had already launched. She began to shake.

Turning around, she stared at eight terrified people, two more that were emotionless, and one that was ready to kick some ass. She smiled. Kai. All of them had their harnesses locked—except Pelham and Greer.

Pretending to lose her balance, Jeannette reached out to the control panel. And pressed the orange button.

"What are you doing?" Greer demanded, glaring at her.

"Sorry, I'm still a little dizzy after losing gravity for so long."

She started back down the aisle, her finger raking across the control panel. Depressing the blue button. The one that would restart the launch sequence.

She left the intercom muted for now as she paused between Pelham and Greer.

"You need to strap in now," Pelham said. It sounded more like an order than a suggestion.

Jeannette smiled. "Headed there now. Hope Stoneman made it out in another pod."

She had to do this right. She wouldn't get a second chance.

Taking a deep breath, she feigned another dizzy spell and pretended to fall.

"Jeannette!" Kai shouted, fighting against his harness that wouldn't unlock.

Jeannette grabbed hold of both Greer and Pelham's harnesses, yanking them down until they locked in place.

Pelham and Greer fought like demons against the harnesses. Jeannette ran to the control panel and unmuted the intercom.

"Thirty seconds to pod launch initiated. All seats are occupied and all harnesses locked."

She let out a sigh of relief as the hatch door began to close.

Until something skittered outside the pod.

She looked up. Into a swarm of gold eyes flashing through the frosted glass panel. Biodrones! She'd seen enough of them as a field medic on Ku'Tal.

Those biodrone injector ships had finally gotten these monsters into the station's belly! And the hatch was closing too slowly. It would never close in time.

Oh, God—hurry!

Claws raked the floor, the sound growing louder. Closer.

She took a step back, the hatch still closing.

"Twenty seconds to launch," a polite, sweet voice announced, nervous whispers growing louder into shouts.

"Biodrones, Kai!" she shouted.

Dozens of goldish-yellow eyes filled the shrinking circumference of the hatch's opening.

Jeannette stepped back. The sound of claws on tile echoed in terrifying layers. How many of them were out there?

Octopus-like appendages with razor-sharp claws beat against the hatch, others slithering through the slim opening, trying to pull the rest of its body into the escape pod.

With a sharp clang, the hatch closed, cutting off a dozen or more appendages that leaked inky black fluids.

Screams pierced her ears. She turned.

Pelham and Greer had transformed into biodrones, squishy octopus-like forms with flailing spiked appendages.

"Oh, God, no!"

"Red, catch!"

Jeannette turned toward Kai, catching the plasma pistol.

She whirled around, aiming the pistol at what used to be Greer's head, and fired. Three shots until the biodrone was limp in its harness, gushing yellow gobs of burnt flesh and spewing inky fluids.

Amber Bao was next to him, screaming even after the thing stopped moving.

Jeannette turned toward Pelham the biodrone.

Appendages raked across her arms and legs as she shoved the plasma pistol against Pelham's appendaged head and fired. Over and over until the biodrone was a steaming puddle of inky black blood.

"Eighteen...seventeen...sixteen..."

Jeannette rushed back to her seat and snapped down her harness.

"All seats are now occupied and harnessed. Preparing for launch in fifteen seconds.

Kai leaned over and kissed her despite all the inky biodrone splatter.

"That was amazing, Red," he said, that mischievous tone absent, his eyes weak. "As soon as we're both out of the infirmary—assuming this damned pod makes it to Civilization—we're having that first date." He pulled in a labored breath. "Then we'll go talk to Mimi Constantine."

"Why?" she asked.

He was so serious right now. It unnerved her.

"About the EVFs I sent you. Your past and the EVFs of that one recombinant you were so worried about," Kai said. "The one with the odd batch number had a letter in it."

She frowned. "Mitchell?"

He nodded, gripping his harness in both hands. "I compared the batch numbers' DNA profiles. All of them are identical matches to each other—except Peter Mitchell's DNA profile."

Jeannette nodded. "That was expected."

"Not like this, it wasn't."

"Ten seconds to launch," the system announced over the intercom.

"What does that mean?" Jeannette asked, gripping the armrests.

"Eight...seven...six..."

"Mitchell's DNA does have a match though."

"Who?" Jeannette asked, frowning.

How was that possible? He came from RDC.

"Five...four...three..."

"Dr. Orlando Constantine," said Kai. "An exact match. Who also happened to be your research partner when you and he worked at RDC. Not just worked there, but he was in charge of testing and special projects. Super-secret special projects."

Jeannette's mouth fell open and she turned to Kai, staring. "WHAT?"

"Launch sequence initiating. Prepare for launch."

The escape pod rumbled as its engine fired and the lighting dimmed.

"There's no telling what's hidden in that kid's DNA, Red. But Mimi needs to know that Peter is an exact match to her brother, Orlando."

The words pelted her like rocks. Peter Mitchell was an exact genetic match to Orlando Constantine.

This new information might just change everything.

As the escape pod shot into space, she thought about Dr. Orlando Constantine who had frequently used himself as the alpha test subject. Was Peter Mitchell's DNA profile his control copy? Or the final copy of whatever it was Orlando was working on? Keeping something safe, hidden among massive amounts of genetic profiles stored there?

One thing was clear: Peter Mitchell was never meant to be part of the Recombinant Defense Program. He wasn't a malfunctioning recombinant either. He wasn't a recombinant at all. He was a cloned copy of the sensitive, anti-war genius who had been brought up in vastly different circumstances. It made no sense for Dr.

Constantine to create this program when he was so against the war (like she was).

What changed his mind? And why?

Something must have changed in him when the program was launched, but what? Someone was after him, but why? She thought Mimi had mentioned this and the fact that Orlando had died on Ballese. Or was it Naharra? Did she know a lot more than she was telling? To protect her little brother?

Kai was right. They needed to talk to her. Soon.

Because if this got out, whoever had come looking for Orlando Constantine would also come after Peter Mitchell. And they played for keeps.

6

PETER DIDN'T KNOW what to think when Sarge told them that two reclamation stations had been destroyed. The thought of such a place existing made him sick to his stomach. He couldn't believe that there were stations out there like the training base that used to orbit Civilization, but these stations just dealt with dead recombinants. His brain had trouble understanding that one because he couldn't picture so many dead recombinants at one time.

Recombinants had always been treated like property, but he hadn't realized until now why he was given a year to live at the front. Because he had been expected to die. He winced. No, not expected. Meant to die. That was the intention every time a recombinant achieved consciousness at RDC.

It made him sick.

His chest tightened into a knot as he stared out the window of Mimi's restaurant, End of the Line, and watched the horizon, trying to slow down his racing heart and hurried breaths. He held his breath a moment, closing his eyes, and concentrating on the exotic spices drifting through the restaurant. New dishes that Mimi was testing and planned to add to her menu. The spices were warm and smoky against a creamy tomato sauce, but he didn't feel like eating right now.

These reclamation stations horrified him. Nauseated him.

So, whenever a training sergeant—or citizen—got tired of a recombinant, did they just contact this reclamation station and arrange for them to come pick up the unwanted recombinant? Dispose of them like the bags of trash that he carried out to the bin behind the restaurant every night?

As frightening as that thought was, the Antarans attacking Civilization scared him even more. They enjoyed torturing living things, including their own people. But he'd just gotten this life. He'd fought so hard for it. For Diana. He loved Civilization, loved his time here with Diana, and now, he loved spending time with his best buddy, Sting. It was the best life he could ever imagine.

Were the Antarans or UCOE about to end it? All because he apparently had an expiration date?

All he felt right now was anger. At the thought of losing everything he'd worked so hard to achieve. He didn't even know where to begin right now. The training station had moved to Civilization after an Antaran attack, but most of these recombinants and soldiers weren't training. They were put into squads and units and sent out to dig trenches, build encampments, and defend the planet. These recombinants never even got time to adjust. Out of RDC only to have a plasma rifle shoved in their hands as UCOE pointed them at the enemy.

To die first. Instead of actual citizens.

And that thought cut right through his heart.

Tonight, the restaurant's main room was full of people, about twenty or so from Mimi's underground operation, and others like Sarge. Diana hadn't shown up yet. Everyone in the room was discussing the dire situation in the Taus system. And the latest news about these reclamation stations.

Mimi had painted the room in a soft gold color, making the darker earthy colors and gold thread in the tapestries of sultans and desert palaces stand out. Sultans were desert princes, according to Diana. And their palaces looked like a patch of mushrooms in the sand, but the tapestries showed them sparkling with light and bathed in golden moon glow. The black booths lining the room's perimeter had been painted with sparkly gold accents in ornate swirls and vines to match the feel of the Sultan tapestries and the gold, burgundy, and rust silk pillows that sat on the floor for the traditional tables. That Sarge avoided.

Above his head, gold, burgundy, purple, and teal silks stretched across the ceiling, like the open-air market stalls on Earth, according to Mimi. Peter had no idea what that meant, even after Diana showed him some videos of it. But he liked how vibrant and alive those places felt.

The room got louder, conversations becoming a single dull roar as that savory tomato sauce wafted through the room, making him hungry.

Peter and Sting walked through the room lit with flickering gold lanterns that hung over each booth and joined in the conversations—to listen if nothing else. So many bad things were happening. He and Sting kept quiet though. Peter doubted that any of these people—besides Mimi and Diana—would listen to anything he had to say anyway.

What did he know? He was just a dumb recombinant. He'd heard it so many times from sergeants and corporals and lieutenants. Shopkeepers and bartenders. Former recombinants he'd gotten through Mimi's underground. He sighed. And captains—like D'Angelo.

The loud thrum of multiple conversations made the whole room buzz and he couldn't follow anyone's points. Any mention of these reclamation places distracted him, filling him with anger and fear. And dread. Fearing another shoe was about to drop. A UCOE-issue chukka that belonged to him.

A hand fell against his shoulder, startling him. He looked up. Sarge.

"Hey, Peter," said Sarge as he sat down at a small table by the window. "You seem...a little out of sorts."

Peter shook his head, shrugging. "I don't know what out of sorts means," he said, "but if it's about all these recombinant death stations existing, then yes. I'm out of sorts."

Sarge's eyes widened. "Recombinant death stations? What are you talking about?"

Peter shrugged again and looked away. He didn't have the energy to try and piece together all the things he'd heard in the room tonight about these stations. What were they called? Reclamation stations?

"You mean the reclamation stations?"

Peter nodded, eyes narrowing. "I never heard that mentioned until you told us about the ones that had been attacked." He stared at Sarge, feeling so lost by this revelation. "Is that where we're sent when we wash out...where they—kill us?"

Peter bit his lip, fighting down the tangle of emotions he felt. Why had they lied to him? Why had Sarge lied to him? Telling him he had a lifetime when they could send him to be destroyed at any time—to one of these stations?

"Oh, Peter," Sarge said, pain in his voice. "No. They aren't for that. I can only imagine what you're thinking and feeling right now."

"Is that where you'll eventually send me?" He asked, struggling to talk. "When you're all tired of me?"

"Peter—no!" Sarge cried, a shocked look on his face. "Of course not. You're part of our family. The reclamation stations are where the bodies of the dead are sent. It's where they scan and reclaim a dead recombinant's MRC chip, gather data on where and how the recombinant died on the battlefield."

"Hey, Sarge, let me try," said Sting, who walked up behind Sarge and brushed a tangle of blond curls out of his eyes. "Pete, they aren't recombinant death stations. They're called reclamation stations."

"Whatever," Peter snapped, glaring at Sting. "You can call them anything you like, but they end recombinants there. Once people are tired of them."

Sting reached out and laid his hand against Peter's shoulder, rubbing it.

"Those stations take care of all the war dead," said Sting. "And they aren't just for recombinants. Everyone that dies in the war is sent through the reclamation stations."

Peter's eyes widened. "Even citizens?" he asked in a soft voice filled with wonder.

"Yep, Pete—even citizens. Everyone that dies in this war is sent through a reclamation station. They send the bodies back to the families for funerals and stuff like that. They take care of the bodies that don't have family, too. Like us, recombinants."

Peter studied Sting's expression. Sting never lied to him. If all the dead passed through those stations, then they didn't seem quite so bad. Now that he knew every citizen and every recombinant went there.

He sighed. He felt terrible. He hadn't meant to say those mean things to Sarge.

"I'm really sorry, Sarge," he said, bowing his head. "I didn't mean to be insulting. I'm still struggling with a lot of this. And I was afraid that you and Diana were tired of me and—"

Sarge reached over and hugged Peter, an act that surprised him.

"Sarge?"

"Peter, we went to hell and back to get you out of the military," said Sarge, a solemn expression on his face, his arm still around Peter's shoulders. "And to make sure you didn't get yourself killed trying to rescue Sting here. You and Sting are family, Peter. That means you're stuck with us. Forever." Sarge chuckled. "You've almost been alive for two years now, so you have no concept of what forever means. To citizens, that means for the rest of our lives and humans typically live to be a hundred years old."

"What?" Peter gasped, taking a step back. "A hundred years?"

Sarge nodded. "That means all the life you've lived so far plus ninety-eight more years. Since recombinants are progressed to adult age, you may only have about eighty years, but that's still a long time,

Mitchell." Sarge patted him on the back. "You and Sting are like my brothers, Peter. You're family to me."

Sting was grinning from ear to ear. "Does that mean I have to work harder at taunting my little sister?" he asked with a laugh.

Peter and Sarge both laughed. Peter was so happy that Sting and Diana had hit it off so well together. Sting teased Diana at every opportunity and Diana gave it right back to him. Peter knew she was crazy in love with him and he would never love anyone but Diana Temple. But she loved Sting, too. In a different way.

Sarge poked Peter's shoulder with his fist. "I look forward to showing you and Sting all the boring family holidays you're now stuck with, being family."

"I can't wait," said Peter, a smile lighting his face. "I want to see the one where you hang weird stuff on dead trees and burn up your socks in the fireplace. While you wait for some fat guy in red to break into your house and leave presents. After he steals all your milk and cookies."

Sting laughed and rumpled his hair. "Pete, that's not that holiday works."

Sarge groaned. "Yeah, these family holidays will take some time to explain, Mitchell. But we like to celebrate the day that each family member is born, too. Every year."

Sting nudged Peter. "Pete knows all about how special a birthday is—don'tcha, Pete? To a recombinant, that day means everything."

Sting was right. It was the most important thing they celebrated. He nodded finally, his eyes misting with tears.

"What'd I tell you, Sarge?" said Sting.

"I look forward to celebrating those days with you and Sting and Diana," Peter said as he sat down at a table in the center of the room.

"So, Sarge," Sting said, plopping down in a chair beside Peter. "Why did Mimi want all of us here tonight?"

"War's gone south, Stingley," Sarge said in his calm, take-charge military voice. "We've had two reclamation stations and a training base blown up in the Taus system this week."

"That's a lot, Sarge!" Peter replied. "Why would Antarans attack those places? If they just handled dead people? Makes no sense."

"Sure doesn't, Mitchell." Sarge sighed and ran his hand through his dark hair. "Seems like these quick *hit-and-run* missions are more like terrorist attacks than anything else. No one knows why they're happening. That's why Mimi asked us all here. We need to plan for the unthinkable: an Antaran attack right here on Civilization."

"Would it be like Ku'Tal, Sarge?" Peter asked. "Ku-Tal seemed like such an organized assault though. A huge war engine compared to Ballese or these hit-and-runs as you called them."

"It could." Sarge sighed. "They could dig in here and bring the fight to the edges of Sol system. If they overran a fringe base around Jupiter or Uranus, they'd be able to fight a war right on Earth's doorstep. It's terrifying."

"Diana's late," said Peter, glancing around the room.

"She wanted me to tell you that she had a late run tonight," said Sarge, motioning toward the restaurant's foyer. "Said she'd be a half hour late."

Someone pounded on the front door, hammering hard and fast until the urgent sound rose above the noise of the crowd. Mimi, wearing turquoise leggings and a satiny tunic that turned peach and turquoise with the light, got up from a nearby table. Her strawberry-blond hair was clipped into a pile of loose curls at the back of her head.

"I'm coming!" she shouted. "Don't bust down my door."

She yanked the heavy wooden door open that had been repainted a rich turquoise. A bunch of soldiers pushed her aside as they surged into the restaurant, dressed in adaptive field camos. Peter counted them, seven. With plasma rifles. Trained on everyone in the room. They wore UCOE patches on their adaptive camos that quickly shifted from a mix of tan and umber, taking on the field of rich colors in End of the Line. Those camos allowed them to blend into any environment. Uniforms they'd never trusted to mere recombinants.

But watching their camos shift into the purples, gold, teals, and burgundies from the silk tablecloths and fabrics made them look like clowns. And it made Peter chuckle.

Slow, heavy footfalls stomped into the restaurant, reverberating against the tiled floor. Forcing the hint of a smile off his face.

Peter felt the cold fear rise in his throat as Captain D'Angelo, dressed in a forest green officers' uniform, stepped into the room, two more camo-clad soldiers flanking him. A chill brushed across his skin at the sight of D'Angelo.

"Good evening, Ms. Constantine," D'Angelo said to Mimi, his voice a hard, ragged version of D'Angelo's commanding voice before Ballese—before Sarge found him alive with no explanation on Civilization. "An interesting gathering you have here."

D'Angelo glared at everyone in the now-silent room as he threw his weight around, plasma rifle cradled in his arms. He was almost the same height as Mimi.

"I like to think that all my gatherings are at least interesting, Captain D'Angelo. Now, what can I do for you and your—squad? Dining room's closed for my private party. We're doing a food tasting for the new menu."

D'Angelo kept that rifle poised as he walked around the room, studying each person like he was capturing an image of them. It terrified Peter. Especially since D'Angelo died on Ballese before the nuclear bombardment.

"Mitchell, Stingley, hide under the table," Sarge whispered with a hiss, pushing Peter and Sting toward the floor.

Under the long burgundy tablecloth covering the table.

The captain paused when he got to Ron Kraver. The former weapons programmer looked unnerved at seeing D'Angelo back from the dead after Ballese. He stared at Linda, one of Mimi's underground operatives who scowled at D'Angelo as she twisted her long, blond braid in her left hand. He moved to a group of three men —recombinants until yesterday. They watched D'Angelo in uneasy silence.

"Hurry," Sarge whispered.

Peter and Sting slid under the table and huddled against the back of the booth. Hoping D'Angelo would move on past Sarge quickly. It was hot underneath here and Peter was tired of hiding.

D'Angelo stopped in front of Sarge at the table. Several moments of silence ached through the room.

"Sergeant Temple," said D'Angelo. "Surprised to see you here."

The tablecloth fluttered as Sarge's feet thumped together. He must have snapped to attention and saluted that undead monster.

"Why is that, sir?"

Another annoying silent pause by D'Angelo.

Peter saw D'Angelo's black chukkas facing toward Sarge. In front of the table. Blocking his and Sting's escape route.

Peter began to sweat.

"In the company of your countrymen that are committing treason."

"Didn't know that fine dining was now considered a treasonous act. Sir."

Sarge's tone was light but not his sarcasm. He was trying to dial down D'Angelo's stormtrooper approach to the situation. Trying to diffuse any violence that the captain might be contemplating. Peter knew how Sarge operated. In this situation, that was the right thing to do.

Especially with a roomful of people.

Mimi cackled as her voice got louder, a shadow beside Sarge. She was standing on Sarge's left now. Peter saw her shadow, heard the jingle of her bracelets.

But someone locked a plasma charge into a rifle. Boots shuffled across the colorful tile floor, the sound in front of the table.

Had D'Angelo called over soldiers? Or was that monster pointing his loaded plasma rifle at Mimi? At Sarge?

"Things are escalating out there, Pete," Sting whispered.

Peter nodded, getting up on his haunches. Ready to lunge at these soldiers if they threatened Mimi.

And Sarge.

"Pure velvety black. Captain, I've never seen an aura this black before, not even in serial killers. Or dead people. Does the blackness suck in all the light from your chakras just to keep you upright, captain?"

A loud thump. Mimi shifted, stifling a cry of pain.

"What the hell?" Sarge cried, stepping in front of Mimi. "You try that again and these soldiers are gonna be on the floor, D'Angelo. I don't care if you're a captain."

In that moment, Peter felt the mood of the room completely change as rage surged through him in white-hot spikes.

"Apologize," someone shouted, snarling at Mimi.

"You plan to go through me with that weapon, sergeant?" Sarge said with a growl. "It'll be the last thing you ever do."

Boots scraped against tile. Someone shouted. Mimi cried out.

Sarge and Mimi were in trouble!

Peter balled his hands into fists, wanting to beat these soldiers senseless. But he couldn't tell by the boots which one was Sarge and which ones belonged to D'Angelo.

"Don't do it, Pete," Sting hissed, grabbing him by the shoulders.

Peter's muscles tightened, his anger building. At best, these soldiers were recombinants. At worst, they were Antaran hybrids, good for killing everything in D'Angelo's path.

Either way, they were all in serious danger. Especially with nine hybrids and D'Angelo carrying plasma rifles. Most of the room was unarmed, waiting to have dinner and sample Mimi's new menu.

Taking a deep breath, Peter shot underneath the tablecloth. Beneath the next table. Moving around the room until he could see what was happening.

"Pete! Dammit!" Sting's sharp whisper hung behind him under the tables as he followed in hot pursuit.

From a table behind D'Angelo, Peter peered underneath the gold tablecloth.

Mimi pulled herself up from the floor to her five-foot-seven-inch height, standing tall as amusement twinkled in her pale blue eyes.

Two soldiers each held onto Sarge, gripping his arms so he couldn't throw a punch.

"My apologies, Captain D'Angelo," said Mimi, a curious grin on her face.

D'Angelo smiled, moving in front of her, so close that his boots touched the tips of her turquoise flats. Mimi didn't intimidate easily though. She stood her ground. Staring into D'Angelo's dead grey eyes.

"That's better, Ms. Constantine," he said, a triumphant smile curving across his pale face.

"See, when I said your aura was pure velvety black," she said, her face animated, eyes still twinkling with amusement. "I didn't mean it. See, that would be far too bright for an empty-eyed creature that wasn't even human. Or good at pretending to be human. I'll start with the color demon-dark until I find something darker and more desolate."

Gritting his teeth, D'Angelo's face turned red, rage burning across his long face, lines deepening around his mouth and eyes as he reached toward Mimi.

"Leave her alone!" Peter shouted, scrambling to his feet.

"Peter, no!" Mimi shouted, Sarge echoing her words.

"Ah, the dimwitted recombinant speaks!" D'Angelo shouted, a laugh gurgling in his throat. "Not realizing that his presence is just the evidence I need to indict all of you on charges of treason."

Peter smiled. "Found your keys yet? To the repository? Oh, wait…"

All of D'Angelo's detail surrounded Peter, training their plasma rifles on him.

Mimi stepped past the soldiers and wrapped her arms around Peter, holding him close.

"You're crazier than an Antaran hybrid, D'Angelo. This is my youngest brother. Dr. Orlando Constantine. He goes by his middle name now. Peter."

Peter kept quiet, waiting for D'Angelo's reaction.

D'Angelo pointed at Peter. "That's Private Peter Mitchell! He was a recombinant in my unit on Ku'Tal!"

Sarge shoved past the soldiers and stood on the other side of Peter. Anger burned in his eyes. Peter feared it was for him and not D'Angelo.

"I was your field sergeant for that unit, captain. Peter Mitchell died in Ku'Tal's swamps just before we assaulted the depot. Reclamation station records confirm that." He squinted at D'Angelo. "You sure you're all right, sir? The brass might think something's wrong if you can't remember your own report."

"I'll have to contact someone at the Ministry of Defense to confirm that, sergeant," said D'Angelo, clearing his throat. He chewed his bottom lip until finally his attention moved back to Mimi. "I'm sure you won't mind showing yours and your brother's identification cards."

Sarge pulled in a nervous breath, his gaze flicking to Mimi. Peter stared at D'Angelo, acting as calm and unfazed as he could manage. Mimi let go of Peter and turned toward her office.

"Will that get you out of my restaurant so we can get on with our menu testing?"

"Yes, of course, Ms. Constantine," said D'Angelo in a placating tone.

Peter didn't trust anyone that came back from a corpse. Especially when they acted like nothing unusual had happened.

Sarge grabbed hold of Peter's arm and held him in a death grip.

"Bring the prisoner," D'Angelo snapped.

Soldiers moved toward Peter.

"I've got this," said Sarge as he frog-marched Peter past them and followed Mimi into the narrow hallway leading to her office.

Mimi sat down at her new desk, crafted from a burled honey-yellow wood. The new mauve computer chair swiveled as she spun it around toward a tan file cabinet against the freshly painted, pale sage green walls. A dartboard hung beneath a white clock and over a white waste bin. Peter smiled. Diana's touch.

The far wall had a large holographic picture frame that cycled through warm desert sunsets, covered with all kinds of tall green things, tall as a man. Smooth, light green surface covered in bunches of tiny spikes. Mimi called them cact-something or other. They didn't grow here on Civilization, but Mimi always said that this planet reminded her of the southwestern United States. Wherever that was.

He didn't know if Mimi was stalling for time, but she had a couple of purple file folders and padded envelopes in her fist that she laid out on the desk.

"Ms. Constantine, if you are stalling—"

"I am not stalling, Captain D'Angelo. My brother's identification card had to be updated for Civilization. He hasn't been here long."

Finally, she pulled out a green United Countries of Earth identification card with Peter's picture in the upper left-hand corner. His full name was listed as Orlando Peter Constantine.

Mimi handed it to D'Angelo. "Mine's in my purse," she said, opening the top drawer and pulling out a teal purse with purple and pink flowers.

She took out her ID card and handed it to D'Angelo.

"This is fake!" D'Angelo cried, staring at Peter's ID for a long time.

"It's got the official seals and everything, captain," Mimi snapped. "It looks just like mine. I'll call my lawyer here on Civilization. He'll be here shortly for the menu tasting. I can have him serve you with lawsuit papers by the time the salads are served."

Growling, D'Angelo charged out of the small office and into the hallway. Mimi followed, Peter behind her with Sarge on his six, an iron grip on Peter's left arm. D'Angelo stopped at the host station that held stacks of puffy black menu holders. He snapped his fingers at the soldiers spread out through the main dining room.

"All right, men, fall in!" D'Angelo barked as the soldiers pulled back into formation in front of the captain, camos already shifting. "We'll be back after a quick records check."

Peter got in D'Angelo's face.

"Check your own record first, D'Angelo. How odd that you come in here shouting about treason and harboring dead recombinants when your own records show you died on Ballese. Sergeant Temple was your field sergeant. Make sure when you're scanning records that you put yours on top. And don't forget to review the sergeant's report. Wouldn't want to miss an undead Antaran captain cheating the government when he was really dead all along."

An arm slid around Peter's shoulders. He looked up. Sarge.

"You heard Mr. Constantine," Sarge replied.

"Have a lovely evening, captain," said Mimi, smiling. "I don't know exactly how a hybrid spends its Friday nights, but I hope it's lovely—and off-world."

Peter stood tall, anger still swelling through his veins as Sarge stayed at his side, shoulders squared, mouth pressed into a tight, angry line as D'Angelo walked out of the restaurant, his squad of hybrids walking in brisk, measured steps out into the night.

Sarge let go of Peter, hands on his hips, anger burning like hot coals in his eyes. He wagged a finger in Peter's face and Peter braced for a fiery reprimand. Until Sting spun him around and shook him hard enough to rattle his teeth. His eyes were green flames, teeth gritted as he drew back his fist and punched Peter in the face, dropping him to the floor.

Sarge froze.

"Damn you, Pete!" Sting shouted, grabbing him by the shoulders and shaking him again. "They could have killed you tonight! Right in front of me."

Finally, the anger left him and he clasped Peter to his chest, holding onto him tighter than Peter could remember. And he was shaking. Hard. Peter felt guilt burn in his stomach. He hadn't meant to scare Sting. He just wanted to stand up to these soldiers, fight back against the horrible treatment he'd endured his whole life. Like every recombinant. All eighteen months of it.

He was amazed that Sting felt that strongly about their friendship. He'd always figured that Sting would get tired of him, like he'd expected Sarge—and even Diana—to feel after a while. Like a cute puppy that had grown into an annoying adult.

"Don't do that again!" Sting shouted, holding him out at arm's length. "You're my best buddy. I can't lose you."

"Sting's right, Peter." Sarge. "Stop thinking that you're expendable."

"You're not expendable, Peter," said a shaky voice behind Mimi. "You're irreplaceable. And I can't lose you either."

His heart rushed up into his throat. Diana!

She closed the door and stepped around Mimi, rushing to him as Sting helped him up from the floor. Diana threw her arms around him, the heat of her skin so hot against his chest. He didn't think he could love her any deeper than he did in this moment. He slid his arms around her, kissing her hard on the lips.

"What happened in here?" Diana asked and let go of Peter.

She slid her arm around his waist and leaned against him. He ran his fingers down her arm in reassuring strokes.

"Undead D'Angelo just came for a visit," Sarge snapped. "Babbling about treason and roughed up Mimi. I tried to stop him, but the soldiers dragged me backward. Until Peter threw himself between her and the soldier." Sarge put his hand on his hip. "With me and Stingley telling him not to."

Diana leaned up and kissed Peter on the lips until he blushed. "That's one of the things I love about you, Peter."

Sting popped Peter on the back of his head. "What? Getting himself into more trouble by not thinking about what he's doing first?"

Diana chuckled as she ran her fingers through Peter's hair at the nape of his neck in soothing strokes.

"And you, Sting, always protecting the man I love," Diana said with a smile. "That's one of the things I love about you."

A loud rumble shook the building. The restaurant went dark.

"Rats!" Mimi shouted and fumbled toward the door.

Three more times, the building shook. Peter held tight to Diana as he moved toward the front door. He felt a hand on his back.

"I've got your back, Pete," Sting said.

"You always have," said Peter over his shoulder.

"And I always will."

Peter didn't need to respond. Sting knew how he felt. Even now, six weeks after bringing Sting home from Ballese, Sting still randomly told Peter how he still couldn't believe that Peter had risked everything to rescue him.

At last, Mimi shoved open the door and they all spilled out into the twilight slipping fast into night. Something burned on the horizon as lights filled the dark sky. Two UCOE shuttles from the relocated training base and three Civilization port authority skimmers flew toward what looked like several crash landings outside of town. Red and blue skimmer lights raced across the desert sand that looked almost molten from the fires and sirens that screamed away from town toward a huge debris field.

"What happened?" Peter replied as Diana squeezed his hand. "Are those more escape pods?"

"Lots more, Peter," said Sarge, his gaze locked on the horizon. "We've lost another station."

Sting was at his shoulder, Sarge behind Diana as they all silently watched the growing number of skimmers responding. Mimi walked up with Ron Kraver who looked unnerved. Mimi looked frightened, Civilization pitch-dark behind her. Peter had never seen the town dark before. It made him uneasy.

Mimi motioned Ron to follow her as she moved around the back of the restaurant, calling for Sarge.

"We're over here, Mimi," Sarge answered, motioning her toward him.

"David, another reclamation station has been attacked. The one closest to Civilization." Mimi's usually bright and optimistic tone was absent, replaced by uncertainty and concern.

"That's Dr. Kingston's station—hers and Dr. Drew's," said Diana, casting a forlorn look toward the desert and all the emergency lights.

Sarge made a sour face. "Damn! Not another one!"

"There's so many," Peter replied, pointing at the trail of wreckage burning across the desert.

"They're single-flight automated escape pods," said Mimi. "Every single pod was launched just before the station was destroyed, an auto-flight module programmed with coordinates and enough fuel for a single flight. There have been nearly a dozen landings so far. Most of the pods are damaged and barely reached their destinations."

"Are we going to set up triage at the restaurant, Mimi?" Diana asked.

"Yes, we are," she said. "I've sent Ron and some others to turn on the restaurant's generator. Once we can support a triage, I'd like you, David, and Ron to contact port authority and UCOE forces and alert them about the triage location. And ask about Dr. Kingston and Dr. Drew."

"You got it, Mimi," said Sarge, squeezing her shoulder.

She smiled. "Don't know what I'd do without you and Diana, David." She reached over and patted Peter on the cheek. "And this one's solid gold. Peter, I'll never forget you standing up for me with a dozen plasma rifles pointed at your head." She laid a hand on Sting's shoulder. "And this one was right on Peter's heels, ready to back him up."

Sting nodded. "I was three steps behind when Pete jumped out. Thought one of us should hold our cover a little longer."

"Peter, Diana, and Sting, you're with me setting up triage," Mimi ordered. "Everyone else, get moving."

Peter rushed alongside Diana, Sting on his right as they followed Mimi toward the restaurant, still dark, to prepare for all the casualties. Peter knew there would be almost as many as the training base when it was destroyed. He hoped that Dr. Kingston and Dr. Drew were safe in one of those pods in the desert.

7

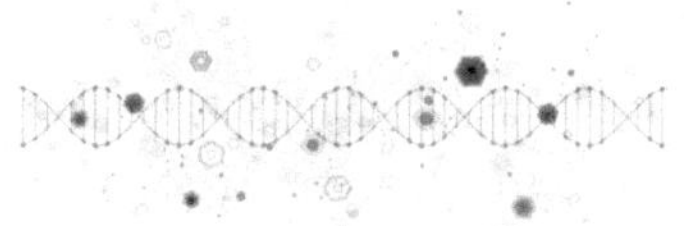

DARKNESS. Heavy smell of burnt fuel and flaming brush filled the air. Choking, Jeannette gasped for air.

Shadows moved around her in the smoky haze, voices all tangled together, shouting. Sobbing. Lights flashing and pulsing in reds, blues, and whites.

"Red?" a distant voice called to her. "Red, answer me! We're on Civilization. Hang in there."

Warmth. Pressed against her hand.

She opened her eyes to slits. The handsome, hazy image of Kai Drew hung over her, unfastening her restraint harness.

"What happened?" she sputtered, coughing.

"Easy," he said, taking her hand and getting her onto her feet. "I've got you. Let's get you out of here first."

Jeannette nodded, staring into his weary face, blue eyes looking so tired and in pain as Kai slid his arm around her waist and helped her up as the other reclamation techs and specialists escaped from their harnesses. Kai helped her toward the hatch. The hatch release lever blinked red, catching Jeannette's attention.

"Kai, there's the release lever," she said, pointing.

"Can you reach it?" he asked.

That had to hurt. Asking her to pull the lever for him. She knew he had injuries, but there hadn't been time to assess his condition when the station lost gravity. He didn't want to let on that he couldn't do it himself.

"Sure, a little closer please."

Kai moved toward it and steadied her as she grabbed the lever. And pulled.

Air hissed, composite rasping as the hatch's membrane-like cover released its seal and slid back. Releasing the outer door that lifted toward the dark sky.

Kai leaned a little on her as they stepped out into the sultry Civilization night.

"Move and you die!" a gruff, frightened voice shouted.

Spotlights danced across their faces in blinding white beams. Illuminating the ring of soldiers with plasma rifles pointed at them. One of them, a tall, stocky man with light brown hair, cut high and tight, and a thick jaw, moved slowly toward them. He wore a dull olive uniform and panned his rifle back and forth, hard brown eyes glancing from them to a small terrain grid dangling from a lanyard around his neck.

"Hernandez, scan the pod for MRCs and hostiles and report. Now!" the man shouted, motioning someone toward the smoking escape pod and burning brush beside it.

"On it, Sarge," said a lanky, dark-haired soldier clad in dull tan camos.

Hernandez shouldered his rifle and moved toward the pod, turning on the grid hanging around his neck. It began to chirp. A slow, staccato sound that made Jeannette's skin crawl.

"Identify yourselves! Now!" the sergeant shouted, green laser sight flashing on Kai's forehead.

The air was thick with smoke, husky with an almost sage-like smell that mixed with the acrid stink of fuel. Jeannette sighed. And death—a smell she'd never forget. Ever.

What happened out here?

Kai didn't move a muscle. "We're ten techs and specialists from Reclamation Base 343-AOD," he announced with almost a shout. "It was attacked by Antarans tonight. A hit and run. With UCOE forces hot on their asses. I hope they chased them all the way back to hell where they came from."

"Your name. Now!" the sergeant demanded, his eyes looking a little wild. A little unhinged.

"Reclamation Specialist Dr. Kai Drew. Beside me is Dr. Jeannette Kingston. She doesn't have an MRC to scan. There are two more specialists inside, Dr. Amber Bao and Dr. Amit Gravinder—"

"Sarge!" Hernandez called out. "I've got nine MRCs on grid. No nasties. Identifications check out. I've got visual confirmation of Drew and Kingston that match the database. Stories check out."

"Scan these two again," said the sergeant, motioning toward her and Kai with his rifle. "We have to be sure this time!"

"Roger that, Sarge!" Hernandez stepped closer, holding out the grid in front of him.

The grid didn't make a sound.

"Sergeant," said Kai, turning toward the antsy soldier. "You should know that we got in the escape pod with twelve people. But there are only ten now."

"What?" the sergeant's eyes widened. "Explain."

"There were dozens and dozens of biodrones on the station," Jeannette replied. "I barely got the hatch sealed in time. When I turned to go back to my seat, two of the specialists shifted out of their human forms and became biodrones."

"Jeannette took them out before they could get loose and kill us though," said Kai.

"Only because you tossed me that plasma pistol," she replied, not wanting to take all the credit.

If he hadn't thrown that pistol to her, those things would have eventually gotten loose and killed her and everyone else. She shuddered, realizing how many times they'd stared death in the face tonight.

"They're clean, Sarge," said Hernandez.

"We're clear, everyone. Disengage and stand down, awaiting orders. Hernandez, call for medevac for this pod."

At last, the sergeant seemed calmer.

"Roger that," said Hernandez, his fingers tapping across his scanning grid.

Kai helped Jeannette toward the sergeant as most of the soldiers swarmed over to the next escape pod.

"Sergeant, what happened here?" Kai asked, glancing around the dark plains. "It looks like a massacre."

Jeannette counted more than a dozen flaming escape pods that had carved burning ruts through the umber and red sands, setting brush alight. Dozens of dark, unmoving shapes lay across the area, burnt and smoldering. Soldiers and other uniforms swarmed the area, medics and other medical personnel carried people out on backboards to medevac skimmers flashing red lights all along the edge of the plains. Toward the town of Civilization that followed the river from the spaceport to the end of the shuttle line.

Where Mimi Constantine's restaurant stood.

"It was," the man said, his voice trembling, jaw clamped shut, eyes haunted by whatever had happened here.

Sirens shrieked past, air hoppers landing, skimmers sliding along the terrain, kicking up sand and dust into the haze of smoke. Off to her left, she counted at least five more pods that had smashed into Civilization's desert plains. Soldiers made their way toward their pod next.

"We lost a dozen or more soldiers, Doc. The first ones never even knew what hit them."

"Oh, God—biodrones," Kai said, his voice trailing off. "Inside the escape pods."

The sergeant nodded again and rubbed his hand over his face.

"First escape pod was full of them. You're the first full pod we've found." His mouth quivered, eyes misting. "And we didn't get them all. Damned things can replicate. If they unleash forces of the magnitude that was on Ku-Tal…"

Kai sighed. "Jeannette and I were both medics on Ku'Tal."

"Then you both know what we're up against," the sergeant said, glancing at the next escape pod. "Could use two more experienced medics. Check in at triage."

Jeannette sucked in a breath. Civilization was becoming the new front…if they survived the initial invasion force. Without Civilization, nothing could stop an Antaran incursion into Sol.

And Earth.

"All right, unit, fall in!" the sergeant shouted.

"Where's triage?" Kai asked.

"A restaurant in town. Called End of the Line. I have another medevac skimmer that's just arrived—"

"A restaurant and triage, nice!" Kai said with a chuckle. "I can sit down to a nice dinner after taking care of all the patients."

The sergeant laughed and pointed to a skimmer hovering nearby. "Climb aboard that skimmer. They'll get you to Mimi's place right away." He unshouldered his rifle, looking tense again. "Let's hit it, soldiers! We got more pods to check. Grids on!"

The sergeant and his unit rushed out across a dark patch of terrain, toward the next escape pod.

"You okay, Red?" Kai asked in a quiet voice.

Jeannette nodded. "Let's get out of here before any more of those biodrones show up."

She and Kai walked with slow steps toward the silver skimmer. The night was cool, flaming wreckage guttering all around them as the wind whipped across the open plains. She helped Kai up into the sleek four-seater that looked like a missile and climbed in after him.

"You those medics that Sarge wanted taken into town?" asked the tall, lanky man seated in the front seat.

"Yes, that's us. Drew and Kingston. Take us to End of the Line, please," Jeannette replied.

Kai collapsed against her shoulder, breath heavy, skin radiating heat. She laid the back of her hand against his forehead and his neck. He was burning up!

"Skimmer part of the date, Kai? Or are you hurt worse than you're trying to hide?"

"Busted," he said, his voice trailing off.

She held him close, her mind rushing through everything that had happened at the reclamation station. The sudden loss of gravity. And then the freefall when it came back only to float through the upturned chamber again. She shuddered at the hundreds of eyes staring back at her through the escape pod's hatch as she'd closed it. And the two specialists who had sabotaged their pod's launch and then turned into biodrones right in front of her. She hadn't had time to even think about that, much less process what had happened. That would come later, but one thing was crystal clear: someone or something didn't want her and Kai to leave that station alive.

Kai groaned and she stroked his hair. "You were pretty amazing out there, Kai. Got us all to the escape pods. And kept us from being killed by friendly fire on arrival here."

"Last I looked, you were taking on biodrones and whatever the hell those two specialists were. You got the launch sequence restarted, too. You were the hero, Red, not me."

She chuckled. "Okay, I'll split it with you."

"Split what?" he asked, his face scrunching in confusion.

"I was going to buy you a hero's dinner at End of the Line, but I guess we'll just split it then."

"Damn, I never know when to keep my mouth shut, do I?" he said with a smirk.

"I hope you never do, Kai. That's one of the things I like best about you. Not taking shit from anyone."

"Most of the town is dark from a power surge, but we've kept it dark as a protective measure," said the driver. "Hospital and End of the Line have power inside and generator backups."

"Good news," said Kai. "In case this is an incursion by the Antarans, we should at least make it hard for them to find us."

"You know it," said the driver. "We definitely don't want to make it easy for them, do we?"

"Make it easy for them to die maybe," Jeannette added.

The skimmer rushed along the river and turned left as the dark transit shuttle track curved off to the right. Toward the shuttle port.

And there was Mimi's restaurant, a homey, two-story building, its umber, sandstone, and river rock walls still standing. The elegant, curved, and gabled roof was untouched and the wide set of concrete steps were pristine as they led up to a large, heavy wood door that had been painted a crisp, bright turquoise. The door hadn't even been scratched.

Two medevac skimmers stopped in front, off-loading several patients on backboards and carrying them inside. A young man with pale blond hair and pale blue eyes held open the doors as the medics carried them into the restaurant.

She grinned. Peter Mitchell.

Tall and lanky. In jeans and a dark grey T-shirt. At twenty-three, he still looked like a teenager, his bright sense of wonder intact after bringing his best friend back from Ballese. Diana had kept her up to date on everything that had happened. Seeing Peter calm and relaxed made her day, especially since she'd helped him escape the military. A place he didn't belong.

She helped Kai out of the skimmer and he leaned on her as she struggled up the stairs.

"Here, let me help," said Peter, rushing down the steps.

He stared at her a moment and then smiled.

"Dr. Kingston? From the training base?"

"You have a good memory, Peter. So good to see you."

"So glad to see you and Dr. Drew survived that attack," he said.

She laid her hand against his forearm. "So glad to see that you came back safely from Ballese. With your best friend."

Peter blushed and stared at his feet a moment. "Thanks," he said finally.

He took hold of Kai and picked him up across his shoulders in a fireman's carry, hefting him up the stairs and inside. Jeannette followed.

Inside was measured chaos.

Tables converted into beds, beds on the floors, IV stands, scanning equipment, and three overwhelmed doctors. They had Civilization Hospital embroidered in blue on their white lab coats. The overhead light was steady and bright, smell of hot coffee, blood, and minty germicide permeating the air.

"Three doctors and four nurses came from the hospital to work triage," said Peter as he laid Kai on an empty bed and covered him with a sheet. "So, you're in good hands."

"And I'll be your fourth, Peter."

"That's great, Doc," he replied.

His eyes still sparkled with wonder. She was so glad to see that the world hadn't taken that from him. She'd never met anyone like Peter. His sense of wonder was magical and had changed how she saw the world. And herself.

"I'll get Mimi so you know where to start. Once you've been assessed, too." He frowned. "You've been through something terrible. I see it in your eyes."

She nodded.

"They can twist your mind and tear you apart, Doc," he said, his face burning with resolve. "But they can never get at your humanness. Your light. That's what they want from us, but their darkness just suffocates it. Remember that."

A chill fluttered down her spine. If anyone knew the Antarans and what they wanted, it was Peter Mitchell.

"I will, Peter," she said in a quiet voice.

He rushed off, weaving between beds and people and then disappearing into the kitchen.

Jeannette moved over to Kai and checked his pulse. A little high.

Understandable after what they'd just gone through. Including being rushed by dozens of biodrones and two planted biodrone hybrids in the escape pod. Hadn't been a fun night so far. Her arms and legs hurt from the biodrone spikes. She felt a little feverish, but the wounds weren't deep. She'd be fine.

She brushed the black hair out of Kai's eyes as he looked up at her.

"This hasn't been a fun date, Kai," she said, clicking her tongue.

"No?" he said with a chuckle. "You don't like questioning your mortality while running for your life because everything wants to kill you on your first date?"

"No," she said, "and it's your fault."

He was grinning at her now, playing along. "How's it my fault again?"

"If you'd had the courage to ask me out sooner, this would have been our second date."

"So, no biodrones and other things wanting to kill us until the second date. Got it."

A dark-haired woman wearing tortoiseshell glasses, hair pulled up under her white skull cap and mask moved toward Kai. She carried a datapad and wore a white Civilization Hospital lab coat, a green blouse, and tan pants underneath.

"I'm Doctor Lin. Tell me what happened to you." She pulled her stethoscope to Kai's chest and listened first before running a mediscanner across him.

"We escaped the reclamation station attack," said Jeannette. "In an escape pod that was just as dangerous as the imploding station."

"Which one?" Doctor Lin asked.

"Which one?" Kai snapped, looking shocked.

"Two others were attacked in the last few days," Doctor Lin replied, getting Kai to sit up while she listened to his lungs.

"That's three destroyed," Jeannette said in a quiet voice, the cold fear creeping back again.

"If we don't hold those bastards here," said Kai, "they'll roll through Sol in a few months."

"I hope we even have that much time," said Mimi Constantine, crossing her arms. "Dr. Jeannette Kingston, welcome back. You finally bringing your man to the restaurant? Complex aura, complex man. Lots of red, tempered by yellow, and deep blue underneath. Strong and loyal. We need more smartasses to fight these slime devils."

Kai flashed a ghost of his most charming smile and nodded toward Mimi. "I like her. Like a smooth shot of whisky in the dead of winter."

Dr. Kingston propped her hands on her hips, her grey lab coat and light-yellow scrubs ripped and stained black from the biodrones.

"Hey now, what am I?" she asked Kai, frowning at him.

"You, Red, are a snifter of fine cognac to be sipped and savored on a stormy autumn night by the sea," said Kai as Doctor Lin rolled over an imaging scanner.

"Lay back down, Mr.—"

"Drew," he answered. "Doctor Kai Drew."

"Wow, you're both doctors?" said Doctor Lin as she placed the stand against the table. "Glad to have you here."

"It's how we met," said Jeannette, remembering the first time she saw him. Six feet tall, lean runner's build, he wore grey scrubs, those electric blue eyes haunting against that jet black hair. Being a smartass as he'd turned toward her in the breakroom. All beige except for the pleather blue chairs and the rainbow of scrubs from all the women buzzing around him.

Hitting on him. Hard.

Kai was the hottest man she'd ever met. He made her heart pound into her throat and her hands shake. Back then, she'd been afraid to even speak to the man, especially with so many women swarming all over him.

She smiled, remembering how he had leaned toward her and extended his hand, and introduced himself.

"Doctor Kai Drew. Just transferred from a reclamation station out near Ku'Tal."

Shaking his hand, she'd smiled and said, "Doctor Jeannette Kingston. Welcome. Let me know if you need any bug spray. For the swarm."

He had laughed as she walked toward the coffee machine. His gaze never left her as she poured herself an almost cold mug of coffee sludge and pretended to drink it.

Doctor Lin flicked on the scanner and used her handheld datapad to transfer settings to it. The scanner whirred up and began scanning as it hummed down the track to his feet and back again.

She felt someone tugging on her lab coat. Kai.

"Doc, this is Doctor Jeannette Kingston. She's gonna need someone to look at these wounds. Biodrones spikes. Wounds aren't deep, so nominal venom injection. Sometimes, an adverse reaction can lead to anaphylactic shock though. Or venom fever."

Someone gently gripped her upper arm. Jeannette turned. Diana Temple.

"Diana! It's wonderful seeing you again. Finally with the one you love."

Diana's gaze snapped to Peter standing behind her, his arms around her waist, holding her close.

"Thank you for everything you did for him." She took his hand in hers and laid his hand against her cheek. "For us. He's all mine. Forever."

Peter grinned, his shy gaze falling to his feet. "She's the only woman I'll ever love, Dr. Kingston."

Diana spun around and kissed him hard in the mouth. He kissed her back with a slow, gentle kiss that left Diana looking breathless.

"Seeing you, two together and so in love makes me so happy, Diana," said Jeannette.

"Mimi asked us to get you settled in one of the beds so your biodrone wounds can be assessed," Diana explained. "I set up one beside—Kai, isn't it?"

Jeannette nodded. "Yes, Kai Drew. Lead the way."

"Running out on me, Red?" Kai called out to her.

"Not yet," she said with a laugh. "I've gotta see how our second date goes."

Kai laughed as Diana and Peter led her toward the table-bed behind him.

"Same, Red," he said in a soft voice. "Second date will definitely be interesting, won't it?"

"It better be, Kai Drew," she said with a groan as Diana helped her out of the grey lab coat and under a sheet. "You've gotta top this one."

"Don't think this can be salvaged," said Diana, holding up the battered and stained lab coat.

"It's a biohazard with all the biodrone fluids," Jeannette replied, letting her head sink back into the soft pillow. "Incinerate it."

Diana left, holding the lab coat with thumb and forefinger. Peter lingered beside her bed, looking anxious and concerned.

"What's the matter, Peter? You look worried."

He nodded, his voice barely above a whisper. "What happened out there?" he asked.

She sighed. "Kai and I work at a reclamation station close to Civilization. Earlier in the day, we were attacked by Antaran ships. The station was hit hard. We lost a lot of people in that attack." She closed her eyes, shuddering as the memories churned behind her eyes. "It was terrible. We lost gravity. Then everything went into freefall when it came back." She sighed. "And then it went out again. But we got safely to our escape pod and strapped in as biodrones stormed our pod before the hatch closed. We had two more in the pod after that, but they looked human."

"Caregivers!" Peter said with a gasp, his face turning pasty white, his pale blue eyes wide.

She squinted at him. "Caregivers? What does that mean, Peter?"

"I don't know exactly what they are, but they can shift form. They're more intelligent than their biodrones. They were trying to create a hybrid recombinant on Ballese—that's what they wanted me, I mean, Sting for. A hybrid recombinant that bleeds red blood."

Jeannette gulped in air, the thought terrifying. All of those gold-eyed biodrones massing in the hallway toward the escape pod. They were easy to figure out. They had one goal. To kill. Period. But shapeshifters appeared human until it was too late...that thought was terrifying.

"Did you see caregivers, Dr. Kingston?" Peter asked.

She shook her head. "I'm—I'm not sure, Peter. They looked human, but they bled like biodrones. Black inky sprays of blood. And they had tentacles."

Peter's mouth fell open and he stared at her for a moment. "That's uh, close enough, Doc. Sounds more like hybrids. I need to tell Sarge about this."

"As soon as Kai and I are back on our feet, we'll happily tell you every detail that happened at the station."

"Peter!" Mimi called from the kitchen. "I need your help please!"

He smiled. "Gotta go. Feel better soon, Doctor Kingston."

"Be safe, Peter," she said as he rushed off, worry shining in his eyes.

She sighed. Regretting that she carried more bad news, especially for Peter. But they had to know everything to keep him and Stingley safe and out of Antaran hands. Or the UCOE government's hands.

Especially their hands.

8

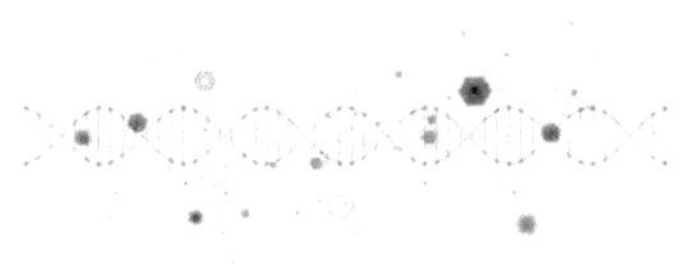

PETER RAN BACK to the restaurant's back room, quarters that he shared with Sting. He yanked open the door and piled inside, his heart racing, the old fear rising in his throat. He'd heard the whispers, listened to Dr. Kingston's account of what had happened on the reclamation station. Saw the slashes all over her. Biodrones! Caregivers!

First, undead D'Angelo and now biodrones—and caregivers—loose on Civilization.

In the faint light from the hallway, the blue walls and curtains were serene against the constant sea of umber and red outside the window. But tonight, with everything blacked out except the restaurant's triage area, the night was thick and dark and foreboding.

His grey canvas lace-up boots squeaked against the cool, ivory-tiled floor. They were a present from Diana who called them high-tops. Chuck-somethings. It took him some practice to tie the laces (he'd never seen them before), but the springy soles felt good against his feet. The room had a faint, nutty coffee scent from the half-full white mug of Karaban coffee he'd left on the white wooden nightstand beside his bed. Coffee wasn't his favorite, but he was learning to appreciate it. Especially with sugar and milk in it—and chocolate.

He glanced out the small window into complete darkness. And it was unnerving. Not seeing the town's colored lights or the bright white glimmer of the shuttle track arcing across the desert toward the shuttle port's blue and white brilliance made him uneasy. All of it was blacked out.

The sight of all that darkness made his skin crawl.

He reached toward his neck, almost expecting the lanyard of his scanning grid to be there, but his fingers brushed across the silver chain and the half-white half-black god symbol that Sting gave him before he took Peter's place on the Antaran ship that night. Peter gripped the round pendant in his fist and squeezed his eyes closed at the memory, at the terrible ache still twisting his insides.

His best friend in the whole world. He sucked in a pained breath. He'd come so close to losing Sting forever.

Sometimes, he shouted himself awake, afraid that rescuing Sting had just been a nice dream he'd had, a datadump as fragile as the tiny red desert flowers that popped up after a short rain shower. But looking over in the night and seeing Sting fast asleep in his bed made it all better.

And he'd fight any and all of those Antaran things that tried to take him back again.

He dropped to his knees and slid out the long, wooden chest under his bed. Mimi had given it to him for his things. He didn't have much. Flicking up the latch, he opened the lid. The box was partitioned in half, one long compartment for his plasma rifle and four smaller compartments where he kept his other things—including his scanning grid. The one he'd carried back from Ballese.

In the middle compartment, he pulled out the datapad, small orange notebook, and strange iridescent gear thing he'd taken from Dr. Constantine's lab when he'd found it on Ballese. There hadn't been a chance to bring up the datapad, notes, and the gear-thing—

much less the lab—to Sarge or Sting or Diana. He put the device and orange notebook back in the box underneath the datapad.

Peter grabbed his rifle and scanning grid and laid them both on the bed.

He had no choice. There was no reasoning or negotiating with any of the Antarans. Except Nikoam, they were all liars and killers. And he'd defend Diana, Mimi, Sarge, and Sting with his life if it came to that.

He shouldered his rifle and then picked up the iridescent gear device. It was about five inches in diameter and a strange gleam radiated through its translucent layers.

The door behind him snapped open.

He shoved the gear thing back into the box and closed the lid.

"Pete! Did you hear about what happened in those escape pods?"

Sting dropped down beside him, looking surprised to see the plasma rifle on his shoulder. He wore a black T-shirt, tan camo pants, and black recombinant-issue chukkas. He smelled like soap and sand, curly blond hair windblown.

"Guess you heard," Sting continued, pointing at the rifle. "Apparently, most of those pods hit ground with a full complement of biodrones inside. They killed a lot of techs and soldiers tonight. A lot of those things escaped though, Pete. They're roaming free."

Peter froze. The situation was getting worse by the moment.

He stared at Sting. Sweat beaded across his upper lip and dotted his forehead, his curly blond bangs shorter than this morning. He'd cut them himself again. Sting hated hair in his eyes. His green eyes glinted with excitement. For the hunt, Peter knew. After what those bastards did to him on Ballese, Peter couldn't blame him for wanting to exterminate every last one of them.

Sting reached out and put his hand on Peter's shoulder, squeezing. "You know what we've gotta do, don't you, buddy?"

"I'm with you, Sting," said Peter with a nod. "Let's run patrol. See what we can stir up in the dark."

He slid his scanning grid's lanyard over his head and swiveled his rifle strap across his chest.

Sting grinned and reached under his cot, taking out his rifle and grid. He also grabbed a small cardboard box and dumped it on the blue quilt covering his cot. Peter grinned. Dozens of charges for their rifles and two tan ammo bags. He and Sting stuffed their ammo bags with cartridges and slipped the bags across their bodies.

"Let's do this," Sting said with a growl as he rose to his feet.

Peter slid the wooden box back under his bed.

"I've got your back, Sting," said Peter.

"You always do, Pete," Sting said, bumping him on the shoulder with his fist.

Sting reached for the doorknob, but the door flew open. Sarge stood there, arms crossed, dark glare cutting right through them.

"Where the hell do you think you, two are going?"

"Out for a beer?" Peter replied.

Sting snickered. Even Sarge's angry expression softened.

"Look, Sarge," Sting began. "We know about the escape pods and the escaped biodrones. Hell, there might even be caregivers out there. Two were sighted on Dr. Kingston's escape pod."

"Caregivers?" Sarge's face pinched, anger darkening to vengeance.

Sarge had a score to settle with those caregivers just like Sting did. So did Peter. For all the horrors he'd seen at Ballese. And what they did to Sting.

Peter shrugged. "May have been hybrids. Either way, we were going to run a patrol around the restaurant." Peter gripped his plasma rifle in both hands. "Make sure D'Angelo and his Antaran buddies don't get inside."

"Fifteen minutes," said Sarge, hands on his hips. "A perimeter scan. If you're both not back in fifteen minutes, you'll be looking for me on that grid, Mitchell. Stingley. You got that? I didn't get tortured on Ballese to bring you and Stingley back alive only to let both of you get killed in Civilization's streets. You, two got that?"

"Yeah, we're five by five, Sarge," said Sting, a grin springing to his face.

Sarge grabbed Peter by the shirt collar and pulled him close. "And if Diana hears about this, we're all in deep debris, Mitchell. So, don't let her find out."

Peter smiled. "Believe me, Sarge, I fear her anger more than those biodrones."

Sarge nodded. "All right. Dismissed. Fifteen minutes."

Peter nodded and elbowed Sting. They rushed around Sarge and moved toward the kitchen. And the restaurant's back door.

Peter slipped into the quiet kitchen and glanced out the window at the dark alley and darker streets beyond it. Without his grid, there were thousands of places to be ambushed.

"Turn on your grid," Sting said in a quiet voice. "Turn on syncing."

Peter grabbed his grid and flicked on the power. He tapped through the life-sign signatures until he found the biodrone physiology and enabled terrain discoverability, letting it map the surroundings as they patrolled. He turned on the sound, testing the low chirp. He paired his grid with Sting's.

"Ready, Sting. I'm on flank."

"Roger that, Pete. I'm on point. We'll patrol a fifteen-meter perimeter." He grinned and ruffled Peter's hair. "Just like old times."

Peter set the scan perimeter to 30 meters just to be sure.

Reaching out to the door handle, he pushed the door open, letting Sting slip outside first. He closed the door behind him and turned around with his rifle clutched in both hands, grid dangling around his neck.

Moving with slow, measured steps, Sting crept into the alley.

"Skimmer's parked along here," Peter whispered. "Scanning."

The skimmer appeared on their grids about two and a half meters to the right of the door.

"Roger that, Pete," Sting whispered.

Peter paused, letting the pervasive black night and the smoky fog from the burning escape pods soak into all his senses. He pulled in a breath. Listening for the skitter of talons. Watching for the glint of gold eyes in the pitch-black haze.

He sniffed the cool air, smelling ash and grease. He concentrated on the wind as the sharp smells of fuel and burnt wires wafted across the river and drifted through town. He had almost a sixth sense for these biodrones now, one he'd developed on Ku'Tal and refined on Ballese. He searched for that trace of honey sweetness on the wind, but not even a hint of syrupiness tanged the smoky night air.

Sting held up two fingers and motioned them forward, around the right side of the skimmer, and down the alley.

Peter followed Sting's path, grid in hand as he swept the area for biodrones.

The alley circled around the back of the restaurant, coming out onto the main thoroughfare through town that forked into four or five side streets. Sting followed the alley as Peter kept his grid in motion. Around the handful of skimmers parked along both sides of the alley.

Ash and embers carried along the cool wind, drifting down like the snow on Ku'Tal.

Sting side-stepped some stacked crates and Peter followed. Around to the front of the restaurant. End of the Line was the only light shining for as far as he could see. Except for the green tracers cutting through the darkness. And red trails of light from UCOE's fighter pilots chasing down enemy ships over Civilization.

How big was the skirmish up there? An infinite army or an advanced scout?

Peter tugged on Sting's sleeve and pointed up at the sky.

Sting looked up, watching the red trails of light arcing toward the desert landscape. In the distance, the desert burned. It made Peter sick to his stomach to see what was happening to the place he called home. The only real place he'd ever known since escaping the military.

With a nod and a poke, Peter followed Sting onto Civilization's main street. The river was a black mirror reflecting the battle overhead in puddles of red and white that ran parallel to the dark, empty street. Sandstone buildings lined both sides of the street, some smoothed with something like colored plaster and others with sandstone blocks.

"Anything, Pete?" Sting whispered.

"Grid's clear," he answered.

Peter hadn't been in most of these places. Except the mercantile across from the restaurant, the Treehouse Pub a block or two down the street, and a bakery two doors down that made fresh, yeasty rolls and bread rounds with garlic and spices baked into them. Diana promised to take him to more of these places and show him what they sold or made.

Peter kept his grid scanning in a steady arc, moving it from side to side as Sting motioned him ahead with two fingers.

But he felt something close. Watching.

Locking step with Sting, Peter stepped forward, expecting his grid to light up at any moment.

Sting moved forward with slow, measured steps, his plasma rifle slung low on his hip, grid in his left hand.

Fear began a slow trickle of cold into his fingers. His mouth went dry. Taste of ash and sand against his lips.

The night was a sudden dead calm. The wind died. Whisper of voices silent. No rustle of doors. No thump of footsteps. Not even the hush of skimmers along the river. The hair on the back of his neck stood up.

His heart beat faster as he took a step down the empty street. Scanned. Another step. Scanned. Nothing.

Dammit! Something was out here. He felt it. Something close. Watching. Calculating.

He sniffed the air.

Beneath the ash and sand and cool of night wafting across the street, he smelled it.

A trace of honey.

"Sting, stop!" Peter said in a loud whisper, pulling in a breath.

Sting froze as Peter moved toward him until his shoulder was against Sting's as they both scanned the perimeter, grids arcing through the darkness.

"What is it, Pete?"

He glanced over his shoulder and back toward the river.

"Traces—something sweet."

"My grid's clear," Sting snapped.

Peter pulled in another breath, hands cradling his rifle as he let the grid fall against his chest. He searched the night for that hint of honey sweetness.

Something just above the smell of dry and burning brush. A brief whiff of sweetness clung to the smoke.

"So's mine, but Sting, the sweetness, I—"

The first chirp was so faint, Peter almost missed it.

He grabbed his grid and crouched in the street, pulling Sting down beside him.

His heart hammered his rib cage, breath coming in short gulps. There was no cover. Nothing to slow them down. Not even a wooden crate. Sweat clung to his upper lip, across his forehead.

"Movement, Sting," Peter whispered, at Sting's back now. "From the north...moving south." He pointed. "Behind those buildings along the river."

He could barely make out the outline of rooftops and fences.

Sting's grid began a slow, staccato chirp.

Peter bit his lip, gripping his rifle with both hands.

Listening for movement. Shuffle of tentacles. Scritch of talons. Something he could target!

"I've got a ghost echo, moving south, Pete. Shifting south–southwest."

His heart pounded into his throat. Fingers turning cold, fear spreading through his chest. He glanced down.

Ghost echoes splashed across his grid. The chirp's staccato rhythm pulsed louder. Faster.

On one knee, Peter swiveled north, rifle raised as the chirp became an insistent whine.

Sting crouched in the street beside him, shoulder against Peter's, rifle raised.

Gold eyes flashed in the darkness.

Peter set himself.

Writhing dark things surged toward them, talons raised. Biodrones!

Peter fired. Orange flash of plasma arcing. The first biodrone collapsed in the street about five meters away. Smoking goo.

Sting squeezed off three shots, felling another one.

But the first one clawed itself up from the dust and inky fluid staining the street. Two eyes becoming four. Limbs multiplying. Separating. Moving.

One became two. Coming at him again.

Peter's mouth fell open.

"Sting..."

One leaped at him, talons just missing his throat.

He unloaded on it and the one behind it, firing again and again. When both of them lay in the street, he burned them both into a puddle of molten blackness.

"Pete, they're gettin' up again!" Sting shouted.

"Keep firing until nothing's left!" Peter replied, turning.

Two more came at him, shadows on blackness.

He pounded them back with a continuous burst of plasma. But every severed appendage began to replicate!

Frantic, Peter ejected a spent charge and slammed another one into the chamber. He burned every squirming, taloned tentacle into paste.

"Obliterate the tentacles!" Peter shouted. "Before they regenerate!"

Two biodrones regenerated right in front of them.

Peter fired, catching the biodrones in a crossfire as Sting opened up on them. Burning them all to sludge.

Three sets of gold eyes came at them from the east. Three more from the north.

"I'll take north!" Peter announced, scrambling to his feet, rifle raised.

"I got east," Sting said, grinning.

Peter mowed down the three biodrones as they screeched and disintegrated, splattering black inky blood and leathery mottled skin all over him. Sting brought down the three from the east and Peter helped him destroy any remaining tentacles.

Three more skittered out of the dark like buzz saws, gold eyes shining as Peter fired again.

Three more dropped. Three appendages rose from the hot inky mess, lunging at him.

Peter side-stepped one, turning it into more sludge, but the other one sliced across his shoulder, talons hooking into his shirt as it careened backward.

Knocking the rifle out of his hands.

It dragged him across the street as more eyes glimmered between two dark buildings.

"Pete!" Sting shouted.

Talons hooked into him from all directions. Eyes. Dozens of gold eyes surrounding him, talons raised.

Cutting. Slicing. Tearing.

Footsteps pounded across the street, plasma rifles pumping orange bursts into the tangle of biodrones as they wrapped tentacles around Peter's arms and legs. Dragging him closer. To more hungry gold eyes. And sharp talons.

Peter screamed! Clawing. Punching. Kicking.

Two more and another and another until biodrones rushed up from the river bank and swarmed him on all sides.

Gold eyes flashed. Talons flailed.

"Die!" Sting shouted, emptying an entire charge.

More plasma fire erupted. Until it rained black fluid and burnt flesh.

Through the chaos, lit by plasma fire, Peter saw D'Angelo in a skimmer just below the river bank.

"We know you have it," D'Angelo said to him from the river bank as he moved toward him. "And I'll tear it out of you—or them—bit by bit if I have to."

"Pete! Oh, God—PETE!"

"It's up to you how this turns out. Orlando."

Orlando? D'Angelo really believed he was Orlando Constantine?

A hailstorm of plasma fire ripped through the squirming, slimy masses of tentacles and eyes. Sting ejected the spent charge and slammed another into the slot. And opened fire.

Peter counted two—three rifles.

In a deafening roar, plasma arcs cut through bodies and appendages. They tore through the mob, cutting across Peter's arms and slicing into his jeans.

His body had gone stiff, his limbs unresponsive. He forced his arms up to cover his head, the exertion painful as he gritted his teeth against the pain. He was drowning in muck and spew.

"Keep firing until none of 'em gets up!" Sting.

Peter groaned. Drowning in darkness, dead biodrones, and severed, quivering appendages.

Until hands grabbed him under the arms and pulled him free as more plasma fire turned the remaining biodrones into slush that mixed with the dust and sand when the wind rose.

The hiss of a skimmer whispered in the silence, speeding away, the sound headed down the river. Toward the shuttle port.

D'Angelo.

Peter felt sick. What did he have that the Antarans wanted?

"Pete! Oh, God, Pete!"

Sting sucked in a breath, his chest heaving as he dropped to his knees, slapping away debris and muck. "Talk to me! Please tell me you're not dead! Please, Pete!"

"Ron, keep a lookout. Easy, Sting, let me help."

Sarge?

"Roger that, David," said Ron. "Don't know if we can take another swarm of those things."

Peter felt hands against his shoulders and under his legs. Lifting him out of the muck of death piled in the street.

"Pete, if you're dead, I swear I'll kill you!" Sting.

"Sting, let me at least help carry him," Sarge. Somewhere off to his left.

Everything burned and ached, the breeze intensifying, chilling his skin. He felt it tingle against the cold air coming off the river as everything turned dark.

"Help me get him up the stairs, Sarge."

Someone took hold of his feet. The contact ached something fierce, but he didn't have the energy to cry out.

Light gleamed around the edges of his eyelids, voices colliding together into a painful thrum against his head.

Then the tugging started. Against his boots, his jeans. His T-shirt. All of it fell away. He felt warm water slathering his face and hair, his arms. Someone held his left hand. Someone else gripped his right shoulder.

Warm water pressed gently against his face, around his eyes. Someone lifted one of his eyelids and shined a light across his eye. Moving it from side to side.

"Pupils are sluggish, not tracking as well as I'd like." A voice he didn't recognize.

"He's got as many plasma wounds as he has talon strikes," said another voice he didn't recognize.

"Good thing most are superficial."

"He's got some partial paralysis, reaction to the venom," said another voice.

Peter tried to open his eyes, but they didn't want to respond. He tried to speak, but only a squeak came out.

"Let's get him cleaned up and these wounds dressed."

The voice sounded funneled and far away as he felt himself

slipping into the dark streets, D'Angelo standing over him, rifling through his pockets.

———

SOMETIME LATER, Peter shouted himself awake.

He bolted upright, but strong hands pressed him back down against the makeshift triage bed. He was back inside Mimi's restaurant. He squinted at the shadow standing over him, his vision blurry. Curly blond hair. Worried green eyes. Sting.

"Sting?" He tried to sit up.

"Whoa, not so fast, Pete." Sting let out a breath he'd been holding, his worried look turning to annoyance. "Dammit, Pete! You scared the ever-livin' hell outta me! Again!" Sting laid his hands against Peter's shoulders and eased him against the bed again.

"Sting!" Peter said in a hoarse voice.

"When those damned biodrones dragged you out of the street, I was losin' my mind!"

Peter shuddered at the memory of all those slimy, squirming bodies and appendages flailing against him. Stench of burning flesh and cloying sweetness. Putrid stink of sticky black blood spewing all over his face and on his hands. He rubbed his hands against the sheet, trying to erase the feel, the memory.

"I—couldn't do any–thing," Peter said, his mouth not wanting to create the right sounds. His whole body felt sluggish, like it couldn't react. The slightest move was work. "Where's...my—rifle?"

What was wrong with him?

"Take it easy. It's safe, buddy. Like you. I was trying to shoot 'em all, but there were just too many. And you were just too close. Then Sarge and Kraver came around from the front of the restaurant, firing."

Peter tried to smile. "Guess—it'd been fifteen minutes, huh?"

Sting laughed, reaching out and gently ruffling his hair.

"Good thing. I wasn't sure what we'd find in all that sludge." He patted Peter's arm. "The docs all gave you an anti-venom shot, so you should be moving better soon."

"Good," said Peter with a sigh. "Could—barely. Move out there."

This was strange. He'd never been affected like this by a biodrone before.

Sting looked up. Diana, her eyes teary, stepped to Peter's left and took his hand in hers, a crisp white bandage encircling his arm to the elbow.

"Peter, you scared me to death," she said, bottom lip quivering.

Tears tracked down her face, her beautiful warm brown eyes flecked gold in the light. He tugged her toward him and kissed her, despite the sluggish muscles.

"Don't cry, Diana, I'm...all right."

"You'd better be, Peter Mitchell."

He forced his mouth into a half smile. "I am. If they'd—wanted to kill me...I'd be dead."

Sting stared at him. "Yeah, you're right, Pete." His face was pensive now.

Something about this whole attack felt wrong. Contrived. Like those things had been sent there. For him. As a show of force. To intimidate him.

He remembered D'Angelo standing there on the river bank with a skimmer. What was it he'd said? Something about wanting something Peter had. And he'd called him Orlando. Why? Was it that strange gear thing he'd taken from Dr. Constantine's lab on Ballese? Or something else?

"Why didn't they—kill me, Sting?" Peter asked. "They're biodrones. Created—only to kill."

"I don't know, Pete," said Sting, his gaze falling to the floor. "I've never seen them try to drag someone off like that. Not even on Ballese in the testing grounds. And definitely not on Ku'Tal."

"Only when the—caregivers called them—off me on Ku'Tal," Peter replied, his words coming easier now.

He wanted to bring up D'Angelo and what he'd said, but not

here. Not now. Especially in front of Diana. He didn't want her to worry. Or Sting. He needed to talk to Sarge. Alone. Something was very wrong here and he didn't know what to make of it. He also needed to fess up to Sarge about finding Dr. Constantine's lab. He hadn't told a soul about the device and the datapad with all the notes. He'd been unconscious and out of his head when they brought him back from Ballese. Everyone had come back injured and then Sarge was back at the job.

He sighed. But after what happened tonight, no one was safe on Civilization like before. What he needed to know most was if this was an advanced scout for the Antarans or was it a last-ditch effort to get hold of him for some reason? It had to be that device. What else could it be? He was a recombinant. He didn't own anything of value. He had no education. What about him made the Antarans come after him again? Especially after Ballese.

Was it revenge for destroying their work on Ku'Tal and Ballese? The genetic repository?

Something told him it was bigger than that. Bigger than one recombinant hunted by biodrones.

Sarge was his best chance to make sense of this. He swallowed a breath. Before something terrible happened.

One of the nurses clad in dark blue scrubs with Civilization Hospital embroidered in gold on the left side stopped beside him. The nurse was a slight man with brown hair and dark eyes.

"How do you feel?" the nurse asked.

"Sluggish, but other than that, I'm fine," said Peter, pulling himself up to a sitting position.

Sarge walked up behind the nurse. "Doctor Cho released him to two days bedrest, so Sting and I will get him down the hall to his room.

Peter frowned. "Two days? But Sarge, I—"

"No buts, Peter Mitchell," Diana snapped, hands on her hips. She turned her gaze to the nurse. "Sting and I will make sure he stays in bed."

"On it," said Sting, taking hold of Peter's right arm.

Sarge stepped up and took hold of his left arm. Together, they got him on his feet. All he had on were his grey boxers. They had cut away his jeans and T-shirt.

Walking was a new exercise in futility. He tried to put one foot in front of the other, but his legs didn't want to obey.

"Stop stalling, Mitchell," said Sarge, struggling to keep him upright.

"I'm not, Sarge, my legs aren't listening to my brain," he said, frowning as he stumbled.

Sting caught him. Footsteps clacked against the tile as they lifted Peter into his arms and carried him to his room. Diana hurried in front of them and opened the door. She turned down the blue and green quilt and sheets and they laid him on his bed. She started removing his grey canvas boots. The high-tops. He reached over and ran his fingers through Diana's hair, stroking the back of her neck.

"Thanks, Diana," he said.

He glanced up at Sarge and Sting, both of them looking apprehensive.

"Thanks for the rescue, Sting. Sarge. I owe you both for saving me like that."

Sting let out a snort. "Let's see, you risked your freedom—and your life—to come to Ballese and get yourself captured to save me. And get me out of the military. And let's see, you also saved my ass from a bunch of cascade mines on Ku'Tal. And you saved our subunit from washing out when Drake accidentally shot you with a live plasma round during our final sim test. That means I owe you at least two more saves, buddy."

Peter smiled but looked down at his hands.

"And let's see," said Sarge. "You carried me out of the swamp when the unit stepped into a minefield. And you carried my injured ass out of that depot repository—whatever it was—all the way to a safe house. And you followed me to Ballese to watch my back. I think I owe you a couple too, Peter."

"You'd have done the same for me out there," said Peter, glancing up at them. "And I'd do it a hundred times over for all of you." He pulled in a breath. "Sarge, Sting," he reached out and stroked Diana's hair. "And Diana. I mean that."

Sting snatched a pillow off his bed and threw it, hitting Peter in the face.

"Enough of this mushy shit. Diana, make him rest while Sarge and I go on patrol with Kraver."

Peter threw the pillow back onto Sting's bed. He reached over and pulled Diana against him, wrapping her in his arms as he slid the quilt over them.

9

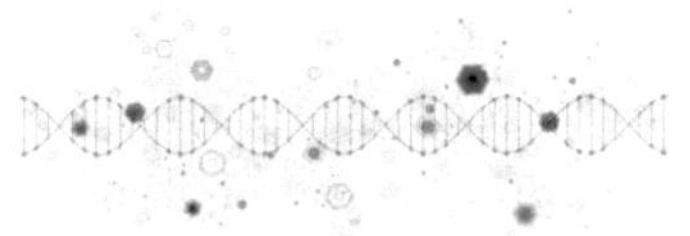

AFTER JEANNETTE WAS TREATED for minor injuries, she and Kai assisted with triaging patients until well after two in the morning. Exhausted, she and Kai collapsed at one of the restaurant tables, the place in shambles, chairs and colored pillows shoved into corners, tables strewn haphazardly throughout, and bags of dirty sheets setting by the front door. The place smelled like bleach and patchouli as Mimi Constantine sat down at the table.

She plopped a bottle of pinot noir on the table, three wine glasses, and a datapad.

"Thanks for pitching in," said Mimi, dressed in black pants and a green blouse, her strawberry blond hair tied up in a red paisley scarf. "I've got a couple of rooms upstairs. Plenty of room for you both to sleep."

"Thanks," said Kai. "Much appreciated since our beds went up in flames today."

Jeannette nodded. "Yes, you're too kind. Especially since all our clothes and things were on that station."

Mimi reached toward the open wine bottle and filled three glasses. Jeannette slid one glass over to Kai and picked up another one. She took a sip, letting it roll over her tongue, the red wine rich with hints of warm chocolate and blackberries.

"That's very good," said Jeannette, setting down the glass.

"So, do we have any counts on survivors yet?" Kai asked and took a sip of wine. "From what I heard, most of those escape pods were full of biodrones."

"It's true," said Mimi, staring into her glass. "Someone said there were about two dozen survivors from the escape pods. Some of the shuttles made it off the station before it crumpled. The station didn't go up in flames though like they expected. It might be a huge salvage operation or they may attempt to repair it."

Kai made a sour face. "Repair it? It's hosed. They'd never get that mess operational again. Salvage some of it maybe."

"I just hope we won't have more of those biodrones on our doorsteps," said Mimi. "David and Ron put together patrols after Peter almost got dragged off by them."

"Peter was lucky," said Jeannette. "Just minor wounds and some plasma burns. A good night's rest and he'll be fine." She took another sip of wine, her gaze falling to the datapad that Mimi laid on the table.

"So, I hear that your man here wants his MRC removed," said Mimi, glancing at Kai.

Jeannette nodded. "Yes, if you wouldn't mind."

"I'd be grateful," said Kai. "And I'll pay you for your time. A donation to the cause."

"Happy to oblige," said Mimi. "But why don't we talk about what you really want to know."

"What?" Jeannette studied Mimi's pale blue eyes, unable to read anything behind her pleasant demeanor.

"I've seen the EVFs, doctor. Yours and Peter's." Mimi stared at her, an apprehensive expression on her face.

"How?" Jeannette asked, shaking her head.

Kai fidgeted with the stem of his wine glass, staring at the dark wooden table.

She watched him squirm for a moment. "Kai..."

"Your man here shared them with me. Only to help you. He says you haven't been able to bring yourself to watch them. But I had to see them for myself—to see Orlando—before I knew where to start."

Jeannette sighed. Sooner or later, she'd have to view them, but right now, she wanted to know about her connection to Orlando Constantine. She could barely remember him. It all felt so distant. And so hazy.

"I need to know how I connect to your brother, Mimi," she said, her hands beginning to shake. "And I have to know how connected I was to—" She took a deep breath and held it a moment then released it. "To the Recombinant Defense Program. My God, did I actually help them create these cloned soldiers that we're sending off to die by the thousands? And treat them like cattle."

Mimi reached over and laid her hand on Jeannette's. "I get it, dear, believe me. I wouldn't be doing what I do if I didn't feel the same way. Orlando was...caught in the middle. Like you, I'd imagine. Both of you were lied to about the nature of the program."

Jeannette couldn't understand how her younger self could have signed onto to such a monstrous endeavor. It went against everything she believed as a doctor, to do no harm.

"Orlando was trying to find another way forward," Mimi continued. "He'd been researching some artifacts in Taus, things much older than the Antaris Nation. A forerunner race that left behind astounding technologies, but no one seems to know what they do or how they work. Decrypting their language is proving elusive. Everyone dismissed these technologies as fantasy. Everyone except Orlando."

Ancient technology from a lost highly technical civilization? She'd seen some opticals of the ruins found throughout the Taus system, intricate mechanisms and circuits that were mind-boggling. Complex matrices and connections. Power sources a complete mystery.

"Every chance Orlando got, he led expeditions to sites on

Naharra and Ballese and the other Taus planets. He told me he was close to a breakthrough. That was just before—"

Mimi paused, choking up, tears welling in her eyes.

Jeannette squeezed her hand. "It's okay if you don't want to keep talking about it."

Mimi shook her head. "Before he was killed on Ballese when Antarans overran the colony." She sighed and picked up her wine glass, taking a drink. "Every time I look at Peter, it's like glancing into the past, into my little brother's eyes."

Jeannette pulled in a breath. No time like the present. She had to know about Peter's DNA profile.

"I don't know how to tell you this, Mimi, but you are looking into Orlando's eyes. I discovered that Peter Mitchell's DNA is an exact match of your brother, Orlando's DNA."

"What?" Mimi cried, thrusting her hand over her mouth.

"Peter's recombinant batch number always bothered me when I was investigating the errors in the MRCs. His batch number was exactly the same as the others in his group, but his number had an O in the middle of it. A letter. Now, I don't know how or why, but Orlando cloned himself and hid the genetic profile in with the other recombinant batches. So, it got—produced along with the other batch."

Mimi sat back in her chair, looking overwhelmed. "I've met plenty of recombinants in my day and we've been able to reintegrate lots of them into life after the military. But I have never met a single recombinant like Peter Mitchell. Ever."

"That's because, technically, he's not a recombinant," said Kai.

Kai was right! By all rights, UCOE didn't own Peter's genetic pattern.

"That's an excellent point that Diana—and Peter—will love to hear," said Mimi, her eyes brightening. "Besides, he doesn't behave like a recombinant. Well, neither does his best friend, the one he rescued from Ballese. Stingley. Y'know, he looks a lot like...oh, no." Her expression darkened. "Oh, my, God...Orlando, you didn't."

Jeannette stared at her. "What's wrong?"

"Orlando and I were just kids when my oldest brother, Beckett died on Mars in a training accident. He was a star pilot. Damn it, Orlando! What did you do?"

"Do you think he created a genetic profile on your other brother, too?"

Mimi nodded, grabbing her datapad. "I thought there was something familiar about Sting."

She flicked on the datapad and paged through screen after screen. Jeannette took a long sip of her wine, glancing at Kai who just shrugged and drank his wine. He was on his feet, but shouldn't be, she knew. He'd tried to hide the broken ribs and fractured left wrist, but she made him take a long break while she tended to the other patients. He was dead on his feet, that wine the only thing keeping him up right about now.

"I knew I still had an image of him in his uniform. Tell me what you think?" Mimi said, turning the datapad toward Jeannette.

His light blond hair was cut short, keeping his curly hair in check. His face was boyish, bluish green eyes bright. He was no more than twenty in that picture. With his hair shorter, John Stingley would be an exact copy of Beckett Constantine.

Because he was.

"But that means that Sting isn't technically a recombinant either," said Jeannette.

"Technically speaking," said Kai, glancing from her to Mimi, "Peter and Sting are brothers." He chuckled. "Your brothers, Ms. Constantine."

"Okay, I was not prepared to have this conversation," said Mimi, rising from her chair. "Not without a lot more wine." She refilled her wine glass. "I'm not sure how I feel about any of this right now. I'll admit, I had an instant affinity with Peter, but I thought it was just his aura and that childlike sense of wonder of his. That made him seem like the little brother from my childhood. Since both of my brothers are gone. But this?"

Jeannette watched her drink deeply from her wine glass as she paced around the table.

"I can't imagine how strange this must be for you, Mimi," said Jeannette. "To have both dead brothers cloned and then run into them suddenly...I don't even know what I'd think."

Mimi nodded. "In some ways, Peter is the best of Orlando, like he was before the war. Before he became a xenogeneticist, before he started working for the government." She sighed, her eyes welling with tears. "Before he signed onto the Recombinant Defense Program...and became obsessed with the artifacts. But Peter is unique despite being Orlando's genetic copy. His sense of wonder is irreplaceably unique."

"I couldn't agree more," said Jeannette.

She hoped nothing ever changed that about Peter. Ironic that such an innocent was produced by something as brutal as the Recombinant Defense Program. And despite the RDC and his time spent fighting at the front. He didn't get to be a child. He was barely treated like a human being. He entered this world at twenty-two with no education—except the skills he'd need to fight and die at the front.

Recombinants were expected to die. They were projected to live a year at the front. And automatically destroyed at five years. Yet, Peter Mitchell evolved despite all of that. And so did John Stingley. Was it their genetics? Or something else harder to pinpoint. Like that connection between them? Peter's love for Diana Temple?

Mimi set her glass on the table and picked up the datapad. She flicked it on and pulled up some files.

Jeannette knew very little about the Taus artifacts. A rare handful of Earth's researchers had brief excursions to the artifact sites on Naharra (before UCOE ordered the nuclear bombardment that led to the creation of Naharra rules). There was some information from the Ballese expeditions until the Antarans destroyed the colony. Naharra had already been lost. Farnas and Karaba had much more exploration time, but now, those planets were in jeopardy, too.

Like Civilization.

"Mimi, I do have some memories of Orlando," Jeannette replied. "I remember him talking about this forerunner race that predated the Antaris Nation and how fascinated he was by their tech and the artifacts they left behind. And I recall that he took some leave and spent some time on Naharra and Ballese. But I have no memory of any of his results or findings."

Mimi picked up her wine glass and took another long sip.

Kai rose from his chair and stretched. "I think I recall him mentioning something about it in one of your EVFs, Red. Some sort of ancient engine or apparatus."

Jeannette frowned. "I wish I could remember."

She had vague memories of working with Orlando, a much older version of Peter Mitchell. She remembered that he had become almost obsessed with the artifacts and their purpose. And she recalled his growing paranoia, claiming that he was being watched. And followed. But that was the extent of her memories of him. Memories with vague surroundings, an almost generic lab, sterile, and blindingly white. White walls, white floors, white tables—and white coats. Her MRC had whitewashed the memories and filed down all the rough edges until they were useless.

She sighed and picked up her wine glass, taking another long sip.

"My MRC sanitized most of my memories that involved working with Orlando, Mimi. What I do remember is Orlando becoming more and more obsessed with the artifacts. And paranoid, claiming that he was being watched. Followed. Filmed. We were already working on an apparently secret project that I have no memory of, but whoever was following him didn't seem connected to the Recombinant Defense Program. Could his obsessive and paranoid behavior have been an effect of the artifacts?"

Kai shrugged. "It's possible. Those were desperate times before UCOE got the first recombinants fully deployed. Especially if Orlando had discovered something about those artifacts that could win a war."

"Perhaps he knew more about them than he let on, at least to me anyway," said Jeannette.

She refilled her wine glass, her brain on fire with possibilities and what-ifs, but there were too many holes in her memory to connect any of it. It was like a bunch of tangled, knotted strings.

"Maybe I can help with that?" Mimi slid back into her chair, her light blue eyes animated, a smile rising on her lips. "Before the colony on Ballese was destroyed by the Antarans," she said, her voice sounding hoarse but excited. "Orlando sent me some encrypted optics through the physical mail, hidden inside an old book. Sent it media rate, so it took forever. He said that the optics were insurance, just in case anything happened to him."

What could Orlando have sent his sister that was so important? That he'd have trusted to arrive by space barge sometime in the next century. Jeannette chewed her bottom lip, her mind alight with possibilities.

"Well, what was on the optics?" Kai asked. He took another sip of wine, his gaze darting from her to Mimi.

Mimi shook her head. "He told me to hide them. And only decrypt them if he was dead and the war was lost."

Jeannette felt a shiver of dread rush along her spine, a heaviness settling on her chest. That sounded ominous. And terrifying.

"So, self-replicating biodrones destroying reclamation stations and landing on Civilization would be a really good reason to open those files, Mimi," said Kai.

He leaned forward, elbows propped on the table. His left wrist was in a blue cast and he looked so tired, working off impulse power after the long, crazy day they'd had.

"I agree," said Jeannette. "If these biodrones were the advanced scouts, then a Ballese-like attack may be imminent here."

"I was afraid you'd say that," said Mimi, wincing as she set down her wine glass.

She patted her datapad, red fingernails tapping the optics slot. She released the small optics disc and held the clear rainbowed circle between her fingers. It was about two inches in diameter and iridescent, an old technology, but that might have been intentional to hide its importance.

"Decrypt it," said Kai, his voice commanding, "Let's see what's on it. We need all the help we can get right now."

Mimi glanced at Jeannette, looking for her to respond, too.

Jeannette nodded. "Let's find out what Orlando needed to keep so safe. It might help us defend Civilization...and home system."

They needed something to bolster their ranks and if nothing else, to slow down the Antarans. Long enough to turn the tide against them.

Mimi slid the optics disc back into the datapad and pressed her thumb to the biometric scanner, launching the decryption algorithm. It took several minutes to authenticate, requiring Mimi to give a voice imprint match and answer several security questions.

"I can't imagine what could be so important on that optics disc that would require that many layers of security," said Kai, shaking his head.

He reached over and laid his hand on Jeannette's, squeezing.

"How you holding up, Red? You've been up about...thirty-seven hours—give or take."

"I'm okay," said Jeannette. "I've got another hour or two left in me." She studied his weary face a moment, remembering all those late nights in med school and as an intern. Not to mention working in the ER. Like him, she'd get through it.

They waited, the silence mounting. It seemed like hours and most of that bottle of pinot noir before the optics disc ejected. Strange symbols flashed across the datapad's screen, scrolling downward at lightning speed.

"What the hell is that?" Kai demanded. "It looks like Antaran code."

Mimi shook her head, still watching the screen. "I have no idea. But I wouldn't know Antaran code if it smacked me in the face. Are you sure it's Antaran?"

Kai nodded. "I'm sure," he said, squinting at the screen. "But it's like a mutation of it somehow."

"An older version," Jeannette added. "Like it preceded the current Antaran script. A forerunner?"

"Maybe," he said with a shrug. "Maybe your brother took it from those tech sites he found, so if the Antarans got hold of the data, they wouldn't understand it?"

"Good theory," Mimi replied, watching the screen fill and scroll with page after page of unintelligible symbols.

They waited for several minutes until the symbols stopped flashing. The screen blanked and a message scrolled onto the screen.

"The engine is now online and in a wait state, awaiting peripheral integration and input. Cipher is active. Ready to connect inputs and engage cipher."

At the bottom of the screen was a note. "Sis, I know what they're after. It's an ancient engine that makes our recombinant defense program look like child's play. Work with JK to understand my colony lab work. You can meditate on it in the chapel. All my love, Orlando."

Kai scrambled backward. "Holy shit! That wasn't a decryption sequence! That was a launch sequence! What did it just do?"

He exchanged worried glances with Jeannette and Mimi, shaking his head.

For the first time, she saw Mimi look flustered.

"I—I don't know. It was just supposed to decrypt the disc, not run anything. Oh, Orlando, what did you just make me do?" Mimi was shaking now, staring from the screen to Jeannette. "Doctor Kingston, only you know what he was working on."

Jeannette bowed her head. Her MRC knew. Guess she had no choice but to challenge those memories head-on and see for herself what had happened.

"I'll have to suck it up and view the EVFs taken from my memory replacement chip," said Jeannette, shaking her head. "It's the only way I'll understand what Orlando was working on back then." She pointed at the datapad. "Including that."

Kai was at her back now, hands rubbing her shoulders. "We've got to take a look at this recombinant's DNA, Red. Mitchell. I can guarantee that Orlando hid things in the kid's DNA. Maybe there'll be a clue to what we've just launched into action?" He sighed. "And which side he was working for."

Mimi rose from her chair, pacing now, her face pale, fingers clenching and unclenching.

"Orlando's no traitor! He believed in the Recombinant Defense Program in theory, but what went into practice went against everything he believed. That much I know."

"How?" Kai snapped, arms crossed against his chest, cradling his broken wrist. "How can you be sure?"

Mimi's face darkened, eyes narrowing as she shot back an angry glance at Kai.

"He bankrolled the startup of my entire recombinant underground operation and supported it until—" Her voice cracked and she bit her lip. "Until the Antarans rolled over Ballese."

Kai moved over to Mimi and gripped her hands. "I'm not trying to brand your brother as a traitor or anything," he said in a quiet voice. "Just trying to understand his motivations and goals. What he was fighting for—or against? It would help us piece together this puzzle."

"Thank you for that," Mimi said, nodding, eyes misting. She squeezed Kai's hand and let go. "It's something I need to understand, too...otherwise, I won't be much help to you."

Jeannette remembered Orlando becoming more and more disillusioned with his work, but *the work* was gone from her memory, only that vague sense of floating whiteness that had been the Recombinant Development Center remained. She also remembered him quitting the program. Going to Ballese. She frowned. Had he quit or just stopped showing up? She sighed, rubbing her forehead. Or did they fire him? She couldn't remember. But her MRC did and those answers were somewhere in the EVFs that Kai had grabbed from it.

As Mimi laid out the timeline of forming her recombinant underground for Kai, Jeannette's thoughts slid back to the recombinant pool of genetics. How each biogenetic profile UCOE created had been enhanced by splicing in targeted artificial RNA sequences. Folding and pairing collections of short helices to create double helices that were amalgams of desired traits and behaviors. Switches to turn off the expression of undesirable qualities. She'd called it Frankenstein Genetics.

How was Orlando's *encrypted* data connected to the xDNA sequencing running through Peter Mitchell's genetic profile? That had been an exact copy of Orlando's genetics. She was almost certain that Orlando had hidden information encoded in DNA inside Peter's recombinant pattern. Genetic computing, especially its processing and storage capabilities, was still highly theoretical and experimental.

And illegal in citizens.

No one would care or look for it in an endless stream of constantly changing recombinant genetic patterns. Or notice a handful of recombinants that didn't match their stored behavior types exactly.

That had a year to live at best.

There had never been a recombinant washed out at five years. Because they never lived past that first one.

For whatever reason, Peter Mitchell stood out. Badly.

He was highly intelligent, observant, and loyal. Sensitive, innocent, but stubbornly persistent. He was Orlando's best image. Sting stood out, too, his genetics based on Orlando's risk-taking astronaut brother, Beckett. Sting had physically and mentally outperformed every recombinant he encountered. Besides that, he was even-tempered, courageous, and tough. And fiercely loyal like Peter.

Together, Peter and Sting made an unstoppable team. Their

bond of friendship—kinship—was enviable. It ran deeper and closer than brothers. And it was unbreakable.

Had Orlando meant to physically clone himself as sort of a backup data repository (or Sting) for his research? Or had that been an accident? A case of being his own test subject gone awry.

Or did he need both genetic patterns for some purpose?

Without Orlando's notes and data files, it was all useless speculation. Reviewing every nucleotide in these genetic profiles would take years. Even comparing Peter's genetics to Sting's would take a long time and some serious processing power. She'd need more computing power than anything available on Civilization. It would require several nodes across the solar array.

The loud thump against the restaurant's front door startled Jeannette.

Mimi moved toward the door. But the door swung open before she got there.

Jeannette got to her feet as a stocky fifty-something woman with brown hair and angry hazel eyes stepped into the restaurant, in dress blues. Colonel Eloise Stanton. Her face was puckered in a scowl as she looked down her nose at Mimi and took in the entire room.

"I was told this was the triage station for the reclamation station emergency," she replied in a low alto voice that rasped a bit as she spoke, her diction precise, almost overstated.

She stared at Jeannette and Kai in surprise for a moment.

"Doctor Kingston, Doctor Drew, what are you doing here?" She turned her angry gaze on Mimi. "What are my reclamation specialists doing here in this makeshift triage unit?" she demanded.

"Barely surviving the attack on the station and the biodrones inside the escape pods," said Kai, his gaze dark and his temper short. "We volunteered to triage patients that survived the attack."

Stanton said nothing. She didn't even respond to Kai as her gaze fell onto Jeannette, a long, withering glare, but Jeannette was beyond being intimidated by this woman. There were much better paying jobs right here on Civilization. She wouldn't participate in any more of Stanton's attempts to intimidate or control her.

"And what about you, Doctor Kingston?" she asked, watching her with an unblinking gaze as she slowly stepped toward Jeannette. "What are you doing here?" She held out her arms. "And where are all the patients? And—the recombinants that were brought here."

"Like Doctor Drew, I was helping in an emergency after escaping the imploding station," she said, doing her best to keep her words focused on specifics. "And those biodrones that wreaked havoc on the survivors' escape pods are now loose in Civilization's streets."

"What about the recombinants?" Stanton asked again, her tone impatient. "Several were seen and...treated here. Where are they?"

Stanton put a hand on her hip, her bureaucratic mask positioned perfectly, but Jeannette saw the monster beneath it.

"What recombinants?" Kai asked with a shrug. "We didn't treat any recombinants."

"Regardless, our heavy losses are a terrible tragedy," Stanton said like she was reading a script. Badly. "We must carry on in their names and fight the good fight. Give their deaths meaning."

Jeannette bristled. "There is no meaning period in senseless death," she said, rising from her chair. "And even less in losing more in meaningless skirmishes in the streets of Civilization."

Stanton scowled at her, but Jeannette stood her ground. She had no trust left in the colonel and at this point, she was out of a job. She had nothing to lose this time.

"Until further notice, you and Doctor Drew have been transferred to reclamation station 951-DGO. We don't yet know if your current station assignment will be repaired or replaced. You are expected at station 951 in two weeks. The shift coordinator assured me that they had ample space on third shift for two talented reclamation specialists such as yourself, Doctor Kingston, and Doctor Drew."

Third shift. Jeannette glowered at Stanton. Evil bitch.

"That's the station near Ku-Tal," Kai replied, glaring at Stanton. "The new one they built after the other one got blown up."

A wry smile twisted Stanton's gargoyle-like features. "Yes, and the new facilities are state of the art, I hear. They will help you both do your jobs much more efficiently, I'm told."

"So, the new station'll implode fifty percent faster than the previous one?" Kai replied.

Jeannette held in a bitter chuckle.

Mimi walked toward Colonel Stanton and led her to the front door, escorting her out of the restaurant. "Well, Colonel, if you'll excuse us, we have to check on the last of the triage patients and turn this place back into a restaurant."

"I hope the biodrones get her," Kai remarked and kicked a table.

Jeannette watched Mimi close the door and lock it.

"You know what, Kai," Jeannette began, turning toward him. "I'll turn in my resignation before I let her dump us into the belly of another one of those space crypts and bury us."

"Agreed," said Kai, looking sullen. "I'll be damned if I let her sweep us and our data into a black hole. And another third shift."

"That was an awfully fast turnaround for reassignment," said Jeannette. "She didn't even know where we were. Or if we'd even made it out."

Kai cast an angry glance at the front door. "She looked very surprised to see us. Like she'd expected us to be dead. And what the hell was that about recombinants?"

Kai was right. Stanton did look surprised to see the two of them. She moved closer to Kai.

"What do you think about us requesting to remain at our posts at the current station?" she asked. "If we route it out of her hands, we could get clearance to remain."

"And royally piss her off? Oh, I'm totally in," he said, the twinkle returning to his glass-blue eyes. "She seems like she's in a big hurry to get us out of here. I mean, get rid of us."

"That's what I thought," said Jeannette. "So, let's request to remain at the temporary location here on Civilization until a decision about the station's future is made. Stay and make her life as painful as possible."

"As much as that pleases me," said Kai, the smile slipping from his face. He looked concerned, his voice turning quiet. "I really want to go back out to our current station and see it for myself. Something just doesn't feel right about this. Biodrones. The timing. How it all went down. And she just waltzes into the restaurant after biodrones swarm the area. Like it was planned, y'know?"

Jeannette nodded. "I felt that way, too," she replied. "There's no way those Antaran injector ships could have put that many biodrones through the hull that quickly. There were too many UCOE ships routing them. And those last two specialists that boarded our pod at just the right moment. They weren't even on our shift. It just felt— staged."

"Yeah, that's the word…staged," said Kai. "With the intent to assassinate all of us in that pod. You and I weren't supposed to survive that attack, Jeannette. But there's more to it than that. And the only way we can prove it is to get back aboard the station somehow. Find evidence that shows it was staged."

Jeannette studied his pensive face, gaze far away as he chewed on the events at the station again. He was right. Something didn't feel right at all. They needed to take another look at the station. Find evidence that proved Stanton was involved in something nefarious.

Before something worse happened. Like an invasion force landing on Civilization.

Mimi walked over to the table, arms crossed, worry creasing her face.

"She kept asking about recombinants," said Mimi. "I want to know why."

Jeannette nodded. "It was peculiar. Not sure why. She's never been interested in recombinants. Even when she tried to bury our report on overused insertions of reconditioned MRCs. We finally got it into some concerned hands at UCOE, but so far, no changes have been made."

"How many reclamation stations use recombinants as part of their staff?" Mimi asked.

Kai shook his head. "None that I've heard of...plenty of dead ones coming through though. Stanton didn't have any on staff at our station either."

"First thing tomorrow, we get a lift up to the station," said Jeannette to Kai. "See what's happened for ourselves."

"Agreed," said Kai with a yawn. "For now, we need some sleep."

"First D'Angelo and now this Colonel Stanton," said Mimi, her gaze still on the front door as she moved toward the hallway that led upstairs. "Civilization may be getting too hot for me and my restaurant operation." She sighed, rubbing her hands against her tunic. "And for Peter and Sting. They're not safe right now. I'm concerned. Especially after Stanton showing up here, asking about recombinants."

Jeannette and Kai followed behind her.

"Why do you say that?" Jeannette asked.

"Because," Mimi replied, her pale blue eyes looking haunted. "That woman had no aura. None. It wasn't even black like D'Angelo's. It was just plain not there. I've never met a human being without an aura." She stared at Jeannette and gripped the railing. "I don't think that woman is human."

A chill rushed down Jeannette's spine as she stared at Kai in shock. Was Mimi right? Was Stanton something other than human? Looked like it was time to find out.

10

PETER DREAMED OF BALLESE. And Naharra—a place he'd never been. A dark, smoky landscape. Rocky outcrops, basalt and ebony cliffsides, craggy pocked soil the color of ash. A desolate red sky. Skeletal trees. A thick grey haze hung like apparitions, the air smelling scorched and heavy. Mountains rose on all sides. Dormant volcanoes.

And a stone path winding up toward a rugged cliffface. On a windswept plateau.

A rocky entrance. Pulsing with life.

Circuits came alive in the ashen soil, honeycombed plates partially buried in the powdery earth. Bright blue and green and red trails led toward a smooth glassy enclosure.

And a dark doorway.

He stood in front of the doorway, arms stretched toward the red sky, feet planted in the soil that kicked up whorls of dust around him. Lightning flashed through the gloom. Crackling like a whip as it split open the sky. Striking the plateau. Causing the glass enclosure to glow with eerie red and blue brilliance.

And the black door. Became translucent.

He gazed through the smoky panels that turned clear. Into the hall of endless glass enclosures, spheres, stretching endlessly into the dark. Deep into the rocky cave.

You are the cipher, said a voice in his ear. *You are the key.*

He blinked. Seeing someone standing in each of the endless enclosures. They all had his face. His eyes. They stepped out of the spherical chambers, moving toward the door in unison.

Dozens. Hundreds. Thousands.

Shifting. Into writhing tentacles and spiky talons. Hundreds and hundreds of gold eyes.

Horrified, he stared down at his arms. As they stretched and lengthened into tentacles.

Peter shouted himself awake.

Diana lay asleep beside him in the silent, dark room, wearing a baggy lavender T-shirt.

He pulled back the covers and sat on the right side of the bed, sweating, shaking. He drew in a deep breath, glancing at the clock on the nightstand. 0502. He glanced over at Sting's bed.

Empty. Still on patrol with Sarge, Peter assumed.

The dream had been so real. Terrifying. He shuddered, pressing his hands to his head.

That's when he saw the pale blue light at his feet. Pulsing underneath his bed.

As quietly as he could, he bent down and slid the wooden box out from under his bed. With careful, quiet movements, he opened the box.

Inside, beneath the datapad and orange notebook, a blue light flashed. And red and green lights strobed across the datapad.

Peter reached in and picked up the gear thing. It made a soft clicking noise, the light a steady, blue pulse. Whatever this thing was, it was active now. But how? It had no switch. No way to turn it on. He had no idea what it did and he hadn't had a chance to even look through the notebook, much less the datapad. That was now turned on and actively doing—something.

In his hand, the device thrummed, almost like a purring cat, the blue light cycling into long, short, and continuous pulses.

What was this thing? What did it do?

He felt its rhythmic waves that vibrated through his spine and every part of his body until he had trouble separating himself from the vibrations.

It took work for him to slide his hand away from the device.

He pushed the device back underneath the glowing datapad and closed the box. Quietly, he slid the long box back underneath his bed and slid underneath the covers again, but the vibrations continued. Even when he turned on his side, they persisted.

He tried to close his eyes, but he couldn't fall asleep with those rhythmic bass waves emanating up through the mattress and into his hands and feet. His legs. He groaned. His brain. He glanced over at Diana, turned away from him on her right side, lavender T-shirt sliding up her thigh. Her breaths were soft and deep.

She didn't seem like she felt any of those vibrations.

Every time he closed his eyes, he saw the world with the smoky red sky and jagged black mountains. Like a part of him had been there before. A place he didn't recognize. That he'd never seen before now.

He felt strange. Like the vibrations were coming from inside him. He felt like he'd drank too much Karaban coffee and no matter how hard he tried, his thoughts wouldn't turn off and his eyes wouldn't close.

He needed to talk to Sarge.

The man would probably be furious at him for not telling him about what he'd found. He didn't understand most of the things in the orange notebook or the purpose of the gear thing. And he hadn't dared to turn on the datapad. Why it turned on by itself frightened him. What if it did something to him? But he hadn't turned on the gear thing either. It started glowing and pulsing on its own.

He sighed. At least, he didn't think he'd done anything to turn it on. There hadn't been a switch or toggle to flip.

The door to the room rattled open.

Peter closed his eyes as he heard Sting slip inside. He heard Sting put away his rifle and climb into bed against the other wall. He wondered if Sarge needed someone to spell him or Kraver on patrol. If he didn't fall asleep soon, he'd get dressed and grab his rifle and grid. Didn't want Sarge getting ambushed out there.

Sting settled under the covers and in moments, Peter heard his soft snores in the quiet. Sting was probably beat after so much patrolling. Sarge had to be dead on his feet, too. Peter cringed. While he slept. It wasn't right.

Sighing, he slid out of bed and fumbled for a pair of jeans and a light blue T-shirt. He pulled on grey socks and his grey high tops. After grabbing his ammo bag from under the bed, he slid out his plasma rifle, thrust his grid lanyard over his head, and opened the door softly. He glanced back, making sure he hadn't woken up Diana or Sting, and crept out into the dark hallway to find Sarge.

The restaurant was deathly quiet. All the lights were off, not the sound of a single footstep. Peter slung his rifle and ammo bag across his body and turned right into the dark kitchen. Toward the back door.

He leaned against the door, staring out into the dark, not a single light shining throughout the town. He wondered if the military had patrols nearby or if they had their hands full guarding the shuttle port. Had they left Civilization to fend for itself?

Slowly, he opened the back door. It creaked open into the dark alley, Mimi's silver skimmer was parked to the left.

He stepped outside, closing the door, and crept across the alley to the skimmer. He crouched, grid on silent, watching for biodrones.

Fear rose in his throat, his skin crawling at the memory of them dragging him across the sand toward the river. He shuddered. And undead D'Angelo. Even as a lieutenant, that man had been terrifying.

On Ballese, Peter had done his best to keep out of the man's line of sight as much as possible.

How many D'Angelos were walking around in UCOE's forces and among the recombinant units? The thought terrified him.

No movement in the dead calm of the streets. The eerie silence made him queasy. Where were Sarge and Ron?

For a long time, he crouched behind the skimmer, watching for any sign of a patrol. But not a single echo of footsteps touched his ears. The grid screen was clear. He sniffed the air for even a hint of sweetness, but the wind was soft and dry, heavy burnt smell scrubbing away anything else.

He got to his feet, locked a charge into his rifle, and crept along the skimmer's silvery edge to the wall. Pressing his back to the wall, he flattened against it, glancing into the main street, at his grid.

No movement. No sounds. But it would get light soon, turning this pitch darkness into a soft grey.

Peter slid around the wall and crouched behind another skimmer parked along the side of the restaurant. The pearly white skimmer reflected his image back to him as he froze. His light blond hair was tousled and needed combing, his pale blue eyes drooping from lack of sleep, his face pasty. The bandages across his arms and neck were tinged red and probably needed changing.

He watched the street. And the curve of the river as it slipped behind the buildings across the street and circled along the transit track's dark black-on-black shape looming in the night. In the distance, even the spaceport was dark.

He wondered what had happened at the port. And why no one had come to the town's aid. Everyone had been left to fend for themselves. Had the miners just gone into one of many underground shelters or had they all rushed to the spaceport to catch the next available transport off-world?

Ahead, a long, freestanding wall cast a fluid black shadow across the street with nothing to break up his path. And nothing to use for cover.

He took a deep breath and looked down at his grid. Clear.

Letting his breath filter out slowly, he gaged the distance to the restaurant's front door.

Less than thirty meters, but he'd be exposed the whole way.

Closing his eyes, he fought down his fear and tried to slow his quickening breaths, concentrating on getting to the restaurant's turquoise door.

He counted to five in his head. And crept out from behind the pearl white skimmer, crouching, both hands on this rifle.

Halfway to the door, the red dot of a laser sight flashed against his chest.

He dropped to the ground as a plasma blast sizzled past his head.

"Sarge? Ron?" he called. "That you?"

"Mitchell?" a voice called out. It was Sarge.

"Yeah, it's me."

Anxious footsteps tapped toward him as he got to his feet. Sarge grabbed him by the shoulders and pressed him against the umber sandstone building.

"What in hell are you doing out here?" he snapped in a half-whisper, still gripping his shoulders. "I almost took your head off." He motioned two fingers over his shoulder. "We're clear."

"I thought I'd come out and spell you," said Peter.

"You're supposed to be sleeping, Mitchell," Sarge replied with a growl, motioning him around the front of the restaurant. "And resting."

Peter hurried behind Sarge, moving fast and quiet until he got to the front door. Ron crouched behind some crates and makeshift barricades, plasma rifle scoping for Antarans. Peter dropped down behind the barrier beside Sarge.

"I'm fine now," he whispered. "Have you seen anything in the streets?"

Sarge shook his head.

"Nothing since those biodrones ambushed you and Sting. But there's been plenty of action at the port and beyond the town.

Where the escape pods landed. Everything's in chaos right now. Areas are cut off. Communication lines are down. Even some satellites destroyed. We're on our own until reinforcements arrive. They're mobilizing, but I doubt we see anything for hours—maybe a day."

Peter leaned against the sandstone wall behind the barricade, guilt burning through his stomach. He felt bad about everything he hadn't told them yet. Sting. Sarge. Diana. Especially about the lab on Ballese. He had to tell them.

"You okay, Mitchell?" Sarge asked, staring at him in concern. "You really should go back to bed and rest. Ron and I've got this until morning."

"Sarge," Peter began, staring down at his feet. "Something happened when the biodrones attacked."

Sarge's tired face pinched, a mixture of dread and concern. "What are you talking about, Mitchell?"

"As the biodrones dragged me out of the street, toward the river, D'Angelo was there. With a skimmer."

"What?" His face flushed. "Why am I just now hearing this?"

Peter sighed. Sarge would love what else he had to tell him.

"D'Angelo believed that I was Mimi's brother. Called me Orlando. Said he knew I had something and that he'd take if he had to rip it out of my chest."

Sarge was quiet a moment, shaking his head.

"What the hell does that mean?" He rubbed his forehead with his hand. "I'm still trying to figure out if this is retaliation from Ballese or if it's the whole damned Antaris Nation coming down on us."

Peter fidgeted, staring at his rifle, his stomach doing flip-flops. He had no idea how Sarge would take the next thing he needed to get off his chest.

"Sarge..." he began, glancing up at the dark-haired man, his kind brown eyes turning stony.

Peter sucked in a breath. God, Sarge was going to be so pissed at him.

"I'm listening, Mitchell," he said, reverting to his military persona.

Peter shifted against the wall, adjusting the angle of his plasma rifle. "There's something else I need to tell you."

"Go on," he said, his tone becoming anxious.

Okay, no more stalling, he told himself, letting out a sharp exhale.

"Something happened on Ballese that I haven't told you about yet." His stomach did somersaults and he couldn't look at Sarge now.

"Oh, shit," Ron said with a hiss. "Can't wait to hear this."

Sarge already looked pissed, his brown eyes filled with anger as his mouth pressed into a grimace.

"Remember that first night when we were taking turns guarding the campsite?" Peter asked, pushing ahead.

"I remember," Sarge snapped. "Go on."

"See, instead of sleeping, I slipped out of the camp to scout the area. Find where they might be holding Sting."

He still couldn't look at Sarge.

"I was afraid you'd do that," Sarge replied, his anger cooling. "Lucky for you, I didn't find out until now. Is that what you wanted to tell me?"

Peter swallowed a breath and shook his head.

"There's more. Well, see, in the colony ruins, I found this place. It had all these god symbols on the wall."

Sarge leaned against the wall beside him, his gaze flicking from the street and back again.

"I remember that place. It was a nearly intact chapel where any and all religions worshipped there. So eerie without anyone there to use it."

Peter nodded. "I was so surprised by all the god symbols and I wandered around to each one, looking at them all. That's when I found this..." Oh, God, Sarge was gonna hate him for keeping this quiet until now. "This trap door."

"Trap door?" Ron replied, glancing back at Peter. "You seriously found a hidden door in there?"

"And didn't tell us!" Sarge snapped, his gaze turning fiery again.

"Hear me out first," Peter said, holding up his hand. "Then you can get mad at me. See, I thought maybe that's where some of the colonists hid during the attacks."

"A survival shelter?" Sarge asked.

Peter shrugged. "Maybe? So, I went down into it. Sarge, there were all these computers and machines and lights. And there was this big metal door that had a place to put your hand for scanning. So, I did. It called me Dr. Constantine. And it opened the door."

Sarge grabbed his left arm. "Dear God, Mitchell! You found Dr. Constantine's lab?"

Ron swiveled around, staring at him now. "Mitchell, do you have any idea how long Mimi's been looking for that lab? Searching for his research data."

He shook his head. He had no idea.

"Seven years," said Ron, leaning against his rifle. "She gave up after our little excursion when D'Angelo invoked Naharra rules."

"What'd you see, Mitchell?" Sarge asked, still gripping his arm.

"I don't really know what any of it was, Sarge. Lots of computers and lights, but I didn't know what they did. Or how they worked."

"A shame," Sarge said with a sigh. "There's no telling what was lost down there."

Peter dragged his foot through the sand on the landing, behind the barricades as he glanced out at the dark and quiet streets. So empty.

"Well, see, Sarge, there was this glowy gear thing on a desk. Next to a datapad and a handwritten notebook. I kind of...well, I sort of stuck them in my pockets and brought them back here to Civilization."

"Mitchell!" Sarge shouted and immediately lowered his voice. "It's been almost two months since we brought you back half-dead from Ballese and you're just now telling me that you might have brought back some strange artifact! And you have no idea what it does!"

Peter cringed. "Sorry, Sarge. There was never a right time to mention it."

"I wish you were still a private, so I could put you on KP duty for the rest of your life!" Sarge shouted, pointing a finger at him. "Where is it?"

He motioned toward the restaurant. "Inside, but there's uh... more."

"What?" Sarge's face was red, his eyes were molten flames, teeth gritted. He'd never seen Sarge so angry before. "How could there possibly be more?"

A heavy sigh escaped from his lips as he looked Sarge in the eye. There was no turning back now. He had to know the rest. He hoped Sarge didn't punch him in the face after the next bit.

Peter was trembling now, terrified that Sarge would bust him in the mouth.

"Well, at about oh five hundred, I woke up and found the gear thing pulsating with light. And the datapad had um, well—it sort of turned itself on, too."

Sarge went ballistic, grabbing him by the shoulders and shaking him.

"WHAT? Some random alien relic you casually threw in your pocket is now active and doing who knows what? And you're just now casually telling me about it? I wish I could toss you onto garbage detail! And cleaning out the latrines! For the duration!" He shook him again. "You show me this thing right now! Do you hear me, Mitchell? RIGHT now!"

"I hear you, Sarge," he said in a sad voice, feeling so stupid now. "I'm really sorry I screwed up. I didn't think. At all. I just thought it was important and picked it up."

Ron sighed. "I'll cover patrol. Go make sure Mitchell's device isn't a nuclear warhead or an Antaran homing device." He cleared his throat. "Or something worse—if that's even possible."

Peter bowed his head. He hadn't meant to cause any trouble. The gear thing and Dr. Constantine's records looked important. He hadn't meant to keep anything from Sarge or the others.

Sarge's expression was still molten. He pointed at the restaurant door. "Inside, Mitchell. Now."

"You don't want to wake up Sting and Diana, do you?" Peter said as he opened the front door. "Or Mimi?"

"Now, Mitchell," he said through gritted teeth, still pointing. "I'll be back, Ron."

Ron just nodded and turned his gaze back to the street as Peter went back inside the restaurant, Sarge right behind him.

He tiptoed through the main dining room, still in disarray, and moved to the short hallway that led to his and Sting's room. Sarge was at his elbow as he opened the door into the dark room where Sting slept soundly. Diana lay unmoved in Peter's bed as he bent down and reached under the bed.

Already, the rhythmic bluish glow had set the ivory tile floor alight as he slid out the long wooden box and lifted the lid. Inside, green lights flickered on and off from the datapad as he picked it up. Underneath, he pulled out the orange paper notebook and the glowing gear. He turned around, holding them out to Sarge, the datapad resting in his palm.

"Welcome, Dr. Constantine," said a voice from the datapad. "It has been 1.9 years since your last session."

Peter almost threw them into Sarge's hands. But Sarge's mouth was open, staring at him with wide eyes.

"Sarge?" he said in a half-whisper, confused by the surprised look on Sarge's face.

"Mitchell, your hand's—glowing."

Peter gasped and stared at the blue glow traveling along the fingers of his right hand, pulsing blue then green then red and back again in sequence. He shook his head and rubbed his hand against his leg, but the glow didn't rub off. But the glow kept rising up his arm, to his elbow, up his shoulder, pulsating in time with his heartbeat.

His gaze flicked over to Sarge, panic rising in his throat. "Sarge, what's happening to me?"

Footsteps pounded down the hallway. A fist rapped on the door.

"Temple, you in there?" Ron.

"What's up, Kraver?" Sarge asked, staring at Peter as he held the notebook and artifact in his hand, the datapad on top.

"We've got company outside."

"Anyone we know?" Sarge asked.

"Biodrones. Shitloads of them."

11

DAVID SHOOK STINGLEY AWAKE. "Sting, gonna need some help out here."

Sting came awake quickly, staring bleary-eyed at him.

"On it, Sarge," he said in a sleepy voice, sitting up in a tan T-shirt and red boxers.

As Stingley scrambled to dress, David turned to Mitchell, whose fingers up to his right shoulder still pulsed with the strange glowing lights. He grabbed Mitchell's rifle and pushed it toward him. Dear God, what had Mitchell unleashed from Ballese? The prospects were terrifying.

"Can you still use your hand?" David asked, studying the frightened young recombinant.

Mitchell squeezed his right hand into a fist and opened it again. He shrugged.

"I don't know what's happening to me, but I can still use my arm."

"Grab the rifle then. Before Kraver's surrounded."

Reluctantly, Mitchell grabbed his rifle and rushed ahead of David and Sting out into the hallway. Sting pulled on tan camo pants and black chukkas, plasma rifle in his arms, ammo bag back across his chest.

Grid chirped a heart-slamming staccato surrounding the front door.

Mitchell was the first one out the door, rushing behind the left side of the barricade, Stingley beside him.

David dropped down beside Ron and squeezed off a burst of plasma fire, catching two biodrones that surged up the stairs toward them.

Mitchell fired, right arm still glowing as he took down two. Stingley squeezed off well-placed shots, taking down each biodrone while Mitchell opened up on them, burning away any chance of severed talons replicating into more biodrones.

David swung his plasma rifle in a slow arc, sighting biodrones rushing up the stairs. One, then two, both falling to his plasma bursts. Ron took the distance shots, picking off several before they got close to the stairs.

The horizon was beginning to lighten, the dark night beginning to lift into a predawn greyness. Daylight might put them on equal footing with these Antaran biodrones.

He glanced up at the sky, looking for any more flaming trails from escape pods, but there hadn't been any for hours, the distant wildfires still burning, giving the air a sweet, smoky scent as more biodrones surged toward their barricade. He hadn't seen any reinforcements yet either. Or Antaran ships on the horizon. Just the plasma fire and explosions burning at the spaceport.

David had expected to mobilize with the unit of recombinants he'd been training, but everything was in chaos now. His comunit was on, but so deathly silent that it was terrifying. He'd tried to call into his unit. To his squadron. To the base at port. But all he'd gotten was static.

And from what Kraver told him about the rocky landing he and Mimi's underground crew had getting onto the planet's surface, David feared that there'd be no way to leave the surface soon. Was that what the Antarans had planned all along? Trapping them all planetside and then unleashing an army of self-replicating drones to massacre them?

Someone or something knew how to shut down every mode of defense or escape on Civilization. Herding all of them into this corner of town to be taken down by biodrones. Cutting off the military and port authority. Plunging Civilization into chaos. And what had happened to D'Angelo after he'd tried to kidnap Mitchell? To take something that fruitcake insisted was inside Mitchell?

Seeing the glow on Mitchell's arm made him reconsider D'Angelo's threat. Was there something inside Mitchell, implanted by UCOE at RDC? Or on Ku'Tal?

He shuddered. Or on Ballese?

Still, he couldn't help feeling like these biodrone attacks were a smoke screen for something else. Where were all the Antaran ships? Ready to roll over Civilization and crush it to dust like they claimed they could accomplish on Ballese.

Was it just a cover to get hold of whatever Mitchell had pulled out of that lab on Ballese? His stomach ached at the thought. Was all of this destruction timed to disguise them trying to get hold of Mitchell? That's how this attack started. He'd never seen biodrones drag off a living recombinant before. They'd swarmed Mitchell, but they dragged him toward the river instead of eviscerating him.

He winced. Where D'Angelo waited in a skimmer. That had to be it. The Antarans were after Mitchell and the tech he'd brought back. Tech they'd failed to locate in the ruined colony.

Somehow, David had to protect Mitchell at all costs. He gritted his teeth. If he didn't kill Mitchell first.

"Pete, what gives with the glow on your arm again?" Sting asked, squeezing off a volley of shots that splattered two more biodrones and stopped two others in their tracks.

"Wish I knew, Sting," Mitchell said, shrugging as he laid down a line of fire across the steps.

David raised an eyebrow. "Again?"

Mitchell targeted biodrones on the stairs, his plasma charges exploding them into blackened, shriveled bits at the bottom of the stairs.

"Happened at the ruins north of here the first time," Sting replied, torching a biodrone that reached the top step. "But it went away."

David felt the slow burn roil through his gut. The gloves at the pub. They'd hidden it from him that day.

"All three of you lied to me at the pub, didn't you?"

"Sorry, Sarge," Mitchell said with a moan. "I didn't do anything to cause it. We were all touching those ruins, but they only lit up when I touched them."

"What a minute!" Ron shouted. "You mean those old ruins actually lit up when you touched them, Mitchell?"

Mitchell nodded. "I don't know how or why, but yes."

What was happening with Mitchell? Was it because of those things he'd brought back from Ballese? Or some other reason? He'd grill Diana and Sting about this later. If they all survived this latest biodrones attack.

"Where'd it come from this time, Pete?" Sting.

Mitchell shook his head, firing at two writhing tentacles. "From something stupid I did on Ballese."

"Pete, you were awesome on Ballese," said Sting, his green eyes turning sad. "Does it hurt?"

Sting picked off another biodrone rushing the barricades.

"Nah, it just tingles," said Peter, shooting the flailing appendages of another dropped biodrone to prevent it from replicating into more. "Wish it would stop."

As unnerving as the glowing pulses of light were, David knew that Mitchell now stood out like a spotlight. Had that been the intention somehow? Or had Mitchell just stumbled onto something that should have been left alone? Without seeing this lab for himself, he could only speculate. And now that Naharra rules had been invoked on Ballese, David had no idea when anyone could land on Ballese now. Probably not in his lifetime.

David targeted a biodrone that rushed past Kraver's missed shot and surged toward Mitchell. Taking it down before it reached the barricades.

First Naharra. Now Ballese. Would UCOE keep nuking planets until they ran out of them in the Taus system? What about Karaba and Farnas? Agricultural worlds, both of them. Feeding lots of people in both systems. And Civilization with its precious rare metal ores allowed for new advances in technology, hopefully, something that might actually end the war instead of perpetuating it indefinitely with an endless supply of aggressive—but human—killing machines. After obliterating all of Earth's tech early on in the war, the Antaris Nation had reduced the war effort to old-fashioned boots-on-the-ground campaign.

He wanted something that would send these monsters back to hell or wherever they came from. As deep into the Antarus system as they could be flung. Far away from the edge of Taus. Where Naharra stood dark and silent for all these years.

And now, Ballese.

The front door of the restaurant opened and Diana, dressed in jeans and a red T-shirt rushed out and dropped down beside Mitchell at the barricades. A plasma rifle in her arms.

"Morning, Peter," she said, smiling, and squeezed off a burst of plasma that brought down two biodrones.

"Diana!" Mitchell cried, looking alarmed at seeing her next to him. "What are you doing?"

"Defending my home. My people."

Mitchell burned down one more biodrone. And another.

"It's just like shooting darts, isn't it, Diana?" Sting asked, grinning as he laid down a line of fire along the stairs, bringing down two more.

She flashed a smile at Sting. "Sure is. Lots more satisfying, too."

Three appendages shifted, becoming full biodrones right in front of them.

David fired a burst at the first one, Ron burning down the second one. Diana took down the third one.

"Peter?" she replied, touching his right arm. "What's this weird glow? Is it some sort of battle armor or something? You didn't go back to those ruins, did you?"

"No, of course not!" Mitchell replied.

"Talk about it later, please," David ordered. "We've got bigger problems than Mitchell's glowing arm."

"Easy for you to say," Mitchell snapped, firing off another burst of plasma that raked the stairs, catching two biodrones.

Sting laughed, burning down another biodrone.

Mitchell emptied an entire charge on the swarm until only a black puddle remained in the thinning grey hours before dawn. David dropped down beside Ron again, taking out three biodrones at the bottom of the stairs.

"Sarge, what about the back entrance?" Mitchell asked suddenly. "Could these things make it inside from there?"

"Mitchell, flank me and we'll find out," said David, crouching as he opened the door.

Mitchell piled inside behind him as they ran through the main dining room, chairs and tables askew, piles of clean black tablecloths and burgundy napkins laid out on tables. David rushed through the kitchen's double doors, Mitchell banging through them.

Mimi was making coffee as they ran past the fry and sauté stations.

"Morning, David," she said, bringing her white mug to her lips. "Morning, Peter."

"Morning," they both replied as they hit the back door.

And heard the pounding on the other side.

"Sarge! Biodrones! They're trying to break through." Mitchell.

"We can't open that door!" Sarge cursed under his breath. "We'll have to go around."

Mimi pointed behind her.

"There's a window behind that picture," she said, pointing at a large framed print of white and purple wildflowers. "Shoot them from there."

David glanced at Mitchell who shrugged and moved toward the black-framed picture on the sand-colored wall. He took it down and set it on the floor. Sarge unlocked the window and thrust it open. Together, he and Mitchell hung out the window and shot down the cluster of biodrones beating on the back door.

"Why are they all concentrated on us, Sarge?" Mitchell asked, emptying an entire charge on three biodrones beneath the window. "They're just rushing right past every other building."

Mitchell ejected a spent charge and shoved another full charge into the rifle, re-engaging the replicating appendages. Two. Then three.

"I want to blame that activated tech you had no business bringing back, Mitchell," said David, firing off another burst of plasma that fried a biodrone at the back door. "But the biodrones were coming at us before that." He thought for a moment, burning down another biodrone. "Actually, the biodrones started after I found D'Angelo."

"Don't forget about the escape pods from the reclamation station landing," Mimi replied, taking another sip of her coffee. "That's where this damned batch came from."

"That's true," said David as Mitchell caught two biodrones in his sights and laid down a wide arc of plasma fire, torching both of them until all appendages stopped flailing.

"I apologize, Mitchell," said David. "This isn't your fault, but you have definitely not been helping the situation either."

"I know," Mitchell said with a nod as the sun peeked through the grey smoky haze. "I'm really sorry for not telling you sooner."

The first rays of soft, gilded sunlight turned the sandy landscape golden bright as the greyness began to lighten.

"All right, I've had enough of this biodrone business," said Mimi, setting down her coffee mug.

She moved over to what looked like a walk-in cooler on the far wall and opened the door. Behind it was some sort of control panel. She flicked some buttons and pulled a lever.

Electrifying the back door.

"Best bug zapper money could buy. I got the fun size just for this situation."

Biodrones fell in droves as soon as they got close enough to fry.

"Why didn't you do that earlier?" David asked, leaning back inside from the window.

"Too many unaccounted-for people last night," she said. "Couldn't risk frying Peter or Diana when she returned. That should protect the back entrance for now. From biodrones and any damned salespeople, too." She smiled. "And UCOE."

"Thanks, Mimi," said Mitchell, pulling back from the window.

"Peter?" Mimi replied as Mitchell moved ahead of David toward the dining room.

"Yeah, Mimi?" he asked, stopping beside her.

She frowned at his glowing arm. "What's going on with the light effects?"

Mitchell just shrugged. "No idea. Wish I knew. I was planning to talk to you about your brother." Mitchell sighed. "And his lab on Ballese."

Her eyes widened and she grabbed Mitchell's arms, holding him in place. "Peter...did you find Orlando's lab on Ballese?"

Mitchell nodded and held out his arms.

"I brought back some things from there. I've been meaning to talk to you and Sarge about them, but when I woke up earlier, the things I brought back were pulsating with light." He sighed, his gaze falling to his feet. "When I touched the datapad with my palm, it kind of went crazy. Then my arm started glowing."

Suddenly, Mimi looked alarmed.

"When, Peter?" she asked, studying his face, his eyes, her gaze flicking to his arm as she took hold of his right hand. "When did it start?"

Mitchell shrugged. "I woke up about oh five hundred and saw

something glowing under the bed. Shortly after, I told Sarge about it and took him to get the things I found in Doctor Constantine's lab. When I picked them up, my fingers started glowing. Then it went up my arm. I don't know how to turn it off again."

Her gaze met David's this time. "David, I think this is my fault," she said, wringing her hands. "Orlando sent me encrypted optics, but when I tried to decrypt them, it ran some sort of application or script. Could I have caused this? Or Orlando's files in some way?"

"Anything's possible," David snapped. "To be fair, Mitchell didn't seem to do anything but hand the items to me. The datapad seemed to think Mitchell was your brother, Mimi. Could that have launched something, too?"

Mimi sighed and shook her head. "I wish I knew, David. It's certainly possible."

"The datapad Mitchell handed me said that it had been one point nine years since Dr. Constantine's last login."

"One point nine years?" She grimaced, a hand on his arm. "David, that's not possible. Orlando died seven years ago on Ballese when Antarans destroyed the colony."

"Could the software be glitched somehow?" David asked.

"Honestly, David, I know nothing about what Orlando was doing or who he was working for when the Ballese colony stopped responding and UCOE sent in troops to find out why. That was seven years ago, not one point nine years ago."

David studied the grief in her eyes and the concern lining her face. The not knowing, he realized.

"David, the time algorithm on those things from Orlando's lab must be off," said Mimi, waving him off.

Mitchell shook his head. "The lab door said the same thing to me when it scanned my hand and I entered the lab. It said that it had been one point nine years since he'd last been in the lab."

Mimi's mouth fell open. "Peter? Are you certain?"

Mitchell nodded emphatically.

"Or..." David began, "Orlando Constantine isn't dead. He just needs the Antarans to think he's dead."

Mimi's face turned pale as she stared at him in confusion, as if she couldn't quite entertain that possibility.

"While they chase after his clone," Mimi said finally.

She pressed her hand to her mouth and leaned against the counter.

"He must have planned all along to sacrifice his clone." She turned to stare at Mitchell. "Oh, God—Peter, I—"

Tears welled in her eyes and she swiped them off her cheeks.

"Mimi, what is it?" David asked, laying a hand on her arm.

"Earlier this morning, Doctor Kingston, Doctor Drew, and I reviewed the optics files Orlando wanted me to decrypt if the war was lost." She pulled in a heavy breath, her eyes full of pain. "But when I decrypted the files, some program or code ran instead, activating something. I don't know what." She looked directly at Mitchell now. "Whatever it was must have activated the things from Orlando's lab."

David felt sick to his stomach as he stared at the glowing lights pulsating through Mitchell's arm.

"And it activated something inside Mitchell's DNA, is that what you're saying?" David asked, shaking his head. "Something your brother encoded there. To turn on when those algorithms launched. But the question is why. What is it? And what does it do?"

Mimi sighed. "I know what it does," she said, staring into the distance. "Orlando's note said that he'd found something that would make the Recombinant Defense Program look like child's play. Something that could replicate fast. On a large scale. That has to be it."

David studied the frightened stare in Mitchell's pale blue eyes as he glanced at Mimi. And then at him. Poor guy was trying to understand what the hell was going on when he only had a small part of the information. And only a basic understanding of how humans operated.

"David," said Mimi as she reached out and took Mitchell's hand, squeezing it. "I don't know what Orlando had planned, but I do know he was counting on the Antarans to locate and pursue his clone as a sign that he'd found the artifact. Orlando described it as a replication engine. From a race that was a forerunner to even the Antaris Nation." She sighed. "Poor Peter has been his lure all this time."

Mitchell's face turned pale, the color draining from his face.

"So, you're telling me that I exist just so I can be your brother's decoy? Bait for the Antarans? Is that what you're saying, Mimi?" Mitchell looked devastated. He bit his lip and laid a hand over his eyes. "I feel sick."

12

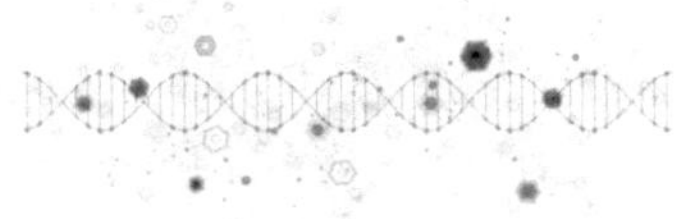

DR. KINGSTON AWOKE in the dark to plasma fire. Startled, she sat up in the double bed with its homey red and white quilt smelling like warm cotton and listened.

Silence. Punctuated by plasma fire.

That meant biodrones were still roaming Civilization's streets. Attacking anything human. But nothing that sounded like the war front had shifted all the way back to Civilization.

If it did, that would put the Antarans on the doorstep of home system. Where several orbital defense stations and the remaining space fleets defended the galaxy's outer edges. With the bulk of Earth's defenses surrounding Earth, Luna colony, and Mars. Where UCOE would make its final stand against the Antaris Nation if the orbitals and long-range ships between Taus and Sol fell.

Defending a galaxy required armadas of ships, dozens of orbitals and stations, and tech. Lots of tech. Not counting the knowledge and experience necessary to launch such a huge operation. And Earth possessed none of these essentials anymore. Especially after the costly start of the conflict and the flagrant overconfidence that had destroyed most of the advanced tech early. Leaving them fighting a twentieth-century war against an enemy with tech that UCOE had never even dreamed of before. The Antaris Nation had out-teched, out-gunned, and out-maneuvered UCOE at every turn. Exhausting resources and obliterating troops.

But somehow, Earth had to find a way to win this war. Because the Antarans would wipe out every single human being if they conquered Sol system.

Jeannette's eyes began to adjust as the small white room began to get light, wooden blinds closed over the south-facing window as she swiveled her feet onto the cool, ivory-tiled floor. Dressing in yesterday's yellow scrubs, she ran her fingers through her short auburn hair and pulled on her shoes. She straightened the quilt and hurried downstairs. Hoping Mimi had some spare toiletries for her and Kai.

Kai was already downstairs when she hurried into the restaurant's main room, tables still in disarray after several rounds of yesterday's triage. Boxes of black tablecloths and burgundy and gold napkins set on tables that had been moved against the walls and stacked against booths. The tiled floor needed to be mopped and sanitized.

Plasma fire was steady at the front of the restaurant now.

"What's happening?" Jeannette called to Kai as he walked out of the kitchen, steaming burgundy mug of coffee in one hand, a plasma rifle in the other.

"Antaran biodrones have been attacking since early this morning," said Kai, taking a sip of coffee. "I'm going out to help."

He set his mug down on an empty table and slung the rifle strap across his shoulders.

"Be careful, Kai," she called as he moved to the front door and jerked it open, ducking outside.

The door slammed shut and Jeannette was all alone in the restaurant.

"Mimi?" she called. "Mimi!"

"In the kitchen," she answered.

Jeannette hurried through the dark dining room to the black double doors and plunged into the kitchen. She found Mimi dressed in grey leggings and a long red tunic, opening a crate of plasma rifles in the store room off the kitchen.

"What's happening?" Jeannette asked, her eyes wide as she stared at Mimi.

"Our location has been targeted by biodrone attacks. Until some help arrives, we're going to have to defend ourselves." Mimi held up a plasma rifle. "Rifle?"

Jeannette shook her head. "I've never even held a rifle," she said.

"Fair enough," said Mimi. "I've called in several of my operatives. They're bringing reinforcements. Still no response from the spaceport authority or the UCOE training facility. Not even a warning siren to take shelter. This whole planet's gone to crazy town."

The horrendous sound of static electricity buzzed nearby. Jeannette glanced over at the back door that kept vibrating.

"Door's electrified," said Mimi, motioning toward it. "Don't go out that way."

Jeannette nodded, feeling confused and frightened. Were they all pinned down in here now? At the Antarans' mercy—and those horrid, tentacled biodrones? What had happened to the UCOE forces stationed on the planet?

"So, you're telling me we're surrounded?" Jeannette asked.

"That's pretty accurate, yes," said Mimi, unloading the stock of plasma rifles.

Mimi grabbed a charge and loaded it into the first rifle and it lit green. She set it aside and loaded the next one and the next one.

"Coffee's fresh in that white carafe. And there's a bag of toiletry items for you and Kai in the bathroom down the hall."

Shaking, Jeannette grabbed a gold mug from the shelf and poured a cup of coffee from the tall, slender carafe. She drank it black. Maybe this was all a crazy dream?

"Is there any way to get off world?" Jeannette asked. "Kai and I need to investigate the status of our reclamation station. See if anything can be salvaged—or learned from what remains. And I need access to equipment there to study more of Orlando's data."

Mimi stared at her a moment. "We could get you off the planet as soon as my operatives arrive."

"When will that be?" Jeannette asked, taking another sip.

"Hopefully in the next four hours—or before those biodrones break through the barriers we set up." Mimi stood up from the rifles and moved over to Jeannette, arms folded across her chest. "We don't know how big a force we're dealing with right now, especially since communication with port authority has been cut. We all may have to fall back toward the spaceport. Or worse, abandon Civilization. Right now, we just don't have any answers."

A rumbling sound shook the building.

Jeannette grabbed hold of the stainless steel counter to keep from falling. Mimi braced herself against the wall as the building shuddered.

"And that would be one of my shuttles arriving," said Mimi, grinning. "Thank heavens!"

As soon as the shaking stopped, Mimi rushed out of the kitchen's double doors. Through the restaurant's dining room. Jeannette followed her to the front door. The sounds of plasma fire had quieted some. Mimi opened the door.

A sleek silver shuttle had landed in the street, two dozen men and women armed with plasma rifles piling out. Flanking the biodrones.

Mimi's operatives fanned out in the street and fired on the biodrones. Together, the two groups made quick work of them, turning the street into inky black puddles of tentacles and talons.

As the streets quieted, Mimi called Ron to the door.

"Ron, have the others set up a perimeter guard around the restaurant while the rest of you take a break. You've been at it for hours."

"I'll gladly take care of that," said Ron. "Hopefully, there won't be another wave of those damned things. Thanks, Mimi."

He hurried away from the door and rushed down the stairs toward the underground operatives. In a moment, Mimi ushered Kai and Diana inside. Peter, Sting, and David backed inside the restaurant, rifles raised, panning the early morning landscape until safely inside again.

Jeannette noticed the strange blue, red, and green glow that had enveloped Peter Mitchell's right arm.

"Peter," she called to him. "What's happened to your arm?"

He shrugged, shouldering his plasma rifle. "Mimi thinks she turned something on when she opened her brother's files."

She turned to stare at Mimi. "You think those files caused this?"

Mimi nodded. "I think Orlando cloned himself to fool the Antarans and throw them off his trail. But I think Orlando intended something more insidious for his copy. This must be some kind of homing beacon."

She shook her head and Jeannette realized Mimi didn't want to discuss it in front of Peter Mitchell. Had Orlando Constantine intended to sacrifice poor Peter to something? To save his own life?

Jeannette thought back to the message she'd seen on Mimi's datapad. Something about an ancient engine that would make the Recombinant Defense Program look like child's play. Had Orlando deciphered some ancient technology? Learned that it had some sort of replication function? Something that could crank out thousands of copies in a very short time? Had he intended to destroy it somehow? Or take it for Earth and win this war?

The thought of such an engine was terrifying. But she couldn't deny that something strange had happened to Peter. She needed to study Orlando's notes to be sure.

"Mimi, did you find anything else of Orlando's?" Jeannette asked. "Written notes? A datapad? Optical images? Anything else that I could review?"

Peter turned back to her. "Dr. Kingston," he said, his gaze falling to the floor. "I brought back a notebook and a datapad from Ballese. Sarge has them."

Jeannette turned her attention to Diana Temple's tall, dark-haired brother, Sergeant David Temple.

"David?" she asked. "Could I review the notes? And the datapad?"

David glanced over at Peter who just shrugged.

"I'll get them," David answered and retrieved them from one of the tables. "Here," he said, holding out the datapad and orange paper notebook. "Just be careful though. The datapad turned on by itself and logged Mitchell in from his palm print."

Jeannette carried the two items over to the nearest table and sat down. She opened the orange notebook.

Diagrams. Page after page of hand-drawn diagrams depicting artifacts unearthed on...her mouth fell open. On Naharra. She didn't realize that Orlando had excavated anything from there.

David walked over to the table and held out something that was glowing. "Oh, and this."

She stared at the strange, gear-shaped item that glowed with light just like Peter Mitchell's right arm. Reaching out, she ran her fingers across its smooth surface. It felt like some sort of glass, but it was warm to the touch. It felt solid. Unbreakable.

She gasped as she gently picked it up and held it in her hands. Was this one of the artifacts that Orlando had unearthed during one of his excavations? Had it come from Naharra? Or Ballese? Or someplace older...someplace farther than the Antaris Nation's worlds? Somewhere out beyond the rim of known space?

Just holding it gave her chills.

Or was it a part of this strange engine that Orlando had been obsessed with? And just how did it connect to the strange splices of RNA that had folded into double helices of traits and stored data? Or to the exact copy that Orlando made of himself in Peter Mitchell. And his dead brother, Beckett, in John Stingley? None of this made sense.

Had the Antarans' interest in Peter Mitchell been a ploy set up by Orlando to trick the Antarans into hunting Peter instead of him?

As some kind of diversion or sacrifice? But Peter's DNA had so much strangeness embedded in its helix. Strings of stored data and weird alien codes edited or inserted. So much of it she didn't understand yet. Data. Instruction sets. And alien code. It wasn't Antaran either.

Did it all go back to the ancient engine that Orlando mentioned? A way to turn the tide of the war? Or make Orlando rich beyond his wildest dreams? At this moment, Jeannette didn't know whether Orlando Constantine was a desperate man being hunted by the enemy who had used his clone as a decoy while he faked his own death or did Orlando have some sort of sacrificial lamb in mind when he'd cloned Peter Mitchell in his own image.

A sacrifice required by this alien engine?

Both possibilities were terrifying. For humanity. And for this unusual young man that was equal parts intelligence, innocence, and wonder. Regardless of what was true, she needed to examine Orlando's work and find out his intentions. Peter Mitchell had endured so much already. She had to find out the truth. He—and Diana—deserved to know.

Jeannette glanced over at Mimi who stood beside Diana and John Stingley and explained about the incoming operatives she'd called in to help defend Civilization. Orlando Constantine was her little brother, someone she loved dearly. And had mourned for seven years. The woman only saw the good in him.

But at this moment, Jeannette didn't know what to think about the man she'd apparently worked with for years (the memories locked away in her MRC until Kai had converted them to EVF). She'd always seen Orlando Constantine as part scientist and part activist. Preserving historical artifacts and the common good. A man who helped build the Recombinant Defense Program and then questioned it.

And she'd supported him in all of those realizations. But why was he desperate enough to clone himself like this? Why were the Antarans hunting him? And why did he let his family and friends believe he was dead? To what end? She had trouble reconciling that decision. Or why Orlando cloned himself. How could Orlando intentionally sacrifice his own clone so he could access some alien technology that might end the war? He'd helped develop the Recombinant Defense Program. He knew what kind of hell those recombinants had gone through. To know all that and still choose to sacrifice his own clone...it made Jeannette furious.

Maybe she'd have even understood and agreed with such a plan— if she hadn't met Peter Mitchell? To sacrifice such an innocent with such a profound sense of wonder? Even for the greater good, it was an unconscionable act to her.

Sacrificed to save a world he would never see?

All for an uncertain technology that *might* help them beat the Antarans? The cowardice and callousness of it all made her sick to her stomach.

Orlando had been against sending cloned soldiers to the war front, a program he made happen, until his own life was in jeopardy. Then he couldn't wait to clone himself and hide, leaving poor Peter Mitchell to suffer and die for him. They weren't androids. Constructs. Machines.

They were human beings.

She needed to analyze and synthesize Orlando's drawings and his data. She would learn what exactly he knew about this engine. And she would do her best to discover what role Peter Mitchell had been intended to play in Orlando's puzzle.

But first, she needed to understand the part that Colonel Stanton had played in this series of attacks. And perhaps get close enough to Captain D'Angelo to learn what he'd become. People didn't just die and come back to life like that?

She shuddered. Unless the Antarans had some advanced technology of their own.

But if they had such a technology, why hadn't they used it on Earth yet?

She had to figure out the connection and expose Colonel Stanton's lies—and her alien DNA. She and Kai needed to get back to the reclamation station. To examine the logs and damage reports, find out how the attack started. See the station for themselves now that the attack was over.

She hadn't gotten a response yet from home system on her MRC report about the overuse of recycled chipsets. And the presence of alien code. Did Stanton have friends in higher places than she'd expected? Regardless, she had to discover what Stanton's end game was, learn what she was trying to accomplish. Why Stanton remained at the reclamation stations rather than at the battle fronts defending home system. And how all of this figured into the Antaris Nation's plans to takeover Sol system.

13

PETER STARED at the multicolored glow that still lit up his right arm, feeling confused and scared. He watched Dr. Kingston's face carefully—and Mimi's—knowing there was something they weren't telling him.

What would they find in those things he'd brought back from the lab? He'd heard Dr. Kingston say something about an engine. Like the one inside a skimmer? Or bigger, like a spaceport shuttle or the troop transports that had dropped him and Sting onto Ku'Tal when he was still in the military? He understood that engines made things move and powered lots of things, but he didn't understand how an engine could create recombinants and biodrones.

The thought still sickened him that Mimi's brother had cloned himself and then allowed Peter (his clone) to be created as a recombinant. Dr. Constantine had to know the horrible life he was dooming Peter to when he added his genetic profile to the recombinant pool. Dr. Constantine created the program. He knew better. He knew Peter was doomed to die on the most brutal battlefield the military had seen in centuries. Having one year to live at best.

But the only thing worse than being a recombinant was Dr. Constantine using Peter as a decoy, destined to be tortured and sacrificed to the Antarans while Orlando escaped. Peter didn't quite understand it all, but what little he'd heard made him angry. At the selfishness. At the lack of compassion. Ignoring the horrors his own clone would face.

And the man didn't care. As long as it wasn't him. Peter felt sick. And furious.

The sound of rumbling echoed outside, shaking the building.

Peter rushed to the restaurant's front door and peered outside. A dozen skimmers and other vehicles thundered along the main road and halted at the street's dead end. In front of Mimi's restaurant.

He gasped, shaking at the massive military presence. Fearing he'd be discovered. And sent back to RDC—to be washed out.

Dozens and dozens of citizens in tan UCOE uniforms—not dull green for recombinants—piled out of the larger vehicles, plasma rifles drawn. And others in civilian clothes. Shiny silver and copper business suits, glare shades covering their eyes as they approached the restaurant in a group of suits.

He closed the door and backed away toward the kitchen.

"Peter?" Diana asked, staring at him. "What's the matter?"Diana glanced at Sarge, shaking her head. "David? What's happening?"

"I'll find out," said Sarge, moving toward the front door.

But the door banged open and the people in the metallic business suits stepped into the restaurant.

"What are you doing?" Mimi shouted, but they moved right past her. "We're closed."

"The planet is under attack by Antarans and under martial law," Sarge said. "Are you here to help defend it?"

A white-haired man in the gold business suit shook his head. "Sorry," he said. "Government agents."

The agent's hair looked like it had prematurely turned white. He looked about forty. Thin, about five foot nine with a square face and strong jaw, he looked a little stern and wiry.

Sarge tried to stop them, but they just shoved past him.

The white-haired man in the gold business suit led the entourage deeper into the restaurant until he got to Peter. The group stopped in front of Peter, the white-haired man removing his glare shades, his small eyes a dull blue, and pulled something out of his pocket. A small black cube floated in mid-air by his head and made a whirring sound as a green light passed over Peter and disappeared when it reached the ground. The black cube glowed green.

"Genetics are a match," said a dark-haired woman in a silver business suit behind the white-haired man. "And as you can see, the tracking unit is active."

"Orlando Constantine," said the white-haired man, stone-faced as he looked up at Peter. "You're under arrest for high treason, theft of highly classified intellectual property, and theft of recovered alien artifacts under the United Countries of Earth Cybersecurity and Terrorist Act of 2137."

Peter's mouth fell open. He'd done none of that. Nothing except exist.

"Identify yourselves. Now!" Sarge demanded, stepping in front of Peter, rifle raised.

Peter's eyes widened and he stared over Sarge's shoulder at the men and their strange attire. They'd take him away and wash him out. Shaking, he took a step backward, shaking his head.

"No, I'm not Orlando Constantine! That's not me! I—I didn't do any of those things!"

The white-haired agent sneered and pointed at Peter's glowing right arm. "The genetics and the glow of the tracker unit say otherwise, Constantine," the man snapped. "We've been looking for you a long time. Did you really think you could just walk off with all that technology? Keep it for yourself?"

"I'm not going to repeat myself, gentlemen," Sarge said again and slid the barrel of his plasma rifle closer.

"Agent Marcus Fitzroy," said the white-haired man, holding up something shiny and gold. "UCOE Intelligence operative. Io Base of Operations."

Peter started backing away toward the kitchen.

"I'm not Orlando Constantine and I don't know anything about what you're talking about!"

The men in the metallic business suits each held up something to Sarge that made him lower his rifle in disgust. They looked like some sort of card or shiny metal thing, something he'd never seen before. They were a shiny gold color like the first agent had and they looked like a god symbol but much larger.

"Cut the act, Constantine!" the white-haired man said with a scowl, gritting his teeth. "You see the badge? I've waited seven years for you to surface. To trip that bioluminescent tracker on your datapad. The one that only your biometrics can trigger. And only your government decryption key can open."

Peter shook his head, holding up his hands. "My name's Peter. Peter Mitchell! I don't know anything about what you're saying!"

Mimi stepped in front of him. "I am Mimi Constantine, Orlando's older sister," she said. "And I can assure you that this is not my 40-year-old brother, Orlando, who died on Ballese seven years ago. Just look at him! He's a kid. A twenty-three-year-old kid."

"Tracker says otherwise, Constantine," said the white-haired man, turning around to the suits behind him. "Probably had some plastic surgery. Some rejuvenation procedures." He nodded at the agents. "Cuff him."

Diana and Sting stepped in front of Peter. "You're not taking him anywhere," Diana said, using her rifle to block the kitchen doors. "He isn't Orlando Constantine."

"You heard the lady," Sting said, pointing his rifle at the men.

Peter's eyes widened when all the people in suits pulled out weapons and pointed them at Diana and Sting.

Sarge jerked his rifle up and pointed it at the white-haired agent's head. Kai Drew joined them. Mimi picked up one of the plasma rifles she'd stacked against the wall. Training it at the agents.

"I'd hate for them to feel outnumbered," said Mimi, pointing the plasma rifle at the white-haired Fitzroy. "At least now it'll be a real old-fashioned standoff."

Peter was horrified. "No!" he shouted. "No...don't risk your lives for me. Diana, Sting—no!"

"Sorry, Pete," Sting said, his rifle trained on Fitzroy. "If they take you out of here, we'll never see you again."

"He's right, Peter," said Diana. "I won't let you go again! I won't lose you."

Off to his right, Dr. Kingston rose from the table where she'd been reviewing the datapad and notebook that he'd discovered in Orlando Constantine's lab.

Peter's mouth fell open as her right arm glowed blue and green and red. Just like his arm.

She stepped up to Fitzroy and held out her arm. "Is this the tracker you're referring to, Agent Fitzroy?" she asked.

He stared at her in surprise for a moment or two. "How did you—"

"Anyone that touches Orlando's unlocked datapad sets off the bioluminescent tracker," she replied and held it out to them.

Fitzroy stared at her and then his gaze flicked back to the datapad and back again.

"Go ahead," said Dr. Kingston, holding out the datapad to him.

Fitzroy hesitated and then reached for the datapad. The moment it rested in his hand, the luminous glow leaked into his fingers, traveling past his wrist and up his arm. Fitzroy sighed and hung his head.

"Everyone, stand down," Fitzroy ordered in a disgusted voice.

Peter watched in amazement as the operatives put away their weapons. Only then did Sting and Diana shoulder their rifles. Then Mimi and Kai. And finally, Sarge.

"Wait a minute," said Fitzroy, staring at Dr. Kingston.

That little black cube appeared again and Fitzroy ran some sort of a scan on her.

"No MRC, but aren't you Dr. Jeannette Kingston?"

She nodded.

"The same Dr. Kingston that was an intelligence operative assigned to Constantine's lab?"

Her face pinched, her gaze widening. "What? An operative? What are you talking about?"

"The genetic scan checks out," said Fitzroy, staring at her. "Don't you remember, doctor? You were going undercover to Constantine's lab, to ensure the success of the Recombinant Defense Program."

Dr. Kingston shook her head, a look of fear burning in her eyes. "No. An undercover operative? For the government? Are you sure?"

Fitzroy nodded. "Of course, I'm sure. It's been eight years, but I still remember the young woman who was almost my wife."

Dr. Kingston stumbled back, staring at Fitzroy like he was a biodrone.

"Almost your wife?" she cried, eyes wide. "I've never seen you before."

Fitzroy sighed. "Was it that bad, Jeannette?" he asked. "So bad that you had to wipe me from your memory, too, like you erased your husband and child."

Peter stared at Dr. Kingston who looked horrified. Dr. Drew looked upset, concerned, but he seemed to keep his distance.

She put her hands on her hips, anger burning in her eyes.

"Let's get one thing straight, Agent Fitzroy, I did not intentionally erase any part of my life voluntarily. The MRC was a requirement of the lab and mandatory for combat medics at the front. And reclamation specialists. I never intended for my husband and daughter to be excised from my memories. Or how she died. I've recovered those memories and I'm working to recover the later ones as well. But I have no memory of you, written or otherwise."

A sadness touched Fitzroy's blue eyes. He studied her a moment.

"We were engaged when you were sent to the Taus labs to assist with the Recombinant Defense Program and gather data on Doctor Constantine, ensuring that the program was successful." He sighed.

"After three years with an MRC, we became strangers. We broke up a year before you went to Ku'Tal as a combat medic."

Dr. Kingston shook her head, looking shocked and frightened.

"I'm sorry," she said finally. "But I don't know you."

Fitzroy nodded, but the pain in his face was evident. He returned his gaze to Peter and Peter stiffened, wanting to run past all these strangers into Civilization's streets. Take his chances with the biodrones.

"So, how do you explain the genetic match with Orlando, doctor?"

Dr. Kingston glanced at Peter and then at Fitzroy again. "Early prototype testing of the genetic profiles in the Recombinant Development Process. We needed to ensure the profile creation's accuracy, so Orlando tested it on himself."

Fitzroy squinted at Peter. "So, he's a recombinant? That means he's AWOL. And you're in unlawful possession of UCOE property."

"He needs to be immediately turned over to RDC," said one of the other operatives. "Doubt they'll be able to repatriate him to the battlefield though."

Fitzroy nodded. "Yep, most likely a washout."

Washout?

Terror welled cold and dark inside Peter. He glanced at the strange people and Dr. Kingston and then gripped his plasma rifle in both hands. Ready to turn it on the first one that moved toward him. He wouldn't let them take him away to be washed out. He gritted his teeth. He wouldn't.

"Sorry to disappoint you," said Dr. Kingston, "but UCOE has no ownership of this young man. He's got Orlando's DNA. That makes him a citizen, not a recombinant."

Fitzroy glared at her. "He came from the Recombinant Defense Program, that makes him—"

"Unfortunate, but it doesn't make him intellectual property owned by a project." Dr. Kingston flashed a quick smile at him and returned her attention to Fitzroy. "Recombinants' genetic profiles are carefully designed and curated. And copyrighted. That makes them technically property of UCOE. And he wasn't part of the project, so UCOE can't claim ownership."

Fitzroy raised an eyebrow. "Copyrighted? Recombinants? You sure about that?"

"Quite," said Dr. Kingston as she glared at the agents. "It's the foundation of the whole program. Look it up, agent. And whether or not you agree with the Recombinant Defense Program, their copyrighted genetic profiles are unique and carefully created for battle and the war front. But Peter Mitchell's genetics weren't designed or streamlined for combat. And his DNA was not part of the copyrighted batches. Or part of the program itself. He is no more a piece of property than Orlando Constantine." She pointed at Sarge. "Or Sergeant Temple for that matter."

Diana slid back a step until she was beside Peter. Her left arm slid around his waist and she pulled him close, plasma rifle still in her right hand.

"He doesn't belong to anyone," Diana said, glaring at Fitzroy. "He's a free citizen just like me. He's also the love of my life and he has rights. He stays here. Where he belongs."

Sting took two steps backward until he was standing on the other side of Peter, still defiant, plasma rifle low on his hip.

"Pete stays here," he added.

Peter couldn't help but grin. The love of her life? He'd been afraid that she would get tired of having him around. He leaned over to her and kissed her.

"I love you, Diana," he whispered against her ear.

Fitzroy's face reddened. "All right, forget about the recombinant!" he shouted. "I can see that he's at least half Orlando's age." He turned his gaze back to Dr. Kingston. "But I'm confiscating this datapad and I want the notes you mentioned. All of them."

Dr. Kingston nodded and walked over to the restaurant table where the orange notebook set, open to the first page. She picked it up, closed it, and carried it over to Fitzroy.

"Thank you," he said in a quiet voice.

"Of course," Dr. Kingston answered.

"We'll need to search the premises," said Fitzroy. "I expect everyone's cooperation. Otherwise, I'll tie up your recombinant friend there in so much legal bureaucracy, he'll be twice Orlando's age when he returns. If he returns."

Peter gritted his teeth, balling his hand into a fist. Would it always be like this? Would he always be undocumented? Would being a recombinant always hang over his head like an axe ready to drop?

"Be my guest," Mimi said, holding out her arms. "We've got nothing to hide here."

She walked over to Peter and patted him on the back. She gripped his hands in hers and he felt something smooth in his hands. The gear thing he'd taken from Orlando Constantine's lab! Quickly, he shoved it in his right front jeans pocket and laid his right arm over it, the glow of his arm hiding the dim light from the gear thing.

Peter moved over to the wall and leaned against it, keeping his right arm pressed against his pocket as he watched the strange government agents in the metallic business suits swarm over the restaurant with scanners and grids and other odd pieces of technology that he didn't understand and had never seen before.

He'd never seen most of the things they carried, but they combed through every single bookshelf, scanned every table, and turned over every chair. They scanned pictures on the walls, examined every part of Mimi's office and the small room that Peter and Sting shared. Fitzroy and one other operative went up the stairs and scanned every single room upstairs while a man and woman in silver business suits scanned the main dining room. One of the suits walked toward Peter.

He stiffened and moved closer to Sting.

The woman moved past him and scanned every inch of the kitchen, including the electrified back door and the hardware that controlled it. Peter tried to act unconcerned, but he was terrified they'd scan him again and find the gear thing in his pocket. He gripped the god symbol around his neck, praying that they'd ignore him.

He tried to control his shaking as he watched them scan Mimi, then Dr. Kingston. Sarge, and Diana next. Kai and then Sting. He kept quiet and tried to blend into the wall, hoping they wouldn't want to scan him again. He let out a breath when the agents in metallic silver business suits put away their scanners and other tech things. They moved toward the front door and waited for Fitzroy to return to the main room. It seemed like half an hour before he returned. He walked over to Dr. Kingston.

"Thank you for your cooperation," he said with a nod at Sarge and then Dr. Kingston. "I'm sorry you don't remember me, Jeannette. Maybe someday you'll check your MRC for the memories of those days and see that there was a time when we were happy together."

His eyes were glassy when he smiled, raising his hand as if he was about to reach out and touch her face. He sighed and let his hand drop to his side.

"Take care of yourself, Jeannette."

"I'm sorry, Mr. Fitzroy," she said, looking sad. "When I volunteered to serve, I didn't know how much I'd have to sacrifice. It was a lot more than I ever imagined. Or agreed to. I wish you well."

Fitzroy nodded, pressing his lips together as he shut off the tracker's glow and turned toward the front door.

"Two military squadrons from the base and one from port authority are now patrolling Civilization's streets for biodrones. And Antaran ships. For the record, there is no active attack on Civilization. The situation was apparently limited to the biodrones injected into the reclamation station escape pods. You're safe for now, but keep a sharp eye out and stay safe."

Fitzroy turned away from Dr. Kingston and motioned the other operatives toward the door. Fitzroy pointed at Peter and Peter froze, eyes wide, hand on the plasma rifle hanging across his chest. Covering the glowing gear in his pocket.

"Recombinant, clone—whatever you call him," said Fitzroy to

Mimi. "Lawyer up and get him legal in a hurry—with an experienced genetics IP attorney. Back home, there's a motion every week to change the laws about cloning and recombinants, but current law says if he's genetically related by one generation—with uncopyrighted DNA—he's part of your family."

Mimi smiled. "Thank you, Mr. Fitzroy. And thank you for your compassion. Something that's in short supply these days."

Fitzroy cast one last glance at Peter as Diana pulled him into an embrace and a smile almost reached Fitzroy's eyes as he turned away. He opened the front door and ushered the other operatives outside. He paused on the threshold, staring longingly at Dr. Kingston for several moments. Peter felt a pang of sadness for the man. He looked a little lost now as he stepped outside, closing the door softly.

But what if other operatives came after him? The decoy. Assuming he was Orlando Constantine?

When the restaurant was quiet again, Peter slid to the floor and dropped his head in his hands.

"Pete?" Sting called, his green eyes wide with concern. He dropped down on his haunches and laid his hand against Peter's shoulders, squeezing. "You okay, Pete?"

Peter felt weak in the knees, his stomach doing somersaults. How could he feel all right ever again when someone else could just walk in here someday, at any time, and call him a recombinant? Then cart him off to RDC to be washed out. Or arrest him as Orlando Constantine.

He wanted to scream and kick the walls and run as far and as fast as he could to get away from here. That man, Fitzroy could take him away with the snap of his fingers if the laws changed and he'd be powerless to stop him. He didn't understand everything the man had said about the lawyers and the legal stuff that just made his head ache.

"I—I can't stay here," he mumbled into his hands, the fear shaking through his whole body now. "They'll just come back a—and take me away. Back to RDC. And wash me out!"

Sarge dropped down in front of him and grabbed hold of his hands, pulling them away from his face.

"Mitchell, I know you're scared, but listen to me," he said, his voice commanding.

Peter grabbed hold of Sarge's wrists and gripped them with all of his strength. "Sarge, don't let them take me," he said. "Don't let them wash me out!"

Sarge shook him. "Mitchell! You're all right, okay? Listen to me!"

He smashed his eyes closed, his breath coming in gulps.

"Mitchell! Listen to me! That operative was bluffing. Do you understand? He knew he had no legal ground to stand on. You heard him when he left. He was bluffing."

Slowly, Peter opened his eyes, watching Sarge as the urge to run trembled through his entire body. He shook his head.

"Sarge, I don't understand. What's legal ground—is that a place? And what do you mean bluffing? What does that mean?"

Sting rubbed his shoulders, trying to get him to calm down. "Pete, you know what bluffing means."

Peter shook his head, glancing from Sting to Sarge. "No, I don't."

"It's like when we were in the training barracks or in our shelter on Ku'Tal. Remember? Playing cards. When you pretend like you have winning cards in your hand and you throw down a big bet. You get everybody else to fold so you can take the pot. Remember?"

Peter squeezed his eyes shut, thinking back to some of those long, cold nights on Ku'Tal. Where they'd play cards on someone's bedroll by the yellow wash of ion light, betting with rations or ammo. Sting had taught him that it wasn't always about the cards in his hands. It was about how he played them. How he made the others think he had a winning hand.

That was bluffing.

His muscles began to relax as he finally understood what Sarge meant. He looked up at Sarge.

"So, you're saying Fitzroy didn't have any good cards in his hand?" Peter asked. "That he was just trying to get us to fold so he could take the pot—er, me?"

Sarge laughed. "Yes, Mitchell. That's exactly what I'm trying to tell you. Without your MRC and a genetic profile developed and copyrighted by UCOE, he can't touch you."

At last, he let out a heavy breath he'd been holding. "You're sure?"

"Yes, Peter," said Dr. Kingston, moving over to him. "Kai and I actually removed yours and Stingley's batch numbers from the computer by overwriting them."

Peter couldn't help but grin. He poked Sting who was also grinning.

"That means we're really free, Pete. Free!"

Peter threw his arms around Sting and hugged him. Really and truly free. It was all he'd ever wanted.

"Let's get this restaurant put back together," Mimi replied, motioning Peter and Sting up from the floor.

Sting ruffled Peter's hair and pulled him to his feet. Into Diana's arms. He melted into her warm embrace, the calm beginning to settle through him again. When he reached Dr. Kingston, he stopped and gripped her hand, squeezing it.

"Dr. Kingston," he said in a quiet voice, "I know how hard it is to have an MRC hijacking your memories. I'm sorry yours took so much away. I know all about how alone it can make you feel. Just know that you have friends you can count on here in Civilization. We'll help you make new memories."

She smiled and laid her hand against Peter's cheek. "Thank you, Peter—you're a gem. That's comforting. I can't imagine how dim this world would be if it lost someone like you. You're a precious gift."

He couldn't help but blush as he followed Sting and Diana into the main room to clean up and reassemble the restaurant for service.

14

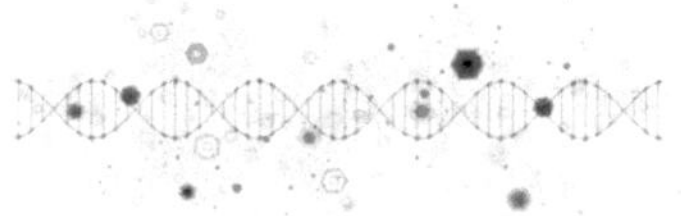

JEANNETTE STARED at the restaurant's heavy wooden door, the memory of Marcus Fitzroy's forlorn expression disturbing. Was any of that true? That she'd almost been his wife—and a government operative? Sent to spy on Mimi's brother, a man she remembered having great respect for, but now, she'd didn't know what to think about Orlando Constantine. Or Agent Fitzroy.

She was afraid to look at Kai, fearing what he might think of her now. He'd been so quiet.

Mimi paused in front of her and it felt like Mimi was staring deep into her soul. Did Mimi hate her now? After hearing Fitzroy's claim? That she'd been a government operative. Sent to spy on Mimi's brother. The brief memories she had of working with Orlando had been as colleagues not as a spy scrutinizing his every move.

"I wish we'd been able to at least look at Orlando's files," said Mimi, her expression sad. "I need to know what it was that we turned on or set in motion. For Peter's sake. Now, we may never know."

Jeannette reached out and laid her hand on Mimi's shoulder. "We'll have time," she said, smiling. "I copied everything over during the standoff. Over to your datapad and beamed it onto backup optics. Oh, and I adjusted Fitzroy's tracker to light up anyone that touched Orlando's datapad after it was unlocked, not just Orlando—and Peter. He'll never know I changed the tracker to light up after anyone touched it."

At last, a smile brightened Mimi's face.

"Thank you from all of us for protecting Peter. I think you already know how important he is to us. Especially to Diana and Sting."

Jeannette returned her smile.

"I had to," she said with a nod toward the lanky blond-haired young man sanitizing tables alongside Sting and Diana. "He's the best in all of us. We can't let that light go out."

Mimi nodded. "Can't argue with that." She stared at Jeannette a moment or two. "Y'know, I'm betting that you walked away from being an operative after working with Orlando. You have a strong heart chakra just like he did. Like Peter does. And I couldn't agree more that losing him would darken the world."

Mimi headed past her into the dining room.

Jeannette glanced up as Kai approached, those electric blue eyes wide.

"Not sure what to believe anymore, Red," he said with a sigh.

She shook her head. "Neither do I, Kai. I have no memory of that man. None."

He held up his hands, his face shadowed with stubble. "Maybe after you've reviewed your MRC memories, you'll have a better perspective on all of this? And maybe me someday."

A sad expression clung to his face, eyes downcast, a frown furrowing his forehead. He took a step back, but she grabbed his arm, pulling him toward her.

"Kai, I can't tell you much about my life before getting an MRC, but now that it's gone, the one thing I know for sure is that I want you in my life."

His face brightened. "You sure about that, Red?" he asked.

"Knowing that I still have my MRC? Knowing you were almost married to Fitzroy?"

She nodded. "Yes, a chance I'm willing to take."

He reached out and cupped her chin. "And if I remove my MRC?"

"Then we'll both still remember this conversation," she said with a laugh.

At last, a smile touched his lips as he moved over to Mimi who was directing Sting and Peter on how to move the tables and chairs back into place.

"Mimi, I'd still like to get this damned MRC removed," Kai said, a hand on the back of his neck. "I sure don't want to be like that poor bastard that left here after being a total stranger to his fiancée."

"Fair enough, Dr. Drew," said Mimi. "As soon as the dining room's back in place, we'll take care of that thing for you."

"Much obliged."

Mimi turned around and glanced over at Jeannette. "You still need that shuttle ride back to your reclamation station?"

Jeannette nodded. "Yes, please. A round trip if possible. Kai and I need to examine the reclamation theatre for clues. Find out what happened."

"Now that we've got patrols in place," Mimi said, motioning toward the door, "that shouldn't be a problem. By the time you return, we can talk about my brother's files and the information he left for us to find."

Jeannette reached into her pocket and removed a tiny optics disc, handing it to Mimi. "I scanned every page of Orlando's handwritten notebook. It's all on here. When Kai and I return, we can formulate a plan once we understand what it was that Orlando found. And what he was after."

"Thank you, Dr. Kingston. I'll get Ron to take you to the spaceport so my team can fly you to the station and back. What's left of it anyway." She laid her hand on Kai's shoulder. "Now then, let's take care of that MRC."

"Gladly," said Kai, studying Mimi as she paused at the kitchen door.

Jeannette reached out and took Kai's hand in hers.

"You better remember everything up to this moment, Kai Drew, when that MRC's out."

He smirked, leaning toward her and kissing her on the lips. "I still remember that you owe me a second date."

"What?" she cried, giving him an incredulous look. "Shooting biodrones outside a fine restaurant wasn't enough of a second date for you?"

He laughed as he turned and followed Mimi toward the kitchen.

"Okay, then you owe me a third date."

"You're on," she replied as he disappeared behind the double doors.

She needed to analyze the strange artifact that she'd given back to Peter to hide from Fitzroy and the other intelligence operatives. It was some kind of part or interface.

Was it part of this fabled replication engine that Orlando claimed to find? Or was it a key of some kind, one that required a cipher string that Orlando had mentioned in his notebook?

She needed more time to review this data that Orlando had left behind, but the strange gear-shaped artifact had originated on Naharra. She was certain of it, judging from the hand-drawn maps she'd scanned from Orlando's notebook. Marking locations.

But she needed to know what this artifact connected to—and how. Was that the only part involved or were there others? Missing and essential to power up some alien engine or replication device? Had Orlando really found a way to turn on this mythic forerunner device he'd claimed to find?

She needed time to study Orlando's schematics and the notes he'd left behind. And she needed to understand how Peter Mitchell fit into Orlando's plan. Was Peter the only living iteration of Orlando's RDC profile or had there been any others before him?

Had Orlando intended for Peter to be arrested and taken apart by government agents, leaving Orlando free to do—whatever he'd been planning? Or had Orlando's purpose been far darker and grimmer than anyone wanted to acknowledge? A sacrifice of some kind? One needed to activate this fabled engine? Or release a monster? All of it to stop the Antarans, but the thought of it was barbaric.

Jeannette had to know and understand, so she could stop Orlando from making a huge mistake that might just turn the war in the Antarans' favor.

15

THAT NIGHT, Peter dreamed of red skies and smoky ashen ground again. He walked through the remains of a forest with skeletal trees scraping bare limbs together like the clicking of bones. The air smelled burnt, charred, the world growing dark as the setting sun's faint warmth barely reached through the smoky haze.

Ahead in the growing twilight stood a stone dais with six bone-white pillars that reached up through the smoky haze, each one illuminated with bright blue lights that cast an outline of a circle onto the dais.

He walked toward the dais and stood in the center of five concentric circles, holding out his arms, his right-hand glowing blue.

As the structure sparked to life, it sent a beam of orange light into the air. The orange light fanned out like lightning crackling across the sky, striking all six pillars. As each pillar lit orange, the concentric circles began to fill with blue light.

As the last pillar illuminated an eerie orange, the entire dais lit up orange and then blue and began to lower into the ground, carrying him down a dark, vertical tunnel and into a cavernous room, its walls covered in a dark, shiny material that looked like obsidian. Like the cool dark metal covering the spires in Civilization's desert. Every wall had strange, glowing symbols and carvings etched into its cool, polished surface. He didn't understand any of the symbols any more than he knew what or where this chamber was located.

On one shiny wall stood a black door with a large, circular indentation in its center.

He walked toward the room, honeycombed floors lighting up with every step he took toward the door. When he studied the indentation, he realized it was large enough for his hand—or the gear thing he'd found in Dr. Constantine's lab. Peter didn't know what lay beyond the door, but the room called to him. Inside his head, until he struggled to resist its call.

Standing in front of the door, Peter pressed the gear into the indentation.

Two doors rumbled open and a strange mechanism loomed before him, at least two stories tall. A round input panel stood in front of the machine with its crystalline enclosures, tall enough for a human—or alien. One large chamber stood in front with a line of enclosures on both sides connecting to the central chamber. All spherical in shape. At least a dozen or more connecting enclosures. All empty. He couldn't count them all.

Something called out to him, pulling him toward the round panel that stood in front of the central crystalline enclosure. Calling to Peter to use the gear, telling him to use it to turn on this great monstrosity of alien technology. He didn't understand what it did or how it called out to him. But it almost seemed sentient, intelligent, telling him to press his hand against the panel. And give it life at long last.

He was the igniter. The cipher. It was inside him. It was how they made him. How Orlando Constantine had made him. In his image. In his altered genetic image. Destined to interface with this strange and terrible biomorphic hybrid machine that was organic, genetic, and cybernetic—and all alien. From a lost race. The device was part living thing and part mechanical—digital, growing, and evolving until he activated it. Bringing it back to life.

Peter stepped inside the central spherical enclosure in front and pressed his hand against the round panel.

Behind him, all the smaller enclosures began to create bodies. The hazy figures changed and evolved until every one of the bodies had Peter's face. Each one took a piece from him until he felt his own body fading away.

Orlando Constantine stood outside the central chamber, pointing, and laughing as he opened the secondary enclosures and let the copies escape with Peter's memories. His future. His life.

Peter tried to scream. Couldn't as other images played across his mind's eye. Ballese. The colony.

He stood in the Ballese colony's empty streets, papers and leaves swirling around the silent buildings. He turned. Finding the chapel in front of him. The place with the god symbols glowed white in the stormy sky's growing darkness. That became a swarm of ships, diving low on the horizon, plasma fire arcing, bombs falling.

The colony burned around him. Buildings crumbled. People died in the streets as the god symbols pulsed with light.

Why didn't the god symbols save them?

As the ships flew low over the street, Peter stared, horrified. Those ships weren't Antaran. They had *United Countries of Earth* printed on their hulls.

Then he knew Orlando Constantine's secret. The reason for him creating a decoy. And why the man was being hunted. The colony on Ballese hadn't been destroyed by Antaran forces.

Peter pulled in a breath, his eyes stinging.

It was UCOE.

Orlando's own people! Orlando let them think he was dead as he burrowed deep into a hidden shelter. So, they wouldn't find out what he saw. What he'd learned.

That UCOE had bombed its own colony.

Peter felt the rage burn through him. All those people! With thousands of years left to live. Citizens! Killed by their own people! People that had leveled an entire colony just to kill—silence—one man that had stolen some alien technology. And witnessed his own people bomb the colony. So, he cowered below while the colonists all died for him.

Why? WHY?

And now, Orlando wanted Peter to die for him. So, he could pose as Earth's savior. Giving UCOE the alien replication device was the only thing that would save Orlando Constantine's life. Stop government agents from hunting him.

But it would cost Peter his life. Because everything in that central chamber got destroyed during the replication process.

The red skies, ashen soil, and smoky haze returned. Where the engine lived. Where it waited for instructions. Waited to replicate whatever entered its chamber. Waited for someone with the key to open the door. Waited for someone with the cipher to build an army thousands and thousands strong. Replication at a rate and scale no one had ever seen before.

On Naharra. Where it all began.

Peter woke himself shouting.

He sat up in bed, coughing, staring at the sun-drenched wall. And Sting's empty bed against the wall. Sting was already up. Because it was morning, he finally realized.

The knock on the door startled him.

"Who's there?" he called out.

"Mitchell, it's Sarge."

He tried to brush the sleep out of his eyes and smooth his hair.

"Come in, Sarge," he answered, his voice scratchy and softer than he'd intended.

Sarge opened the door a crack and stuck his head inside. He looked tired, dark circles under his eyes, his face a little paler than usual.

"You okay?" he asked.

Peter frowned. "Yeah, why?"

Sarge opened the door wider and stepped inside, closing it. He sat down at the end of Peter's bed, the blue quilt askew across it, blue sheets tangled.

"You were shouting in your sleep," said Sarge, but not in a judging kind of way, Peter realized.

The look on his face was concern. Just concern. It made Peter smile.

"Sorry," he said. "Hope I didn't wake anyone else up."

"Mitchell, I'm worried, okay? You've been acting strange since you told me about Mimi's brother and his lab. Well, since all the tech you brought back turned itself on."

"I keep having these dreams," said Peter, straightening the blue sheet across his bare legs. "Bad dreams. But they're his dreams. Not mine, Sarge."

The door opened and Sting entered the room.

"Pete, you're finally awake," he said, walking over to the bed.

He grinned and ruffled Peter's blond hair and then plopped down on his own bed, studying him.

Peter's brow furrowed, his gaze falling onto his best buddy.

"What?" Sting said, holding out his hands. "I want to know what all the shouting and dreams are about, Pete. Since you're tellin' Sarge here about it, you can just tell me, too."

"Fine," said Peter, sighing. "They're not my dreams, okay. They're his dreams."

"Orlando's dreams?" Sarge asked.

Peter winced, nodding.

Sarge cast a sideways glance at Sting who studied Peter's face with a scrutiny that made Peter nervous. Did they think something was wrong with him? Did they think he was broken now? Broken by the strange gear thing and whatever Orlando Constantine had rigged up on his datapad. And now, they were going to try and fix him. For a recombinant, that usually meant pain or worse. Something he couldn't think about right now.

"But I'm not broken," Peter snapped. "You don't need to fix me somehow." He dropped his head into his hands, staring down at the quilt. "I don't know what's happening to me, but I'm seeing his past. His memories. What really happened on Ballese."

The bed creaked as Sting rose from his bed and flopped down beside Peter, a hand on his bare shoulder.

"Pete, we don't think you're broken," he said, shaking his head. "We just think something's happening to you and neither of us understands what that is—unless you tell us."

"Sting's right, Mitchell," said Sarge in his best training sergeant voice. "You're not broken, but some of this technology has..."

His voice trailed off and Peter saw that he was struggling for words. Sarge never struggled for words.

"This tech has done something to you," Sarge continued. "Sting and I are trying to understand it. And help you. Support you."

Peter stared at both of them. Sarge's dark brown eyes were kind and he saw no deception there. Sting's light green eyes were bright, electric, lit with emotion. The same way Sting looked that awful night on Ku'Tal when he'd taken Peter's place as the Antarans' captive.

It made him angry.

Never again. He'd never let Sting take his place like that ever again. It wasn't right. He loved Sting like a brother. More than a brother. And the thought of Sting sacrificing himself again made Peter's eyes well with moisture.

Not Sting. Not Sarge. And definitely not Diana! He'd accept whatever consequences came his way for bringing back things he didn't understand. It was his fault. He'd face it alone, without Sting or Sarge getting hurt. Or worse—killed. He couldn't live with that guilt again. He'd agonized over Sting for weeks and weeks. Now that they were all safe and together, he would make sure they stayed that way.

"Pete...I know that look," said Sting, gripping his shoulder now. "Talk to me. I see your mind racing with something you're not telling us."

Sarge's gaze darkened, his mouth flattening into an angry line. "Talk to us, Mitchell."

Peter sighed. Feeling cornered.

"Something's—happening to me. I don't understand it and I don't know what it is, but I'm starting to know things that he knew. That Orlando knew. Secrets. Bad things. And—" His voice broke and he gulped a breath of air, lifting his face from his hands. His voice came out so small and aching that he could barely finish the thought. "And I think I'm becoming...like...him."

Peter could see the fear shining in Sting's eyes as he shared a frightened look with Sarge who looked unnerved. Sting took Peter by both shoulders.

"Pete, you're you. You're not Orlando Constantine! Just because you have the same genetics doesn't mean you're exactly like him. You didn't live his life. And he didn't live yours."

"Exactly, and no technology I know of can turn you into him, Mitchell," said Sarge, his voice a soft, measured calm that had come from six months at Ku'Tal and a suicide mission to Ballese. "You may be his exact genetic match, but you are nothing like the man. Trust me, Mitchell. I've never met another person like you. And I doubt I ever will."

Peter bit his lip, his eyes stinging at the memory of all those people dying on Ballese. Pointlessly. For no reason. How could anyone live with that?

"All those people, Sting!" he cried, trying so hard not to feel every death, but they ached through his soul as if he'd caused them. "Sarge, all those citizens!"

Sarge shook his head. Another sideways glance at Sting who looked more worried than ever now.

"Mitchell, what citizens? You saw the colony. It was dead. Empty. Talk to me, Peter."

Peter shook his head, grabbing handfuls of the blue quilt as the remnants of the dream ached through him. "All the colonists on Ballese, Sarge. And the original colony on Naharra. They're all dead.

Gone! All of them—killed! Their bodies just left in the streets to rot. I saw it. I saw it all!" He was trembling now, heart pounding into his throat. He could barely speak, his voice so tight and small. "And I think I caused it. All of it."

Sting rubbed his shoulders, trying to calm him down, but it was all so fresh and raw. Orlando Constantine's memories made him ill and he wanted to throw up. Were they his own memories somehow? Either way, it hurt more than anything since he'd brought Sting home.

"Mitchell." Sarge's voice was calm and slow, a steady, soothing rhythm that made Peter concentrate on his words. "Nothing that Orlando Constantine did or does is your fault. Do you hear me?"

Sting just kept rubbing his shoulders.

"Sarge, I—"

"Mitchell," Sarge repeated. "Nothing Orlando Constantine did is your fault. You share his genetics, not his actions."

"But all those people, Sarge!" His face screwed up with pain, the guilt bitter and rising. "They all died while he just hid. He just let them all be murdered above him while he was safe and sound in his lab below." Shaking, he grabbed hold of Sting's forearms. "Sting, the Antarans didn't attack that colony on Ballese. UCOE did."

Sarge's brows furrowed, his lips drawn tight, anger beginning a slow burn in his brown eyes. "Mitchell! What are you saying? My people would never—"

"Sarge, it's true." Peter sighed. "Your own people destroyed the Ballese colony. To kill Orlando Constantine. And they lied about Naharra, too, Sarge. All of it was a lie. Why do they all tell so many lies, Sarge? Why? I just don't understand."

Sarge shook his head, fear beginning to shine on his face as his anger cooled.

"Who lied about Naharra? It was all over the nets, Mitchell. Image after image. Digital footage everywhere of the bombing run over Naharra. The overwhelming Antaran presence murdering the whole colony. The nets showed all the warhead drops. Oh, God—the mushroom clouds…"

"UCOE lied," said Peter, feeling sick and disgusted. "Orlando Constantine lied with them. They all lied about the nuclear attack and fallout on Naharra to keep people away, Sarge," Peter said, his gaze shifting to his former field sergeant. "Orlando helped them fake the radiation readings after UCOE murdered the colony. He worked on the project to build the mock bombs that UCOE dropped. The payloads were empty. To save it. That's why they tried to silence him on Ballese. Why they're still hunting him now."

"To save what, Pete? The planet? Naharra?" Sting asked, shaking his head as the color drained out of Sarge's face. "You're talking so fast, buddy. Slow down and take a breath."

"To save the engine," said Peter, rubbing his forehead. "That's what he called it. It's part machine and part living thing. Older than Earth. Older than Naharra. Older than the Antaris Nation." He moaned, holding his head again. "How do I know these things?" He gulped a breath. "He's been protecting it all these years. From the Antarans. Now from UCOE. But Sarge, Sting—I don't understand why. Why?" He sucked in another gulp of air. "It's calling out to me, Sarge. Out to him. And…" He smashed his eyes closed, not wanting to see their reactions. "And it's changing me inside somehow. The stuff Orlando hid. It's—Sting, it's turning things on inside my body."

Sting and Sarge could only stare at him, fear hovering just behind their eyes.

"See," Peter said in a shaky voice.

He reached under the bed, pulling out his scanning grid. He flicked it on and pointed it at himself. A ghost echo washed across the screen, setting his hair on end and making his stomach drop. What did they do to him on Ballese? And what sort of time bomb had Orlando Constantine saved into his DNA?

Was it slowly changing him into an Antaran hybrid now that Dr. Kingston and Mimi had tripped some buried programming deep inside his genetic code? He didn't understand it all (or any of it), but it was so much worse than trying to escape the military. Or rescuing Sting.

Peter swiped at the moisture leaking out of his eyes and dropped the grid on the quilt.

"Sting," he cried, holding out his hands. "What's happening to me? Am I becoming a biodrone? Or a caregiver like Tevihu?" He shuddered. "Or undead. Like D'Angelo."

All of those possibilities terrified him.

Sarge sat down next to him on the bed and gripped his other shoulder, Sting on his left side.

"Peter, all of this has happened so fast. I don't know what to believe right now," said Sarge, struggling to say the right thing. "But I know you have no reason to lie. Not about this."

Peter knew Sarge was trying so hard in his careful kind of way, but Sarge was out of his element. Sarge knew recombinants. Soldiers. Not this DNA stuff.

Peter rubbed his face, shaking. Terrified to look in the mirror. Would mottled skin and tentacles stare back at him? Or worse, the caregivers' translucent skin that shifted form like smoke on water.

Sarge caught Peter's face and made him look the man in the eye.

"Peter. Listen." Sarge paused, waiting until he had Peter's full attention. "Just because the grid reacts to you doesn't make you a biodrone. Or God forbid, a damned caregiver. That grid can scan a lot of things. I acknowledge that something strange is happening here, but you aren't going to turn into a biodrone, Peter."

Peter sighed. "Are you sure, Sarge?"

Sarge nodded. "Damn straight I'm sure," he said. "Look, I don't exactly understand what happened to D'Angelo, besides him being— well, undead or whatever. But the one thing I do know is that nothing has taken control of you, Mitchell. Except fear because of what's happening with this grid." He let go of Peter. "I don't know how you know these things about the Ballese colony or Naharra, but I think it's time to take this to Mimi and find out exactly what she does and doesn't know about her brother, Orlando." Sarge sighed. "And maybe she can tell us something about this damned engine I keep hearing about."

"That makes two of us, Sarge," said Peter. "Ever since that gear thing lit up and the datapad turned on by itself, I've dreamed about it. I see it every time I go to sleep. Like it's calling out to me. But it's a machine, Sarge. How can it be both a living thing and a machine? I don't understand."

Sting pulled him into a tight hug. "Don't you worry, Pete? I've got your back. No matter what happens. No matter where. I've always got your back. You're my brother, man. Forever."

Peter nodded, hugging Sting back as his shaking began to subside.

"I've got your back, too, Mitchell," said Sarge. "And yours, Stingley. Whatever happens with this insanity, we're all three in it together. Got it? We're family and family sticks together. Don't forget that because I mean it."

"Thanks, Sarge. Sting." Peter let go of Sting. "I never quite understood how it felt to be part of a family. Until I lost Sting. But Sarge, you and Diana and Sting have all taught me so much about family."

"Pete, when this tech stuff hurts you, it hurts me, too," said Sting, sighing. "Just promise me you won't try and protect me again. Like you did on Ku'Tal."

Peter frowned, shaking his head. "What?"

"Don't go trying to save me again by sacrificing yourself! Understand?" Sting's tone was sharp. "I'm not ever gonna let you do that shit again. You got me, Pete? Either we both live or we both fight, but not one for the other. Together or nothing. Got it?"

Peter couldn't help but smile. Sting was the best friend he'd ever had and he loved him more than his own life. Like he loved Diana. And Sarge. He'd do anything and everything to protect them, too. But he knew Sting wouldn't let him if he had anything to say about it.

"Got it, Sting," he said and gripped Sting's hand in his for a moment.

Just then, Sarge's com rang. He jumped, looking startled but relieved.

"Looks like some communications are back online," he said and slid it out of his pants pocket. "This is Temple. What, sir?" Sarge's face turned paler than the ivory-tiled floor. "How many? ETA? Roger that rendezvous point, sir. We'll mobilize everyone that can carry a weapon. Temple out."

Sarge stared down at his comunit for several long moments. Finally, he turned around.

"Sarge, what is it?" Sting asked, rising from the bed.

Peter scrambled out of bed and onto his feet, dressed only in blue boxers. "They're coming, aren't they? The Antarans."

Sarge nodded. "Huge force. Ships. Troop transports—on a direct vector for Civilization. Space Corps' mobilizing units from Ku'Tal and Farnas. And the waypoint between systems." He shook his head. "None of them will get here in time to cut off that damned strike fleet. Training base is deploying every last recombinant and citizen that can handle a plasma rifle. Including the Civilization militia. And I'm calling up Mimi's Underground. Grab your rifles and grids."

"How long, Sarge?" Peter asked, grabbing for the tan camo pants on a hook beside the small white dresser.

"First scouts are minutes away," he said, his voice low and tight. "The entire invasion force? At most? Two hours—give or take." His voice was grim as he moved toward the door. "Dress formal," he replied, opening the door and disappearing into the hallway.

16

JEANNETTE AND KAI called in some favors and obtained landing clearance to gather forensic data from the attack on the reclamation station. The shuttle had to dock via a makeshift airlock due to all the damage, but they succeeded in getting aboard.

Gliding through the black calm of space, Jeannette and Kai tethered against the reclamation station's burned and battered hull. They wore mottled tan and grey envirosuits with mag boots and oxygen backups just in case. The station's artificial gravity felt unstable, like it had that night when the whole thing upended and nearly imploded.

Even now, Reclamation Station 343-AOD listed about ten degrees to starboard as Jeanette and Kai made their way out of the badly damaged launch bay, debris in dark piles along the sides of the bay, the once shiny grey floor burnt and warped. The bay's buckling framework had melted, but emergency crews had reinforced it with orange honeycombed braces to keep the whole thing from collapsing. Red and blue emergency lighting cast eerie shadows throughout the high-ceilinged launch bay, its ceiling a tangle of wires and twisted conduits.

The lighting made moments from that night rush back to Jeannette. She held her breath, the station and the memories unsettling.

The silence was palpable, hiss of their rebreathers a faint echo through the eerily quiet station as they left the launch bay, moving deeper into the structure. Rebreathers scrubbed the air, but Jeannette smelled a hint of burnt polymer and cold ash as she followed Kai into one of the narrow maintenance jump tubes, allowing them to untether and do a slow freefall into the station's lower decks. To the reclamation theatre in the belly of the station where only bodies and conveyor belts moved 24/7.

Back to the place where everything started. Third shift.

Jeannette stood above the opened hatch that swirled hundreds of feet down onto the reclamation floor, mag boots and her tether line keeping her in place. Her stomach did somersaults as she watched the red emergency lights strobe down the sides and disappear, like an old-time flashbulb camera. It felt like looking into the abyss, into the singularity of a black hole.

She braced her hands against the scraped and burned composite walls and waited for Kai to go first.

"Ready to take a leap with me?" he asked, laying a gloved hand against the mottled tan and grey sleeve of her envirosuit, his rebreather vibrating in the stillness, making a mechanical sound as he pulled in another breath.

Jeannette sighed. She didn't much care for heights, but she had mag boots, a tether, and oxygen backup. What could go wrong?

What if they dropped into a vortex of biodrones down there? Or through the bottom of the station and kept on falling?

"Uh, VerticalOne?" he asked again, holding out his hand to her.

Mimi and Kai insisted they use code names. Just in case.

Finally, Jeanette nodded, pulling in a mechanical breath, and gripped his gloved hand a moment.

"I'll go first and you follow," he said, the rebreather muffling his voice.

"Careful, VerticalTwo," she said, squeezing his hand. "We have no clue what's down there now. Not even a visual."

He nodded and she let him go.

Kai took hold of the sides of the tube with both hands. He pulled in a mechanical breath and unhooked his tether line from the main conduit. Swallowing a breath, he flicked a switch on the front panel of his envirosuit. Turning off his mag boots.

He began to drift and grabbed hold of the tube's edges as he peered one last time into the abyss. His rebreather hissed as he pulled in a deep breath.

And dropped into darkness.

Her heart thumped against her rib cage, hands shaking as she counted the seconds. Listening for any noise. The sound of a gasp. Or a whisper.

They were leaping into the complete unknown down there. Expecting to find sabotage. Besides Mimi and a handful of her operatives, no one else knew they were here. They needed to get in and out quick. Scrape as much data as they could and do some quick analysis on the genetic profiles of Peter Mitchell and John Stingley.

Jeannette already had a copy of Orlando's and his brother, Beckett's original genetic profiles to use as controls—gotten from their personal effects. Thanks to their sister, Mimi.

The quickest way for her to gather and analyze the data she needed was to use the station's processing power to isolate control parameters and capture the differences for each. On the station, it would take minutes. Somewhere else? Weeks.

She couldn't wait two weeks until she and Kai were banished to a reclamation station orbiting Ku'Tal either. She had to know now what game or games Orlando was running. But first, she needed to understand what had happened here. At this reclamation station. Find out if there was evidence below of sabotage. She needed to find out what games Stanton was playing, too.

Two century-like minutes passed until Kai's velvety voice echoed through her helmet, a little tinny sounding from the rebreather.

"I'm down," he said in a warm, velvety voice. "Theatre's floor is still intact. I'll be here waiting for you. Just take it slow and easy. But know that this station has been reinforced and stabilized despite her slight tilt."

Jeannette's breath quickened as she moved her feet toward the tube's opening, feeling a rush of cold air as her heartbeat thrummed faster through her chest like a battle drum. She pulled in a deep breath and held it, untethering from the main conduit.

Pulled in another deep breath and held it while she grabbed hold of both sides of the jump tube's opening.

Counting to three, she let go.

And dropped like a stone!

"It's too fast!"

"Switch off your mag boots!" Kai said in an anxious voice. "They're pulling you through the tube."

She blinked twice, calling up her suit's digital interface in her helmet's visor, and flicked off her mag boots.

Her descent slowed.

She let out a breath and gulped at the air as she continued to drop through the dark passage that was like one of those old water slides from hell.

Until she felt gravity disappear. And her body's descent slowed again.

Her body floated as she moved past the last of the strobing red lights and into the dusky light of the reclamation theatre's cavernous well. Still partially lit, the theatre's day-shine lights gave the space an unholy gleam. The lights' strange, cool blue-white hue never seemed to convince her brain it was seeing sunlight.

Through her helmet's suit interface, she toggled on her mag boots as she hovered above the shiny grey floor. With the magnetic field active, the boots pulled her down to the floor.

"And you stuck the landing, VerticalOne," he said with a smirk. "I'm impressed."

She smiled. "Only because you reminded me about the boots."

Kai shrugged.

"So, how do you want to do this, Vertical Two?" Jeannette asked, her words vibrating through the rebreather. "I'd like to run the two comparisons against the controls and capture the results."

"Okay, I'll gather access logs and anything else I can scrape," he replied, his voice echoing through her helmet. "They haven't changed access protocols yet, so I've got a bit more reach. After that, we retrace our steps to the escape pods and investigate along the way."

Jeannette nodded. "Don't take your helmet off. Don't want the cameras picking up any facial recognition. The patterned envirosuits and visors will scramble and deflect any DNA scanning attempts. Rebreathers will hamper any audio voice recognition."

He grinned at her. "These aren't standard issue, are they?"

"Nothing our base station supplies is ever standard issue, is it?" she replied.

Kai shook his head. "Nope, and that's a relief. I was planning on both of us living through this trip." He reached out and laid his hand against her helmet. "And I still owe you a third date."

"Yes, you do," she said with a smirk. "And now, you can't claim it got filtered it out."

His chuckle was a mechanical snap through the rebreather as he turned toward the metal door that led out onto the grid floor of the reclamation theatre.

Mimi had removed his MRC.

Once Jeannette moved away from the jump tube, she turned off her mag boots again, preferring to float above the floor and use her tether line to move ahead as Kai opened the door into the reclamation theatre. For a moment, she could only float there and stare with her mouth open.

"What?" she said with a gasp. "How can this be?"

Every single reclamation station looked untouched. Pristine. Completely unaffected by the attack on the station.

That was impossible!

She and Kai were here when the entire station capsized and then righted itself like a bobber in a hurricane. Only a handful of tools lay on the floor, not even one table out of place. Every single reclamation station was lit with bright blue-white light. Untouched. Unaffected. Green lights on the equipment blinking, ready, and waiting for input. For the next shift.

Like someone had gone to a lot of trouble to put it all back together again. Like nothing had happened.

"Nothing's even smashed," he muttered. "And the belts are still moving...how?"

The thunk and whirr of the conveyor belts was the only sound in the room as the belt system tracked through the depths of the reclamation station and up through the higher levels toward the launch bay. Empty. Running as if they were ready for a typical, awful third shift. Jeannette half-expected to turn around and find a stack of red body bags on the rack beside the processing station.

Kai's face looked pale, concern and confusion burning in those electric blue eyes.

"Okay, let's do this fast," he said, his voice hollow as he slid toward the reclamation station beside the one Jeannette chose.

She worked quickly, signing in with a test account used to calibrate systems, and called up two unlabeled genetic profiles numbered zero and one (Orlando and Peter). She keyed in some parameters and ran the incremental scan that isolated and reported only the differences, running it in the background while the calibration process ran.

As the first profile comparison began counting down completion percentages, Jeannette watched Kai swipe and tap items in the pod's visual display as he dipped deeper into log files, scan data, and repair information. He seemed to have found a trail or two to follow. Hopefully, it didn't lead him down a rabbit hole.

Or worse—a black hole.

She moved across the aisle to another processing station, logged into a systems test account, and called up genetic profiles two and three (Beckett Constantine and John Stingley). She'd saved the encrypted profiles using a public kiosk into a public area of the solar array using temporary accounts with nondescript names that she deleted before arriving here.

Now, all she could do was wait for the incremental change logs to parse and process the results for both profiles comparisons. As soon as they finished, she'd launch an encryption protocol that would alert Ron Kraver to pull them down from another public kiosk. And wipe the kiosk to UCOE defense standards.

Jeannette walked over to the other processing station where Kai huddled, watching data flash past above his head.

"I'm just grabbing everything I can," he said, glancing up at her.

His fingers flashed across the mechanical keyboard instead of the virtual display, his typing loud and frenzied above the tick and birr of the empty conveyor belt climbing out of the reclamation theatre.

"Probably a good idea," said Jeannette, her voice metallic through the rebreather.

She turned. Glancing behind her. No one there. Not even a body bag on the wire-racked shelving.

She felt...almost a presence, expecting someone else to be standing behind her, but she and Kai were alone.

Still, that feeling persisted. Like someone was watching them. Observing them.

She glanced at the visual display on her helmet and pinged the shuttle. Hopefully, it was still docked to the launch bay, waiting for her and Kai to emerge.

"Everything okay, VerticalOne?" asked a woman's voice.

She hadn't met the young woman with short, spiky, black hair before this trip.

"Yes, Stasis. Just checking in to make sure our ride is secure."

"Statis is safe and secure," the woman replied. "We won't leave without you. Over."

"Thanks. VerticalOne out."

Jeanette turned back to Kai who was still touching screens, pounding out commands, and copying log files, and moved over to the first profile comparison. Still running, screen flashing, green and white letters reflecting off the stainless-steel tables. The cool but bright white light that hung above the processing station had a slight oscillation, casting their shadows across the floor like a jerky, stop-motion video.

Frowning, she moved across the dark aisle shadowed by the constant rumble and bump of the conveyor belt overhead and checked her second job. Same result. It would just take time. She had to be patient, but something didn't feel right down here. It made her skin turn to gooseflesh and the hair on the back of her neck stand up.

Kai seemed oblivious to anyone and anything, his focus on log files and events posted. She leaned against the stainless-steel table and gazed up at the conveyor belts. Running endlessly through the deserted station.

The moving shadow above her head startled her.

Her gaze darted toward the ceiling, rafters broken and melted, temporary struts maintaining the cavernous room's structural integrity.

But the black-on-grey shadow shifted and twisted, long tentacles flailing.

Her blood turned to ice.

Two biodrones crouched on the conveyor belts, their mottled, corpulent flesh unmoving despite the bump and whir of the belts, carrying them downward, toward the storage rooms. The only thing lower than the reclamation theatre in this space station.

Dead biodrones? On the conveyors?

"VerticalTwo..."

He didn't answer, his full attention still on scraping every last bit of data from the logs.

"My God," Kai hissed. "Stanton's logged into systems all over this station. Just her account and the automated service accounts. Running all kinds of strange processes. This doesn't make any sense."

Jeannette watched, horrified as two more biodrones appeared on the conveyor belts. And two more. Then three and four.

Then it hit her like a brick, the thought chilling. The station hadn't been overrun by a biodrone invasion.

Someone was creating them!

And Kai had just identified the who. Stanton. She felt a chill against her skin.

She slid her comm out of her pocket and snapped images and grabbed video footage of the biodrones lined up on the conveyor belts. Like they were on a factory output line, moving through production to packaging and shipping. She sighed, her stomach dropping. Like down to Civilization in the guise of an Antaran assault.

Just how much of that attack had been contrived by Stanton? But the one missing piece to all this was why? It was a terrorist act. A treasonous act by a cowardly traitor.

But only if the woman was still human.

Had Stanton been compromised by Antarans?

One of the hybrids developed on Ballese? Or was Stanton one of those terrifying caregivers that Peter Mitchell and David Temple had described? Creatures that could change form and mask a genetic scan.

Worse, she realized.

Not mask, but project a genetic form for the scanners. She'd laughed at Mimi Constantine's comment about the woman lacking an aura, but at this moment, Mimi's observation was the only evidence that suggested Stanton wasn't what she appeared. Well, that and the discovery of alien code in her MRC.

Jeannette sighed. But she'd found that same type of code in the recombinant's affected MRC batches, too. Was it a base-level alteration or something more sinister? Like a time bomb, waiting to explode?

How long had Stanton been compromised?

Regardless of the why or how long, Jeannette knew that they needed to get out of here before Stanton discovered their presence here.

She shuddered, glancing up at the biodrones again. Or those things got activated and sent after them again.

She moved over to Kai and tugged on his arm.

"A few more minutes please," he muttered, still staring at the computer screen. "Someone named D'Angelo is also logged in. With fucking admin privileges! I need to figure out who that is and what Stanton's angle is—"

"Look up," she said in a quiet voice, already knowing the answer. "At the conveyor belts."

She watched his face as he glanced up toward the belts, his eyes growing wide, his mouth falling open. He froze, staring at the biodrones that covered the conveyor belts that rumbled downward toward the storage rooms below.

He glanced down at his screen. Session terminated scrolled across the display.

"VerticalOne," he said in a deadly quiet voice, his gaze flicking from the biodrones passing overhead to his screen. "Get your data. Now. We have to get out of here. Now!"

Jeannette backed away from him and hurried over to the first station. She glanced up at the virtual display. Analysis completed. Encryption in process. The screen flashed and said complete. Then turned red, a message saying file not found.

She smiled. Ron Kraver had already grabbed and deleted the first file.

She rushed across to the second station and pulled the virtual display up to eye level. Ninety-nine percent complete. So close.

"VerticalOne..." he said in a half-whisper. "Time to go."

She shook her head. "I'm one percent from completion on the second job."

His eyes narrowed. "Leave it," he said with a hiss.

Jeannette turned away. "Why?" she asked. "It's less than a minute to completion."

He turned, his eyes burning with fear. "Someone just killed all my processes and forcibly logged me out. Twice."

A chill ran across her skin, stomach dropping as shadows above her head swayed in the processing station's blue-white lights.

She glanced at the completion time on her last process. "Forty-seven seconds left," she said, her voice tinny through the rebreather.

Kai looked up, eyes widening. "Great. That'll be forty-five seconds after we're both dead."

Above her head, biodrones on the conveyors began to stir, talons and tentacles rustling.

17

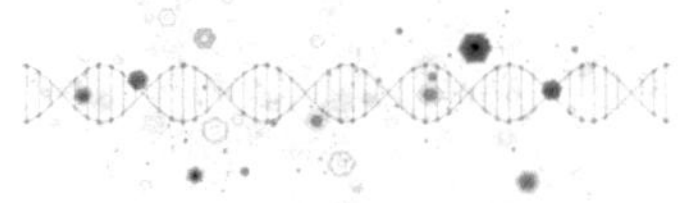

PETER DRESSED QUICKLY in tan camos and a tan T-shirt just like Sting and Sarge wore. Grabbing his dull green flak jacket, he pulled on tan chukkas, fastening the Velcro straps, and grabbed his plasma rifle, slinging it over his left shoulder. He slung the ammo bag across his chest and emptied the ammo tin under his bed into the bag. He grabbed his grid and pushed the lanyard over his head. That's when he saw the orange light pulsating from the pocket of his jeans that lay folded on the white dresser.

He pulled out the strange gear-like thing that felt warm against his fingers as it blinked steadily, reminding him of the homing device Diana had given him before he left for Ku'Tal.

Was this thing some sort of homing device? Something Orlando Constantine had intentionally left for his clone? His useless copy that the man had intended for destruction somehow. Sacrifice? Or a scrap heap. Washed out like so many recombinants before him?

Is that what Orlando Constantine had intended all along, for Peter to only live long enough to draw out his enemies? Lead them down a phony trail that ended with him getting killed or being sent back to RDC for washout? Was that why he even existed? Had he achieved consciousness solely to become Dr. Constantine's decoy? Meant solely to throw the Antarans—and UCOE operatives like Fitzroy—off the man's trail long enough to escape arrest and all consequences.

While Peter took the brunt of it.

He sighed. Like all those people had at the Ballese colony. And on Naharra. All of those people at the first colony had been murdered so Dr. Constantine and his alien engine could live. Was the man's intelligence and contributions (and this engine) so important that thousands should die for him, Peter included?

Peter felt only anger and revulsion toward this man now.

Brother or not, Mimi's sibling was a lying coward. And Peter feared what had already been activated inside him by the man's personal tech devices. Was Sarge wrong? Was Peter turning into something mindless and vile? Like those biodrones? Or worse— something ruthless and hungry. Like Tevihu and the caregivers.

The sound of plasma fire jolted him to action. He shoved the gear thing in his pants pocket and rushed out of the room. Into the vacant hall and through the dark, empty restaurant. Toward the front door. He grabbed the door with both hands and threw it open.

Into chaos!

In the fading light of the setting sun, Antaran ships hung on the horizon like birds of prey over the planet as wave after wave landed in the desert at the edge of town. Unleashing a massive dust storm as roiling masses of biodrones and five remote-directed platforms with large laser guns mounted moved toward Civilization.

Through the streets, squadrons of UCOE forces rushed behind houses and buildings as UCOE tanks plowed across the rocky desert, kicking up sand and drawing explosions as they rolled toward the massing enemy forces. UCOE shuttles began to drop out of the sky, landing between the Antarans and the town. Filled with soldiers.

Waves of recombinants sent to face these monsters.

Peter winced. And die horrible deaths. Like the ones he'd

witnessed on Ku'Tal. Over and over until they would permanently haunt his dreams.

This wasn't happening!

His heart slammed against his rib cage as he watched barricades go up at the edge of town and on every block. In front of every building. Including the two dozen or so stacked around the dead-end street where End of the Line stood, dark and silent.

How many of Mimi's people would die here today?

"Pete!" Sting shouted.

Peter glanced around until he caught the hand signal in the alley that curved around the restaurant. He ran down the stairs and darted around the left side of the restaurant.

In the alley, Sarge, the underground crews, and Sting, wearing his own dull green flak jacket, had gathered alongside two squads of former recombinants. And Sarge's training unit.

Mimi was with them, dressed in a tan flight suit, her hair tied in a ponytail at her nape, plasma rifle under one arm.

Diana and Sarge, in tan flak jackets, each carried plasma rifles and wore tan camo pants and tan T-shirts. Diana's hair was tied back with that familiar purple scarf.

He closed his eyes a moment, the memory of Diana's warm vanilla scent comforting as he'd carried that bright purple scarf against his heart through his entire tour on Ku'Tal. She'd been right beside him on Ballese, too. And he knew she'd be beside him here on Civilization, too.

As he approached, the chirp of scanning grids began.

"Sarge, got movement!" a recombinant shouted.

A dozen rifles raised toward Peter as he reached the barricade.

"Don't shoot!" he shouted. "I'm not an Antaran!"

His grid chirped steadily around his neck, making him nervous and ashamed.

What was happening to him? What did Orlando Constantine's tech do to him? Maybe Sarge and Sting were wrong? Maybe he *was* becoming one of those mindless hybrids?

"But Sarge, the grid—" shouted two recombinants, their heads shaved off to stubble. Their dull green uniforms made Peter shudder.

A year ago, that had been him. And right now, he had everything. And everything to lose.

"Mitchell!" Sarge called, motioning him behind the barrier.

Peter rushed ahead, fearing someone would burn him down with plasma fire before he reached that barricade, but he made it behind and dropped to his knees, rifle clutched in both hands.

"All right, listen up!" Sarge shouted, pointing at Peter. "Everyone with a grid scan Mitchell. Lock in the scan and hit exclude. Now!"

Peter heard a dozen chirps and then silence.

"Happy now?" Sarge snapped. "He's one of us, so shut the hell up and watch for the enemy. It's not Mitchell."

Sting and Diana slid over beside Peter who huddled against the restaurant's sandstone walls, watching for movement.

Grinning, Sting reached out and ruffled Peter's light blond hair.

"See, Pete? Told ya you're not an Antaran." Sting.

Diana frowned, shaking her head. She reached out and pulled Peter close, wrapping her arms around him. He sucked in a pained breath and held her tighter than he'd ever held her before, pressing his face against her hair that smelled like sunlight and rainwater. And her purple scarf. Like warm vanilla. Like her.

"I'll love you forever, Diana," he whispered against her ear. "No matter what happens."

Her eyes turned watery as she held him out at arm's length, fear welling in her warm, honey-brown eyes.

"Peter, you're scaring me," she said, her eyes so wide and frightened, like a hunted deer. "I love you and I don't ever want to be without you."

He kissed her. Gently, but the urgency sent tears down her face. He wiped them away with his thumbs.

"Don't cry, Diana. All I want is to stay here with you and Sting and Sarge." He glanced down at the ground and then smiled up at her through hooded lids. "Breaking dishes with Mimi and helping other recombinants."

Diana smiled and held him close again. "You're all I've ever wanted, Peter Mitchell. Never forget that."

"I could never forget that. Or you, Diana Temple," he said back to her, still smiling, and then kissed her again.

He wanted to tell her about the strange dreams and the weird tech he'd brought back from Ballese and how it made him feel different. But he couldn't. She would worry more and he couldn't stand the thought of causing her pain.

Shuttles and lightflyers shot across the sky. Headed toward the setting sun and the arriving Antaran ships hovering over the town. Explosions and gunfire echoed. The mechanical rumble of tanks and troop movers reverberated through Civilization's deathly quiet streets. Windows and doors boarded up. The air smelled hot like ozone and plasma fire. All across the mining town, plasma fire had erupted. Crackling like lightning. Lighting up the umber sky as it darkened with smoke and the approaching dusk.

There wasn't time to tell her now anyway. And she'd just worry. Like Sarge.

"All right, listen up!" Sarge. "We're serving as the town militia. Providing support and cover for UCOE's front-line advance and protecting this part of the city. We'll hold this position and provide fallback cover for the main offensive if needed. There are more than thirty of us at this post. Soldiers. Veterans. Mercenaries. And citizens. But today, we fight as one unit. Together. To push back the bad guys and keep them from destroying our worlds. Our lives. Starting with this city."

"And send 'em back to hell!" Sting shouted.

"Right where they belong!" Peter added.

Sarge pointed toward three silver shuttles parked in a vacant field beside the distant curve of the transit shuttle track as dusk descended. Less than a block from the alley. "If we're overrun or we have to fall back from this position, get to those shuttles standing by to carry us off-world to safety. Courtesy of Mimi Constantine."

"And I'd rather see us fall back and live to plan another assault before they're entrenched," said Mimi. "There are other ways to fight back than launching a direct suicide run at their main contingent. Remember that. No suicide runs."

She opened two big, metal cargo boxes filled with grenades.

"And here's a little backup, folks. Just in case."

Peter and Sting slid one of the cargo containers close and dropped three of the small grenades into their jacket pockets. With a quick shove, they slid the container over to Sarge and the other recombinants. They all grabbed some grenades and passed the container onward.

A long, dark shadow rushed along the alley as two, small Antaran ships landed, framed by the distant shuttle track. Alongside the river that ran parallel between two of Civilization's main streets.

"Do not engage until I give the order to fire," Sarge commanded as he dropped down behind the barricade and raised his rifle. "Repeat. Do not engage until I signal. Hold position."

But the Antarans were already pouring out of the ships. Biodrones Peter gasped. And caregivers!

18

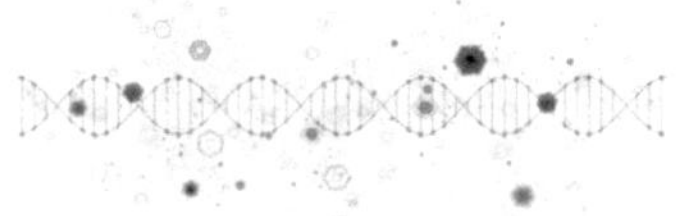

THE LARGE MONITOR screens above Jeannette's and Kai's heads on the theatre floor flickered to life. Stanton stared back at them, hands folded behind her back. Looking calm and serene. The woman's face looked pasty and crinkly around her mouth and eyes and neck, her UCOE dress blues pressed and perfect, gold buttons glinting.

Jeannette blinked on her helmet's visual display and selected *record* as she streamed the video feedback to the shuttle.

"Such a shame," said Stanton, clicking her tongue. "Losing two of my best reclamation specialists so suddenly in this devastating—" She chuckled. "And unprovoked attack."

Her voice echoed through the cavernous grey chamber as tentacles rasped against the conveyor belts above them.

Jeannette glanced at the streaming progress on the second processing unit's visual display. Thirty-seven seconds to completion.

"You mean the attack you ordered?" Kai snapped, his voice rising in layers above the bump and rumble of conveyor belts.

"Me?" Stanton cried, a hand on her chest. "You accuse a loyal officer in service to the United Countries of Earth of orchestrating a treasonous alliance with the enemy? Why, Dr. Drew, your accusation is baseless. And absurd. Why, who would even believe such a tall tale?"

Twenty-nine seconds to completion.

Jeannette accessed the maintenance module for the reclamation theatre, sliding through options. Locating the systems calibration check. Right next to the emergency systems shut down and life support systems shutdown. She remembered Kai showing those entries to her after joking about shutting it down to conserve oxygen while Stanton ran off at the mouth on the loudspeaker.

Twenty-one seconds.

"Baseless?" Jeannette replied, her rebreather hissing. "Absurd? No more than you turning this damaged station into a biodrone production facility for the Antarans, Colonel Stanton. I'm sure home system would love to hear about how this initiative is supporting the war. And see it with their own eyes."

Stanton chuckled, looking so sure of herself.

"It's just the beginning of this war initiative, Dr. Kingston. And there are many more to come. I've already dispatched dear Captain D'Angelo to acquire the cipher that will significantly step-up production of biodrones and—other hybrids."

Jeannette glared at her.

"Tell me, how many biodrones have you already sent down to the surface of Civilization? After you murdered much of the personnel inside their escape pods as they fled the destruction. Like you tried to murder Kai and me."

Sixteen seconds.

"Murder's such a strong word, Dr. Kingston," Stanton said, a smug smile rising on her thin, pasty lips.

Jeannette pulled up the *initiate life support system shutdown* function on the visual display, her finger hovering over it.

"So's genocide," Jeannette continued, her voice tinny. "You're not an officer. You're a monster. And I'm not quite sure you're even human." She turned toward Kai who glanced over at her display, his eyes widening. "Something UCOE will definitely want to hear."

Thirteen seconds.

"Red's right, Stanton," Kai replied, moving beside her. "Much more of a monster than I ever realized." He pointed at the biodrones as they lurched down the conveyors toward the storeroom.

Jeannette held in her smile. He was distracting Stanton. Buying her time to finish the last genetic comparison, grab the files, and shut down life support.

Eleven seconds.

A horrible grinding sound erupted through the reclamation theatre as the entire conveyor system screeched to an abrupt halt. Biodrones fell onto each other as the rumbling thunder shook the grid floor, the conveyors reversing. Sending dozens of awakening biodrones toward the reclamation theatre.

She shuddered. Toward her and Kai.

Eight seconds.

Kai began to sweat, his brow and upper lip glistening as the biodrones traveled out of the storeroom, conveyor belts clanking as they moved upward toward the processing stations. Toward the grid floor.

Jeannette pressed her finger against the *initiate life support shut down* command.

Three seconds.

Air vents and intake valves fell eerily silent all around them and below them. Something Stanton hadn't heard yet.

"Too bad neither of you will live to tell anyone," said Stanton. "Have a lovely death, Dr. Drew. Dr. Kingston."

"You, too, Stanton," said Jeannette as an alarm rang out, red lights flashing overhead.

"Warning," said an overly pleasant computerized voice. "Life support systems have been shut down due to an unexpected process. Please evacuate all lower levels immediately."

"What have you done?" Stanton shouted, her voice echoing through the chambers.

"Honestly, you really have to ask?" Jeannette snapped.

The words, *analysis complete* appeared on Jeannette's visual display. The screen flashed and the message read, file not found. It was done.

The scritch of the first biodrones hitting the farthest processing station echoed through the cavernous chamber.

"Red..." Kai replied, backing away, his rebreather buzzing. "We've got company."

Tentacles flashed beneath the blue-white lights, clacking against the floor. Skittering toward them from the far side of the grid floor.

Grinning, Jeannette grabbed Kai's arm and pulled him toward the reclamation station across the aisle.

"Look! Conveyor belts are headed for the launch bay! Thanks for the exit strategy, Stanton!" Jeannette shouted as she locked the conveyor tracks in place with the systems account.

She and Kai jumped up onto the stainless-steel tables and rolled onto the reversed conveyor belts that would normally carry body bags below the reclamation theatre. But Stanton had them running from the reclamation tables upward. Toward the launch bay.

Crouching, Jeannette and Kai clutched the conveyor railing and turned on their mag boots. Locking onto the moving belts. And unlock the conveyor belt system's current configuration that Jeannette had locked in place.

Stanton had just provided them with a quick shot back to launch bay while struggling to reinitiate the life support systems.

Biodrones slithered across the reclamation tables and spun around, leaping onto the conveyor belts about ten meters behind them.

"Run, Jeannette!" Kai shouted through his rebreather with a buzz.

His boots pounded down the conveyor belt and Jeannette matched his steps as the belt rumbled and lurched up and out of the reclamation theatre and curved around the edge of the station. Toward launch bay. And the awaiting shuttle. If they were fast, they'd get there a couple of minutes before the biodrones.

If they were fast.

"VerticalTwo to stasis," Kai shouted through his rebreather, his breath huffing as he ran, pressing the comm button on his suit. "Stay suited up and open the doors. Get ready to launch. We've got a lot of company on our six and we're comin' in hot on the belts. Over."

Static buzzed through Jeannette's helmet.

"Roger that, VerticalTwo," Ron Kraver's voice. "Holding position. Doors are open and we're ready to welcome your guests off the belts with a fireworks party. Over."

"Steady there," said Kai, grabbing her arm when she stumbled.

Holding her on her feet, Jeannette realized as he stopped running and crouched, arms wrapped around her as the conveyor belt rounded a sharp, steep curve. Keeping both of them aboard and letting the belts carry them around the curve.

Behind them, several biodrones scrabbled closer but careened off the belts, unable to weather the curve.

But there were many more behind them.

When the conveyor belt fanned out straight again, Kai pulled Jeannette to her feet and they pounded down the creaking conveyor belt again as the chute widened into a downward curve, dropping into the launch bay. Jeannette grinned. And into the awaiting shuttle.

She grabbed hold of Kai's arm and together, they leaped off the conveyor belt and hit the dull grey floor where one of Mimi's shuttles revved its engines.

Behind them, more than a dozen biodrones rolled off the belts behind them, mottled skin and talons a blur as they surged toward Jeannette and Kai.

Kai pushed her into the shuttle as the biodrone leaped, landing on his back. He fell, the biodrone on top of him. And the next one and the next one.

"KAI!" she screamed.

Ron Kraver rolled out of the shuttle, plasma fire arcing, catching the next two in its beam.

Jeannette grabbed a crowbar off the floor and launched herself at the biodrones on top of Kai. Talons slashed at his face, bouncing off his helmet, and across chest and legs, slicing gashes through his suit.

The crowbar smashed into the first biodrone's head.

It lolled over to one side, tentacles twitching. Spewing inky black fluid into the air.

The shuttle pilot crawled onto the nose, rifle raised, picking off the biodrones coming off the belt.

Ron slammed the butt of his rifle into the other biodrone on top of Kai while Jeannette bashed the third one's head with the crowbar over and over until it fell away, talons and tentacles curling into black, inky knots.

Together, they grabbed Kai by the arms and dragged him into the shuttle as the door began to close. Catching several writhing talons in the jamb, severing them. The tentacles sprayed black fluid as the pilot climbed back into the cockpit and tapped the thrusters.

The pilot taxied the shuttle away from the swarming biodrones. Into the launch tube.

And slammed the thrusters.

The shuttle shot forward into dark space and dropped, setting course back to Civilization.

Jeannette unfastened her helmet and tossed it to the side as she dropped down beside Kai on the floor of the shuttle.

His breath was ragged, chest heaving as blood seeped across his torn envirosuit.

"Dammit, Kai! You're always trying to save me!" she shouted, tugging the suit off his arms and peeling it down to his waist. Checking for injuries. "And if you're dead, I swear I'll kill you!"

He chuckled, smiling as he struggled to catch his breath.

"Wasn't going to let them touch you, Jeannette," he said, breath huffing.

He was sliced up and bleeding, but he was breathing and trying to sit up. She and Ron helped him into a seat and buckled him into a restraint harness. She needed to get him an anti-venom shot as soon as they touched down, but a cursory examination revealed no apparent puncture wounds or broken bones.

"Thank you," she said, a hand against his face, smoothing his coal black hair out of his eyes, off his forehead.

Leaning down, she pressed a soft kiss against his lips. He grinned, kissing her back with a hard, urgent kiss. Before letting her go.

"Hell, I'd have taken the rest of them on if I'd known you'd react like that, Jeannette," he said. "I can hardly wait for our fourth date."

She laughed out loud as she buckled into the seat beside him and gripped his hand. Ron snorted and moved up front to sit in the co-pilot's seat.

"You, two have weird dates," he said, making Jeannette and Kai both laugh.

The shuttle's comm chimed and Ron answered. "Stasis. Go ahead, Civilization."

Mimi's hard-edged voice filled the shuttle compartment.

"Stasis, Civilization is under attack. Repeat. Civilization is under attack."

Static cut through, breaking up the communication signal.

"Large...force of Antaran—ships...Repeat. Strikef— on... ground—"

"Base station!" Ron shouted. "You're breaking up. We're nearing Civilization. Coming in to assist on the ground. Over."

"Ron, no!" Mimi shouted. "Too many...we're—b...overrun. It's—too...late, it's—"

"It's never too late!" Ron replied. "On the ground in ten with assistance. Kraver out."

Ron turned around, anger narrowing his eyes, his jawline taut. "They're under attack down there. We have to help them. Somehow. They won't last long if they're pinned down in the restaurant."

"Just start passing out the rifles, Kraver," said Kai, pushing his arms back into the sleeves of his envirosuit. "I've got a score to settle with those bastards."

"What Kai said," Jeannette replied. "At the very least, we can burn a path to the shuttle for them."

Ron smiled as he moved toward the ordnance rack at the back of the shuttle. He pulled out six rifles, handing one to Kai and Jeannette. He propped the others by the door along with a big black bucket of plasma charges.

"Game on, then," said Ron, giving the pilot a nod.

19

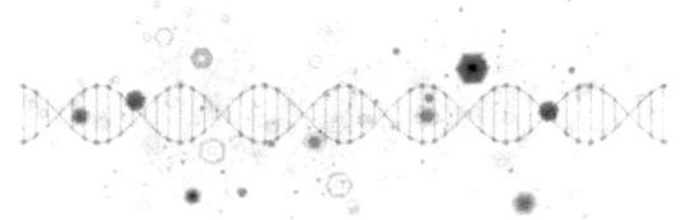

THE SILENCE WAS PALPABLE, the cloying stink of sweetness hanging in the smoky air. Suffocating as biodrones and caregivers armed with rifles moved through the haze-like shadows.

In range.

Peter swiveled his plasma rifle toward the translucent-skinned caregivers that moved silently at a distance as the biodrones clacked into the street ahead of them. They wore tan robes and blended into the umber sand surrounding the town.

The sight of those monsters made Peter's blood boil as he focused his green laser sight on the nearest one's head, wanting to end its existence. But he couldn't pull the trigger yet. Not until Sarge gave the go-ahead.

Just as he started to move his scope, undead D'Angelo emerged from the other shuttle, shouting orders and directing troops. Whatever commanded his body wasn't human, Peter reminded himself. But it was hard. Recombinants learned obedience first and foremost or they never made it out of RDC. By the time he'd reached the training base, it was second nature, the commissioned officers' uniforms an instant, visceral trigger to obey or be destroyed.

Seeing D'Angelo in a UCOE uniform, regardless of what had happened to the man on Ballese, made Peter twitch and squirm as the man barked orders as if still on their side.

He had to keep telling himself that D'Angelo was the enemy now.

"Sarge," Peter called. "It's D'Angelo."

Sarge sighed and rubbed his forehead.

"Damn. Thanks for the heads up, Mitchell. Everyone, D'Angelo may still look human, but he's been hybridized by the enemy. Do not let him through this barricade. He's no longer on our side. Is that clear?"

"Roger that, Sarge," Peter and Sting replied in unison along with the other recombinants.

"He gives me the creeps," Diana said in a quiet voice. "I saw his body cold and stiff on Ballese. He's not in there anymore, but I want to know what's commandeered his body."

"So do I, sis," said Sarge, sliding over beside Diana.

Peter smiled. Protecting her. Because she was his little sister. Not because she was one of only a handful of shuttle pilots left in this group. Just in case something happened to the pilots manning those shuttles. Diana had been training Peter and he had just passed the requirements for his solo pilot's license. He could fly one of those shuttles in an emergency. And so could Sarge.

Peter moved to Diana's right, pivoting between her and Sting until his shoulder was against her back.

"I'm sticking close, Diana," he said against her ear. "To protect my heart."

"Your heart?" she asked, looking confused.

He leaned over and kissed her softly on the lips. "You're my heart," he said. "And without you, mine won't beat. I love you, Diana."

The first chirp of the grid startled him.

The soft cheep ping-ponged across the barricades.

"Sarge, I've got movement in the street," Peter said in a half-whisper. "Six or seven biodrones. Heading southwest. Close. Less than six meters and moving fast." He swallowed a breath and let the grid drop against his chest. "It's D'Angelo."

"Take down anything in range," Sarge ordered, steely-eyed as he lifted the muzzle of his plasma rifle.

"Detecting several caregivers with him," Peter replied. "Four meters and closing."

"Fire at will," Sarge growled.

The first shot echoed in the stillness. A blue bolt of lightning arced over the barricades and fried the first biodrone in range. Sting dropped the next one behind it, too.

Peter raised his rifle, squeezing off a shot that took one of the caregivers' heads off. It dropped to the street, body flopping as thick black blood spattered the street.

The rest of the makeshift squadron opened fire at the advancing Antarans.

Biodrones rolled over the barricades, more than a dozen. With more behind them.

Someone screamed. Plasma fire exploded around them.

Peter threw himself over top of Diana, shielding her as Sting got to his feet and shoved the barrel of his plasma rifle against the nearest biodrone and fired. It exploded in a shower of blackness and blue flame.

Sarge slammed the butt of his rifle into a biodrone beside him and shot it at close range until it was a smear in the alley.

Talons raked across Peter's back and arms as he covered Diana.

He swiveled, bringing up his rifle and shooting two biodrones right in their flashing gold eyes. Blowing them both apart.

And still they came. In an endless line, punctuated with caregivers, D'Angelo watching from a distance.

Peter pushed Diana behind him, against the sandstone wall, and blocked her with his body as he fired off shot after shot. Diana kept firing, plasma rifle gripped tight in her shaking hands. Sting was at his shoulder, squeezing off well-placed shots in the chaos behind the barricades.

It was getting harder not to hit the other recombinants and soldiers, but Sting's relaxed stance gave him an advantage of not firing unless it was a kill shot.

Something bounced against the ground somewhere off to Peter's left. He glanced toward it.

A small, oblong silver thing hit the alley.

"Grenade!" Peter shouted, shoving Sting and Sarge backward as he kicked it toward the street.

The Antaran device detonated, blowing a hole in the street and shattering barricades. Launching Peter into the sandstone wall on top of Sarge and Diana as biodrones and recombinants flew across the alley like rag dolls.

Miraculously, none of the makeshift squadron got hurt. Including Sting and Sarge.

Peter got hit by debris, cutting his face and hands, but he had shielded Sarge and Diana from harm.

Again, another wave of biodrones rushed at them.

Sarge and Sting struggled to pull back the remaining barricades for cover as Peter turned and laid down a line of fire, slowing down the biodrones' advance while the makeshift squadron regrouped behind the surviving barricades.

Another silver tube-like device fell behind the barricades.

Peter lunged for it, throwing it back at the Antarans. A moment later, it exploded, obliterating the front line of biodrones.

Behind him, he heard Mimi Constantine on the comm, calling for backup and assistance on a wide beam.

"Keep your heads down and your wits about you!" Sarge. "We can keep this up as long as they can."

Sting twisted the top of a round hand grenade and rolled it into the street, between the biodrones and a small group of advancing caregivers armed with laser rifles that rushed across the street.

Toward the broken barricades.

The grenade exploded.

Severed tentacles, talons, and black fluid rained against the street. As more moved behind them.

Sarge tossed another grenade into the next group, blowing them into the darkening sky.

And still they came.

Four biodrones surged past the plasma fire and grenades, talons gutting a man on the far side of the alley. And a recombinant.

Peter's grid shrieked and wailed as the line of biodrones careened toward them. But then he saw the ghost echo appear behind them from the east.

His stomach dropped. The Antarans were flanking them!

"Sarge!" Peter shouted, pointing over his shoulder. "More biodrones from the east. They're flanking us!"

Sting whirled and heaved a grenade over the squadron and into the alleyway to the east as the first glint of biodrone talons appeared.

The grenade exploded in a shower of tentacles and sandstone.

"Good call, Pete!" Sting said with a grin.

Sarge crouched by the remaining hunks of stone barricades surrounding the makeshift squadron as half aimed at the flank and the others at the front. Grenades sailed toward both lines as Sarge and the other recombinants emptied the cargo container. All they had left were the grenades in their pockets now.

"Dammit, they've got us pinned down!" Sarge's voice roared above the explosions and plasma fire.

"Sergeant Temple!" a familiar voice shouted, amplified.

Peter shuddered. It was D'Angelo.

"Send out the recombinant and we can stop all this foolishness."

"Which one?" Sarge shouted. "We've got about two dozen over here. With more coming."

"Come, now, Temple, you know exactly what I want," said D'Angelo, his voice thick and gruff as it echoed through Civilization's empty streets.

"No, I'm afraid I have no clue, you being undead and all," Sarge replied. "D'Angelo's dead. So, whatever your name is, know this. We will fight you monsters to our last breath and our last charge. All of us."

"Sarge is right!" Sting.

"D'Angelo!" Mimi's voice rang out above the plasma fire. "Not to ruin your day or anything, but there's a very large antitank gun pointed at you and your ship right now from an inbound shuttle. I suggest you and your wind-up toys shag on out of here and join the real fighting by the spaceport. Otherwise, the house special at End of the Line tonight is gonna be roast D'Angelo with tentacles. Served with a very bitter port."

Diana laughed, Sarge trying to hold his in, but it slipped through his fury.

"Come now, Ms. Constantine," D'Angelo responded. "I see no large-scale weaponry deployed here. Just send out your brother's recombinant and the rest of you can go."

Mimi shook her head. "I love it when the bad guys are so arrogant that they're stupid," she said. "Looked all around us, did ya? North. South. Guess you forgot one very important direction." She pointed toward the sky. "Up..."

A shuttle dropped through the hazy smoke and fired a large pulse of energy that shook the ground and set the nearby brush and buildings on fire.

The shuttle door swung open, a dozen plasma rifles pointing toward the surface, unleashing a shower of blue fire along the squadron's flank. Incinerating the entire force of biodrones that had advanced on their flank. Landing on top of the obliterated biodrones.

Ron Kraver slid the door open and stepped out of the shuttle, huge plasma rifle balanced on his shoulders. Dr. Kingston and Dr. Drew stepped out behind him, plasma rifles in hand. They ran toward the barricades along with the rest of the shuttle crew, joining the firefight.

Sting and Diana cheered.

"You were saying? D'Angelo?" Mimi replied. "I mentioned that your aura is jet-black, didn't I? That's usually a sign of imminent death at someone else's hand. And soon—I might add."

"Really?" Peter said with a gasp.

Mimi shook her head. "No. But I was on a roll with that antitank gun bit." She smiled at Peter. "Ron just called me two minutes ago, said they were in range. Thought I'd push the envelope a little. D'Angelo's envelope. Or dead letter in his case."

Sarge laughed. Peter just stared quizzically at her, shaking his head.

"An old Earth joke, Mitchell," said Sarge. "Before your time."

Peter just shrugged as Ron dropped down behind the barricades, Dr. Kingston and Dr. Drew beside him. All three wore speckled tan and grey envirosuits, helmet visors open. They looked torn and bloodied, but not seriously injured. The rest of the shuttle crew hurried behind the barricades after them.

"Sorry we're late to the party, Mimi," said Ron, nodding toward Dr. Kingston. "We had to extricate our former combat medics from the new biodrone production plant."

Sarge's eyes widened. "What plant?"

"The one in the ruins of Reclamation Station 343-AOD, my former employer," said Dr. Kingston, her short red hair shiny in the waning light.

Biodrones surged around the sandstone building again, talons raised, gold eyes everywhere.

The replenished squadron returned fire, plasma arcs crackling through the electric, hazy dusk, blowing apart biodrones after biodrone.

Until every severed talon and every amputated tentacle became a new biodrone.

"Keep firing until they're fucking pudding or you'll just make more of them!" Sting.

Dr. Kingston grabbed hold of Mimi's arm. "Mimi, they're coming after Peter."

Peter swallowed hard and kept firing, but he couldn't help but concentrate on Dr. Kingston's voice now.

"D'Angelo keeps yelling for us to send him out," said Sarge between shots. "I told him to go to hell."

"We won't let that bastard near Pete, Doc," said Sting, squeezing off a long burst of plasma fire, smoking a biodrone into paste.

"Or any of them," Diana added, burning down a writhing talon in the street that was starting to replicate.

"He's in great danger," said Dr. Kingston. "Stanton said she'd sent D'Angelo after the cipher. Mimi, that's Peter."

"What are you talking about, Dr. Kingston?" Diana asked, looking visibly upset. "What's this about a cipher?"

"I compared Peter's DNA to Orlando's control copy," said Dr. Kingston, firing at a biodrone. "Orlando embedded data and instruction sets into Peter's DNA. And pieces of apparent code that aren't present in any human programming language. It isn't Antaran either. It's in an unknown language that resembles similar construction to the artifact that Orlando discovered on Naharra. A piece of which Peter brought back from Ballese."

Peter could barely concentrate on the biodrones, hearing Dr. Kingston's words. There was something inside him? Had the glowing gear-thing in his pocket set it all in motion? What would it do to him?

Mimi shook her head. "So, what does all that mean, Dr. Kingston?"

Dr. Kingston glanced down at her plasma rifle a moment. "It means that Peter's carrying around some sort of cipher or key in his DNA that opens a door or turns on an ancient replication technology. Mimi, if it falls into Antaran hands, we'll be overrun. This war will be over."

Mimi nodded. "Then we protect Peter Mitchell at any cost. Got it."

"You heard the lady," Sarge shouted. "Protect Mitchell. That's an order!"

"Aye, aye, Sarge!" Sting replied, sliding against Peter's right shoulder. "He's not leaving my sight."

"Or mine," Diana snapped, firing a burst of plasma at two biodrones cresting the barricade.

A fresh wave of biodrones skittered across the alley and swarmed the barricades.

Peter saw them fan out across his grid, appearing north and south. The roof!

He jerked his head up, barrel of his plasma rifle raised.

"Look up! They're on the roof!"

He laid down a line of fire along the top of the wall as a dozen or so biodrones swung down from the rooftops, talons flashing.

Sting tossed up a grenade, sending a bunch of biodrones flying off the roof to splatter against the pavement.

Two more swung down on top of Sarge and two recombinants. Peter threw himself in front of Diana as a talon snapped down toward her chest. His plasma rifle stock took part of the blow, his left shoulder the rest, the talon piercing deep into the muscle.

Sting grabbed hold of the flailing talon and tore it free, incinerating it with his plasma rifle.

"Oh, God! Peter!" Diana shouted, holding onto him as blood seeped into his tan T-shirt.

He winced, still firing. "I'm okay, Diana," he said through gritted teeth.

Ahead, in the smoky twilight, caregivers advanced on them, their forms translucent as they began to shift.

"Ready grenades!" Sarge shouted.

"Fling 'em high!" Sting yelled, tossing two armed grenades at the caregivers.

One of the recombinants armed a grenade, but biodrones drove talons into his chest. The grenade fell, rolling against the remaining barricades.

The grenade blast blew the barricades apart. Showering the squadron in rock and metal.

"Fall back!" Sarge shouted. "Toward the shuttles! Move it!"

Peter glanced off to the west as two more Antaran ships approached.

D'Angelo rushed toward them now from the north. Half of their forces would never reach those shuttles that were less than a block away.

Glancing over his shoulder, Peter saw the shuttle still in the alley where Ron Kraver and the other underground crew members had left it.

He winced. There was only one way to make sure Diana, Sarge, and Sting reached those other shuttles. And safety.

Peter waited, his heart heavy, giving them as long of a head start as he could. It would take Diana and Sting a moment or two to realize he was longer beside them.

Swiveling around with his plasma rifle, pockets stuffed with grenades, Peter turned toward the advancing Antarans.

"D'Angelo!" Peter shouted. "I'm right here! Come and get me if you're man enough!"

Sting's voice echoed somewhere behind him from the vacant field. "Oh, my God...Pete! PETE!"

"Peter, NO!" Diana screamed.

D'Angelo rounded the corner of the sandstone building, caregivers and biodrones at his shoulders. Between Peter and the shuttles now.

"Take him alive," D'Angelo ordered, pointing. "He has the cipher."

Shadows shifted around him as Peter turned, boots pounding down the alley, sounds reverberating as he raced toward the other shuttle's open door at the alley's end.

Skittering of talons and boots filled the silence above his huffing breaths as he leaped inside the shuttle and climbed into the pilot's seat.

He flicked levers and poked buttons, closing the shuttle's main door. Something slammed against the shuttle, rocking it a few moments before the door snapped closed.

With shaking hands, Peter lit the engines and taxied down Civilization's main street as night descended. He hit the thrusters and surged down the street until the shuttle lifted off, rising through the smoke and the haze and the night until the only place that had ever felt like home disappeared beneath him.

Leading the Antarans away from Civilization was the only way to save it. The only way to save Diana, Sting, Sarge, and Mimi.

He glanced down past his bloodied T-shirt, to the orange glow of the strange gear in his pocket.

He'd lead the Antarans to Naharra, where the dreams kept pushing him. Where the ancient engine—part machine, part man—waited.

If he was the key to unlocking this horrible thing that could replicate Antarans by the thousands, then maybe he could also shut it down.

He had to try. Even if he had to give up everything and everyone he'd ever loved to save them.

For the people he cherished, he had to try.

The End of **SPLICE, Experiencing True Purple, Book 3**

The story continues in...

CIPHER, Experiencing True Purple, Book 4

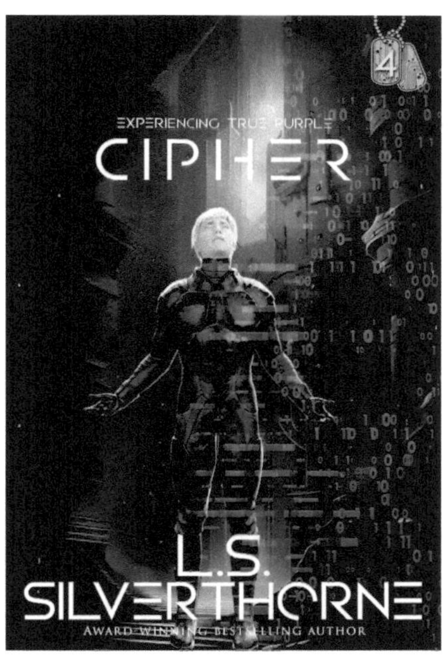

EXPERIENCING TRUE PURPLE
CIPHER
L.S.
SILVERTHORNE
AWARD-WINNING BESTSELLING AUTHOR

Novels by L.S. Silverthorne

Experiencing True Purple series:
RECOMBINANT, Book 1
HELIX, Book 2
SPLICE, Book 3

Standalone:
REDISCOVERY

Writing as Lisa Silverthorne

A Game of Lost Souls series:
Contemporary Romantasy
THE CINDERELLA HOUR
THE PRINCE CHARMING HOUR
THE EVER AFTER HOUR
THE FALLEN HEARTS SEASON
THE RISING SPIRITS SEASON
THE ETERNAL SOULS SEASON
THE ROYAL WEDDING HOUR
THE HEAVENLY HONEYMOON HOUR
THE DIVINE NEWLYWEDS SHOW
THE CELESTIAL COUPLES SHOW
THE ENOCHIAN APOCALYPSE SHOW
THE ANGELIC ANNIVERSARY SHOW
THE PERDITION PICTURE SHOW
Complete Series!

Curse and Crown series:

Epic Court Intrigue Romantasy
THORN & BLADE
STORM & STEEL

The Spiral series:
Dark Contemporary Fantasy
BETWEEN
REPRISE
AVENGE

The Resurrectionist Papers
Paranormal Romystery
GRAVE RECKONING

Standalones:
ISABEL'S TEARS
LANDFALL
PACIFIC BLUE TATTOO

Short Story Collections
THE SOUND OF ANGELS
THE MAGIC OF ORDINARY THINGS
TIMELESS
WINTER'S EMBRACE

FORTHCOMING!

Experiencing True Purple series:
Cipher, Book 4
Renascence, Book 5 (Series End)

WRITING AS LISA SILVERTHORNE

Curse and Crown series:
Flame & Dagger, Book Three (2026)
Frost & Foil, Book Four
Curse & Crown, Book Five (Series End)

The Spiral series:
Ruin, Book 4
Descent, Book 5 (Series End)

The Resurrectionist Papers:
Corpses Delicti (2026)
Stiffed Again

ABOUT THE AUTHOR

LISA SILVERTHORNE, an award-winning author, has published over 30 novels and 150 short stories and novelettes in many genres. She is the author of *A Game of Lost Souls, Experiencing True Purple, The Spiral, The Resurrectionist Papers,* and *Curse and Crown.*

Before you go, you are invited to please leave a **review of this book**!

Reviews are a wonderful way to help an author and share your thoughts with other readers, so **please post yours,** in as many places as possible!

 **ONLINE STORE!**

For Ebook Bundles, book swag, and beautiful
Special Edition *hardcovers (coming soon), visit:*
LisaSilverthorneBooks.com